Lucy's Choice

Lucy's Choice

Kinky Companions 3

Alex Markson

This paperback edition 2020

First published by Parignon Press 2020

Copyright © Alex Markson 2019

Alex Markson asserts the moral right to be identified as the
author of this work in accordance with the Copyright,
Designs and Patents Act 1988

ISBN: 979 8 57 964406 0

Chapter 1 – Lucy

"Hello, Lucy. Come in."

"Hi, Jenny. Thank you."

She led me through the house to the room at the back. I remembered it from my counselling sessions with her years ago. I'd decided I needed to come back.

"Take a seat."

I settled myself in that familiar chair. The room hadn't changed much; nor had Jenny.

"Welcome back, Lucy. As we agreed, I dug out your old notes. But why don't you tell me why you're here?"

I'd prepared for this; had it all clear in my head. But I'd been through this before. It seemed so straightforward, but when you tried to tell someone, it all went awry.

"When I worked with you before, it was about my family. You helped me come to terms with my break from them, but things have changed a bit recently."

"In what way?"

"My father died a couple of weeks ago. He had a major stroke last year. Since then, he's been virtually helpless, and had several more until the one which killed him."

"How do you feel about his death?"

I paused, reflecting on the question.

"I don't know, Jenny. I think that's why I'm here."

We fell into silence, a silence I remembered well. Jenny wanted me to lead; she didn't ask too many questions, just allowed me to talk.

"After he had his first stroke, my mother contacted me. She wanted to meet. Eventually, I agreed."

"Was that a difficult decision?"

"Yes. It came out of the blue and I was suspicious. But in the end, my curiosity got the better of me. I'm still in touch with my sister, and I had the impression something had changed."

"How did the meeting go?"

I described that stilted first meeting; both of us feeling our way. Then the subsequent ones and the awkwardness of Christmas Day.

"Did you attend his funeral?"

"No. At least we all agreed on that. I didn't want to go, and my mother didn't want me there."

"You hadn't seen him when he was ill?"

I shrugged.

"No. My mother thought it would upset him."

"And you?"

"I didn't want to. But now, I'm not sure I made the right choice."

"Why do you say that?"

"I didn't see him for fifteen years. Now I never will."

"How does that feel?"

"At the moment, it's okay. But I worry about how it might feel in the future."

"Is that why you're here?"

I looked at her.

"Possibly. But I'm trying to work through what happens now. With my mother."

"Whether to rebuild your relationship with her?"

"Yes. I'm not sure I want to."

I told her about my doubts. My life was good. A job I loved, a small circle of good friends. My art was flourishing, and I wasn't going to let my family harm any of that.

"You doubt your mother's motives."

"I think Mum and Dad were crutches for each other. They depended on one another. With Dad gone, Mum is suddenly on her own. I don't intend to become another crutch for her."

"What does your sister think?"

I told her about Tim and Annie's situation. How they'd moved away from my father in recent years and how they were helping Mum get back on her feet. When our time was up, Jenny surprised me. Instead of asking me to think about my mother, she asked me to think about my father. What I felt about him now he'd gone. We'd talk about it the following week. Well, that would put a downer on the week to come.

***

Sally arrived on Friday evening; she was staying the night. The first time she'd done so since Dad died. I'd met her a few times over the previous two weeks as usual; for lunch, to go to the gym. And I'd rung her a few times when I'd felt low. She was the one who encouraged me to go and see Jenny.

After she arrived, and we shared a long hug, I pulled away from her.

"It's all your fault," I said.

"What have I done?"

"I saw Jenny on Tuesday."

"Oh."

"She asked me to think about Dad."

"Ah."

"I know why she's done it, but it's hard. There aren't any good memories at all."

Sally gave a hollow laugh.

"I know that feeling; or at least, I did."

"Did?"

"Yea. Remember the last fifteen years? The shadow? I hated my father. Since I've worked on it with Jenny, and with help from you and Marcus, I don't hate him anymore. He's a bit of a joke, isn't he? This mystery man. But think how it would have been if I had been close to him and found out about these fake identities. It would be even worse."

"I see what you mean."

"And now, there's a new bombshell for us to deal with."

3

"What bombshell?"

"I'll tell you later. But what I'm saying is, you need to think about him. Not hide him away, as I did. Look where that got me."

"Yea, I suppose so. Hungry?"

"I could eat."

"Good, I've cooked enough for ten."

I had, as well. I'd be eating it for days. We sat and chatted over dinner. The wine flowed; rather liberally. I relaxed and forgot about my family.

"So, what's your father done now?" I asked Sally.

"He may have had another family."

"What?"

She told me what the genealogist had found. I was stunned. And surprised how calmly Sally was telling the story. But she was right; she had come to terms with her past.

"What are you going to do?" I asked.

"No idea. I'm going to sit on it for a while."

"What does Marcus think?"

"He's being his usual self; letting me think it through on my own first. He'll tell me his views when he's ready."

"Or when he thinks you're ready."

"That's about it."

"You've found a real gem there. For a man."

"I think so."

"Could your dad have had other … women?"

"Who knows? It seems he wasn't exactly a model of fidelity."

I raised an eyebrow.

"Like father, like daughter," I said.

She looked puzzled for a moment, then burst out laughing.

"Oh, God. You're right. I'm unfaithful all the time."

We were both tipsy by now. I got another bottle of wine, and we moved to the sofa. We'd made an unspoken pact to get drunk and set about our task with gusto. A third bottle appeared. When that neared empty, I was largely talking gibberish.

"See," I said. "That's the trouble with straight people."

"What?"

"Every time they fuck, they have a baby."

"That's not true."

4

"Item one; my parents had two children. They only fucked twice."

"You don't know that."

"Do too. Item two; wherever your father went, he seems to have had babies."

"Bit of an exaggeration."

"But gay people don't. We can fuck all the time. No babies."

"You're pissed," Sally said.

"Am not."

"Yes, you are. You want to be careful. Someone might take advantage of you."

She had a wicked look on her face.

"Ooh, yes please."

She put her glass down and took mine from me. I was a bit hazy about what followed. But I remember being naked on my bed, on all fours, and Sally fucking me with a strap-on. By now my balance wasn't great, and I remember falling over a few times. Lots of laughter and giggles, but then that wonderful feeling as she brought me to orgasm, and the gentle aftermath. Lying in each other's arms; cocooned in each other's warmth.

The bliss was broken when I had to rush to the bathroom. I reached it just in time to throw up; violently. I panicked as I saw the colour, but relaxed when I remembered how much red wine I'd drunk. Sally came into the bathroom and checked I was okay. She handed me some tissues and got me a glass of water. Five minutes later, I felt a lot better, cleaned my teeth and used some mouthwash to get rid of the taste. We went back into the bedroom.

"Your fault," I said.

"Me?"

"Yes, if you hadn't fucked me so hard, it wouldn't have upset my tummy."

"Sorry, won't do it again."

"Oh, yes you will. But perhaps I won't drink so much next time."

We lay back on the bed, cuddled in each other's arms and fell asleep. When I woke, I looked at the clock. One thirty. We hadn't moved. Sally was lying on her back; I was lying half over her. I let my hand trace lightly over her skin, enjoying the softness and warmth. My fingers running up and down her body. I decided to see how much I could do without waking her.

I let my tongue rest on her nipple and started to lick it; she moved slightly. I put my lips around it. My other hand was between her legs stroking her thighs, moving closer and closer to her sex. Her legs opened automatically, and I let my fingers trail over her pussy. A little moan made me smile, and I began to run my fingers around her lips. Gradually pressing firmer.

The moaning increased, and I ran a finger over her clit. Her body flinched, but she was still asleep. I circled her hood and her hips rose slightly as she came to meet my touch. Sliding a couple of fingers into her, I used my thumb to gently rub her clit. She was moaning now, and her whole body was responding.

I watched her as she stretched and twisted; all controlled by my touch. It was incredibly erotic. I saw her hand come off the bed and slip between her legs. I wondered what she was dreaming about. I'd been in this position many times; waking from a delicious dream to find myself near orgasm, with my hand calling the shots. She was near too.

When her hand touched mine, already fucking her, her eyes opened, and she gave a little start. Coming to quickly, and seeing me, she relaxed and closed her eyes again. Her body turned and she put her arm around me, pulling me to her. My fingers continued their work, and a couple of minutes later, she came in a flurry of moans and whimpers. And promptly fell asleep again.

The next morning, we were both a little delicate. It didn't stop us making love again, but we were gentle. It was just as good. We eventually got up and made some breakfast.

"Has it been bad, thinking about your dad?" she asked.

"No; I just feel nothing. I'm worried I haven't had any … well, dreadful cliché I know, but any closure."

"Not going to his funeral, you mean?"

"Yea."

"Regret not going?"

"No. But perhaps I should have done something to mark it."

We went quiet for a moment.

"Was he buried or cremated?" Sally asked.

"Buried. Their church doesn't accept cremation."

"Do you know where?"

"Longton Cemetery."

"Perhaps you could visit his grave."

My heart missed a beat. I hadn't got as far as thinking about that.

"What for?"

She looked at me; I knew she'd been through so much with her father. The situations weren't the same, but if anyone understood my feelings, it would be Sally.

"To say goodbye," she said.

It had a certain logic to it. I hadn't seen him when he'd been ill; nor had I gone to his funeral. Seeing his grave might give some sense of finality, but I didn't think I could do it. Sally sensed my doubts.

"Let's go this morning," she said.

She said it lightly as if she was asking me to go to the park. She carried on eating a croissant. Watching me. It was one of those moments where friendship meant so much.

We said nothing as Sally drove. When we got there, she came around to my side of the car and opened the door. She put her arm in mine, and we walked under the arch into the cemetery. It was large, but a quick scan showed us where the recent burials were. When we got there, I saw three fresh graves. Sally unhooked her arm and went over to them.

She checked the name on the first and moved on to the second. She turned to me and held out her hand. I felt rooted to the spot but forced myself to move and take it.

"He's here, Luce. Take your time. I'll be over on the bench."

I mumbled something incomprehensible. She moved away and left me facing my father's grave.

I don't know how long I stood there. My brain wasn't ready to make any sense of my emotions. They swirled around, random thoughts and fragments of memory from long ago. The lack of love; the coldness. The frustration of my teenage years when I wasn't allowed to do what my friends were doing. The final showdown.

When I was ready, I looked around and saw Sally waiting on a bench about twenty yards away. She stood up as I approached. Her arms opened, and I fell into them. We held each other tight and I wept. I let myself go; my whole body shaking as tears streamed down my face. Sally didn't say a word. Again, time seemed to stand still.

Eventually, the crying stopped. I pulled away, and she handed me some tissues. God knows where from. I wiped my face, and she put her arm around my shoulder and led me back to the car. Nothing was said until we got home, and she shut the door.

"Want a drink?" she asked.

"Just a coffee. Thanks."

I sat down, and she brought two mugs in. We sat there holding them.

"You need to go," I said.

"Nonsense. I've told Marcus I'll be late back."

I smiled at her.

"Thanks, Sal."

Eventually, I told her to go home. I had to deal with this. And that meant being alone with it.

***

"Did it help?" Jenny asked.

"Yes. It was the right thing to do. If I didn't see him or go to the funeral, at least I saw where he was. Was able to … pay my respects."

"How did you feel?"

"Relief."

"Relief you'd done it?"

"Relief he was dead. Sounds awful, doesn't it?"

"I'm not here to judge, Lucy."

"I stood at his grave and thought of all the things he'd said to me when I told them I was gay. Things a child should never hear from a parent. He died for me that day, but it took me years to realise it."

"Are you glad you went?"

"It ends a chapter."

"Would you have gone if your friend hadn't suggested it?"

"I hadn't even thought of it."

"That's what friends are for."

"She's a diamond."

"She knew some of the story?"

"Most of it. We've been friends for over fifteen years." I knew I had to tell her. "She's a bit more than a friend."

"A partner?"

"Well, it's complicated, Jenny."

"Okay. You don't need to tell me."

"I know. But I think I should. At least some of it. Because it could be something you need to know."

"If you want."

"She is my lover, but only part-time. She's in a permanent relationship."

"These things happen; it's quite common."

"It's more complicated than that. There's nothing illicit about it. Her partner knows and is happy with the situation. I meet up with them both regularly, and he's a friend as well."

Jenny tilted her head slightly and smiled.

"I must admit, that's slightly less common."

"The other thing is, she has been a client of yours. We thought it only fair to tell you. We assume you couldn't work with both of us."

"Is she seeing me at the moment?"

"No. She finished a while ago. But she may need to come back."

"Well, it's not a problem for now. But you're right. I probably couldn't help you both at the same time. Thank you for telling me, but let's face that if it happens."

Chapter 2 – Marcus

"The Rocky Horror Show's at the Theatre in April," I said. "Want to go?"

"Ooh, yes," Sally replied. "Are we going to dress up?"

I'd already pondered the question. I loved Rocky Horror and quite fancied dressing up. But did I have the nerve? I suspected Sally did. I'd seen that little exhibitionist streak at the play party. She had more confidence now. I was less confident about my physique.

"Possibly," I said. "Not sure who I'd go as."

"I've got one or two ideas. Shall I see if Lucy wants to join us?"

"If she'd be interested."

"I reckon she might. I'm meeting her for lunch tomorrow, I'll ask. What about Mary?"

"Would she go?"

"I have a suspicion Mary's more of a dark horse than I realised. Shall I see?"

"Yea. I'll leave booking until we know."

"Are you still away Thursday night?"

"Yes."

"Do you want me to change Friday?"

"No, it'll be fine."

"Sure?"

Friday night was one of Sal's nights at Lucy's.

"Positive."

"I'll make it up to you on Saturday."

"Is that a promise?"

She came over and pushed me back against the table. Flinging her arms around my neck, she went to kiss me, pulling her head away as I went to meet her lips.

"Mmm. It's a promise. Perhaps I'll be naughty."

"Well, it does come so easily."

She laughed and kissed me this time.

"And isn't it wonderful?"

***

I was away Thursday night because I'd got myself an agent. Well, possibly. He'd got in touch to say he had seen some of my work in a magazine. He then looked at a couple of the books I'd self-published. He liked them and wanted to meet me. I checked and he seemed to be well known and trusted, so I agreed.

I didn't know if anything would come of it. I'd been writing for years. Short stories, short books, and novels. The shorter stuff tended to sell well to magazines and a few websites and the longer stuff I'd published myself. It had given me an income, along with writing I'd done for a few blogs.

But the blog posts were tedious and bored me. After Sally and I got together and I accepted she was going to foot most of the bills, she urged me to stop doing it and get on with the creative stuff.

I knew I wasn't a great author. But I enjoyed it; it gave me pleasure and a sense of achievement. My imagination had always been fertile, and I never had problems coming up with ideas; quite the reverse. They appeared all the time. Sometimes I wished they would stop so I could do some writing.

I drove to London on Thursday morning. I was taking my time. The meeting was in the afternoon and I was expecting it to last a while. He'd also invited me to dinner afterwards. It seemed rude to refuse, so I had decided to stay the night rather than go home. When I arrived, I spent a couple of hours doing a few bits of shopping and grabbed lunch.

I liked Peter as soon as I met him. Jovial, positive, and friendly. I'd spoken to him on the phone a couple of times, but I was old school. You could only see the real person when you came face to face. He led me into his office and talked about my work.

He had been honest; he'd read my books all right. Telling me things he liked and things I could improve. I welcomed his insight. I'd never been shy of criticism. I thrived on it. He made some interesting points; one or two were things I had suspected myself. He asked me lots of questions; I'd expected this. This was an interview, where we were interviewing each other. If this was going to be successful, it had to work both ways. He briefly went through what he could do, and for how much. I'd done my research, and it was all standard.

The meeting didn't last as long as I had expected. By the end, we both thought we could work together. He promised to have a contract drawn up and sent to me. Meanwhile, his dinner invitation took on further meaning when he said he'd also invited a commissioning editor from a well-known publisher, who he happened to have sent my books to. Suddenly, a casual dinner became another interview.

I met Peter at the restaurant, and we were immediately shown to a table. It was achingly trendy, trying a bit too hard. Probably opened six months ago and would be gone in another six months. I looked around and noticed most of the tables were occupied by two people. But I guessed most were business meetings rather than couples. We ordered a drink and looked at the menu. Shortly afterwards, a woman appeared at the foyer and looked around.

"Ah, there's Eva."

He waved and she acknowledged him and strode towards us. A tall woman with long straight hair and wearing what looked like a man's suit. She wore it well.

"Eva, Marcus Foxton. Marcus, Eva Cassini."

We got the introductions out of the way and a waiter took our order. It was clear both Peter and Eva were regulars. We made small talk for a while, all trivial stuff. I was conscious of her inspecting me. When the food arrived, we started, and the talk turned to books.

"How long have you been writing, Marcus?" Eva asked.

"Oh, years. I started when I had to give up my career due to illness."

"Always wanted to?"

"No, not really. Always been an avid reader, but never considered writing. When I had time on my hands, I thought I'd give it a try."

She asked me about my favourite writers, where my ideas came from, how long it took me to write. It took me a bit by surprise; I had thought she'd either like my books or not. But I guessed if they were interested, they'd want to know what they could expect of me.

"How much have you written?"

"Well, I've self-published seven novels, and about a dozen shorter pieces. I also do short stories which get published in various places. Magazines, websites, that sort of thing. I used to write for a few blogs, but I got fed up with that."

"But you've never had anything published?"

"Not by an old school publisher, no."

She frowned slightly but quickly recovered. I knew what publishers thought of those of us who were self-published.

"I've read the two novels Peter forwarded to me. I quite enjoyed them. They could have done with a professional editor, but they're interesting."

I gritted my teeth.

"Thank you."

"Do you have any unpublished material?"

"Yes. I've currently got two novels and three novellas."

"Well, we wouldn't be interested in novellas. What are the novels about?"

I outlined the plots, and she listened quietly.

"Are they in a readable state?"

"Oh, yes."

"Send them to me. I'll look at them. Peter can give you my e-mail address."

"Okay. I will."

"If we took anything on, I presume you'd be happy to do all the promotional stuff?"

"No, I wouldn't."

They both stopped eating and looked at me.

"Sorry?" Peter said.

"I won't do promotional stuff. Perhaps the odd signing. But nothing else."

They looked at each other.

"It's crucial, Marcus," Eva said. "It's the way we'll all make money from your books."

13

"I don't need the money."

They looked at me as if I were mad, although Peter had a faint smile on his face.

"Then why do you write?" Eva asked.

I leaned back in my chair.

"Well, Eva. If you don't understand that, I'd suggest you're in the wrong job."

Peter stifled a laugh with a cough. Eva stared at me.

"But no book sells in any numbers without promotion," she said. "That's what we do."

"But that doesn't need the author."

"Of course it does."

"You sell books by dead authors, don't you?"

"Yes."

"I don't imagine they do many photo opportunities."

Peter laughed openly this time.

"All right," he said. "We have a minor disagreement here."

"No, Peter," I replied. "It's not minor. I have some health problems and I like my privacy. If the cost of selling more books is going to affect either of those, we've all had a wasted evening."

Eva sat still, looking at me. Then broke into a smile.

"Okay, Marcus. Let me see those two novels. If I like them, we can talk further. Deal?"

"Deal."

***

"You don't think anything will come of it?" Sally asked.

She'd arrived home at lunchtime and we were eating in the dining room.

"Peter may sign me, but I don't think Eva's going to want to work with me."

"You're too obstinate."

She smiled as she said it.

"I'm not traipsing around the country promoting myself. You know that's not me."

"I do, darling."

14

"After all, publishers aren't the author's friend. Yes, they help a lot; editing, cover design and so on. Then the marketing; that's the key. But they take most of the money for doing it. They're not interested in the writing; what they want is a saleable product."

"Harsh, but true."

"We'll see what happens. How's Lucy?"

"Not too bad. She's seeing Jenny again, so I'm not prying. You know how it was when I was working stuff through."

"Mmm. Best leave it alone."

"Exactly. Anyway, she wants to come to Rocky Horror."

"Good."

"So does Mary, she jumped at the chance."

"Really?"

"Yea. Apparently, she went to a couple of showings of the film years ago. All dressed up."

"I told her she should publish her memoirs."

"But neither of them is keen to dress up. Lucy might, but Mary probably won't."

"It's not compulsory."

"No. Are we?"

"Haven't made up my mind yet."

I'd walked into her trap.

"Dare you," she said, and I laughed. "And if I remember rightly," she continued, "you never refuse a dare from a lady."

I looked around the room.

"Did a lady come in?"

She whacked my arm.

"I'll think about it," I said. "Still don't know who I'd go as."

"Frank'n'furter."

"Seriously? I think I'm more Riff Raff."

"I'll find the right things for you to wear."

"I'd look more like Lily Savage."

"No, you wouldn't. I'll get something and you can try it. Deal?"

"Deal," I conceded. "Oh, there are a couple of packages for you in the hallway."

"Ooh, I'll look at those in a minute."

There was a wicked glint in her eye. We finished lunch and caught up with our news. She went into the hall and after a few seconds, called to me.

"I'm taking these down. Won't be long."

I cleared the lunch things and brushed the table.

"Darling …" she called from downstairs.

"Yes?"

"Can I borrow you?"

When I arrived in the bedroom, I found her naked and moved towards her.

"No, forget that for a moment," she said. "Clothes off, please."

There were two boxes on the bed, surrounded by several packages of different sizes. Wondering what was going on, I did as I was told.

"Remember we said you didn't have anything special to dress up in? After the play party?"

"Yes …"

I had a terrible feeling I knew what was coming.

"I've bought a few things to put that right. I want you to try them on for me. And don't worry, I've bought one or two things for me. I'll try them on for you."

"Ah. Now you're talking."

She sat on the bed and picked up the first package. Undoing it, she handed me a pair of wet-look boxers. The material was soft in my hand, and I stepped into them, pulling them up. They took some getting on; they were skin-tight. When I finally got them in place, I looked in the mirror.

I'd always been a bit conscious of my physique. I wasn't fat, but I wasn't exactly toned. But they looked all right; they certainly felt good. Tight and a little constricting, with a pouch in the front which had a zip on either side. Handy.

"Well?" I asked.

"I think I'm going to enjoy you dressing up. I like those. Turn around."

I did a twirl.

"Mmm. Those are a definite hit. Now try these."

I took the boxers off; well, tried. It was even more difficult getting them off than it had been to get them on. Sal got a fit of the giggles as I tried to wriggle out of them.

"Good job they've got easy access."

When I managed to get them loose, she handed me another pair. Similar in shape, but made entirely of a transparent mesh, apart from solid seams at the waist and on the thighs. They were also tight and slightly shaped, so they held me in place.

"They're good too, darling," she said. "Do they feel good?"

"Yes. They feel different; it's like I'm putting on something special."

"Now you know why I like dressing up for you. Get them off; still a couple of things to try."

After I'd removed them, she handed me a pair of trousers. Wet-look again, with studs all the way along the side seams. They proved difficult to put on. I had to sit on the bed, and roll them up, feeding them slowly up my legs, and finally pulling them over my bum. I stood and adjusted them as best as I could and looked in the mirror. They did look quite good. They were clinging, but not too tight.

"Well?" I asked Sally.

"Mmm. They're … masterful. Put this on too."

She handed me a top. Like a t-shirt in shape, but a similar material to the trousers, only lighter. With mesh panels at the sides. I pulled it on; again, tight, but not restricting. It matched the trousers well. I looked in the mirror, and Sal came up behind me.

"You look good. Put that on and you can do whatever you like."

She put her hand on my bum and squeezed it.

"It feels good too."

I went to kiss her.

"No. I've got a couple of things to try on."

She went back to the bed and picked up another package. A bodystocking. She spent some time getting into it. It was stunning; a delicate mesh that was transparent, but made you look closely to see detail. She walked to the mirror.

"Well?"

I stood behind her, and put my arms around her tummy, pulling her towards me.

"You look fabulous. But it's a bit frustrating, isn't it?"

Watching me, she put her hands between her legs. I heard the unmistakable sound of Velcro.

"Hey presto. Instant access."

"I might have guessed."

"Well, I didn't want you to rip it off the first time I wore it."

She slipped it off and opened the last package. Something made of black latex. A dress. It looked far too small, but I guessed that was the point.

"Now," she said. "I've never worn latex before. I gather there's a knack to getting it on and off. You'll have to bear with me."

She disappeared into the bathroom with the dress and came back a couple of minutes later having washed it. Spraying her body and the inside of the dress with a lubricant, she slipped it over her head and was able to pull and stretch it over her body quite easily. She made a few final adjustments and smoothed it out.

"Do I take it from the grin on your face it meets with your approval?" she asked.

It certainly did. It was skin-tight, without a wrinkle or a crease, and touched everywhere. Everywhere it existed that is, because it was short, very short. Hardly covering her bum. It was also fairly transparent. Being black, it wasn't immediately obvious. But look closely, and everything was visible. She went to the mirror.

"I didn't think it would be this see-through," she said. "I don't think I'll be wearing it anywhere but right here."

"Sounds good to me."

"You like it?"

"Mmm. Do you?"

She wriggled her body.

"Yea. I don't think I've ever worn anything this tight."

I went up behind her and ran my hands over her; she watched me.

"So, my choices are all hits?"

"Yup. Looks like it."

"Right. How about I choose what you're going to wear for the rest of the day, and you choose for me?"

"Okay. You can stay exactly as you are."

"I thought you might say that."

She looked at me, thinking.

"As we're at home, I want you in the wet-look boxers. You can keep the top on as well."

"Okay, but I'm not sure how long I'm going to be able to control myself with you in that."

Turning around, she put her arms around me and kissed me.

18

"Who says I'm going to be able to control *myself*? Remember I said I might be naughty tonight?"

"Yes."

"I might not be able to wait until tonight."

She kissed me again and started to clear up the packaging, while I peeled the trousers off and put the boxers back on. I followed her up the stairs; quite deliberately. She exaggerated every movement on every step; quite deliberately. It was going to require willpower to wait until tonight.

Chapter 3 – Sally

Marcus had liked the latex dress Penny wore at the play party. She had looked fabulous. I had loved it too. Now wearing one around the flat I could see the attraction. It clung to me; always reminding me I had it on. But it was comfortable too, and easy to wear. I'd expected to keep having to pull it down or adjust it. But it sat in place perfectly.

Whenever I looked at him, he was watching me; it seemed to be working for him as well. And I loved what he was wearing. He'd never dressed up before. I never figured out whether it didn't do anything for him, or if he felt he didn't have the body for it. But seeing him in the tight top and boxers was doing it for me. And I knew exactly what I wanted to do; or rather, him do to me.

I took every opportunity to walk in front of him or bend to pick something up. One of the advantages of him dressing up was he couldn't hide his interest. Those boxers filled out nicely as I teased him. Occasionally, I let him stroke my dress or kiss my neck. But always pulled away before he got any further.

We loved doing this. It depended on us both following the unwritten rules. We could easily have fallen on one another and taken what we wanted. But we both had patience; he'd had it since we'd met, and I'd learned the benefits from him. So, I teased, and he let me.

We both knew at some point I'd push it too far, and he'd take control. I'd be at his mercy; right where I wanted to be. He'd be free to do whatever he wanted. What we both wanted. It led to some of the most mind-blowing experiences I'd ever had.

I didn't tease all the time; that would have been too easy. He may be patient, but he had his breaking point. I did too. I was already nicely warm; imagining what he might have in mind for me. That was one of the appealing things. Our relationship was never one way.

Yes, I was the one who loved pain, but we did switch. I often took control, but that didn't involve much pain. When I was in charge, I used him; used him to satisfy me. It worked for both of us. But when he took over, it was better. He was better at it, for a start. He could melt me with a word, an expression, a touch. Never loud, rarely rough; always erotic. But in a way, I was in control. He read me; could read me like a book. It was frightening sometimes. He seemed to know my mood; what I wanted, what I needed. Slow and gentle; firm and forceful; hard and relentless. He was rarely wrong.

He didn't always give me what I wanted, but he usually played to my needs. It often matched his own. Today wasn't a slow and gentle day. He'd know. And when he was ready, I'd get it.

We cooked dinner together, occasionally running a hand over each other. A touch, a kiss, a look. Dinner itself was a break. Hard play on a full stomach was best avoided. Tended to make you feel sick. We called a truce for an hour; again unspoken.

"I must admit," he said. "When you called me, I thought you'd got some costumes for Rocky Horror."

"No. I've been looking at that. Most of the costumes I've seen have been cheap and tacky."

"Well, I don't think you have to be too literal. "

"How do you mean?"

"I reckon it's better to get into the spirit rather than slavishly copy the original."

"I guess so. Perhaps we go down that path. I still want you in a basque and stockings, though."

"It's the heels that scare me," he said.

"We'll get them well before the day and you can wear them around the house."

"Thanks," he said, rolling his eyes. "That's just dandy."

I was determined he was going to get dressed up; I fancied seeing him in the full get-up. I wondered if it would be a turn on. I'd seen the film often enough. Tim Curry was so hot, but he had the confidence of an actor.

21

We allowed dinner to go down and relaxed, sitting on the sofa, me leaning into him with his arm around me. Comfortable and warm. But I soon needed to tease again. I got onto my knees, kissed him, and laid flat across his lap. My bum in front of him; barely concealed by my dress and clearly visible through the latex. He placed his hand on one cheek.

"No touching," I said.

"You're pushing your luck."

"Mmm. I wonder how far I can go?"

I wiggled my hips. I could feel his cock pressing into me. As I lay there, I knew I wasn't going to want to tease for long. I wanted to get going. The afternoon had had its effect, and I needed to trigger his response. I got up and sat on his lap; his cock pressing into my bum. I put my arms around him and kissed his neck, before resting my head on his shoulder.

"I need a pee," I said. "I'm disappointed, darling."

"Why's that?"

"You didn't stroke my bum."

"You told me not to."

"Since when did you do what I tell you? Wimping out, now?"

I stuck my tongue in his ear and jumped off his lap to go to the loo. When I came back, he was standing in the centre of the room, his arms folded. My heart skipped a beat; it had started. He beckoned me with one finger. I walked towards him and stopped a pace in front of him. Slowly, he walked around me, stopping behind me. I felt him standing close to me; a hand landed on my hip. His other hand gathered my hair, and moved it back, away from my ear. Then he spoke; softly.

"Go to the playroom. Remove your dress. I'm going to enjoy punishing you. One implement tonight; you may choose it. But remember; you're going to feel its touch for a long time. So, choose wisely. Understand?"

I understood. And decided to take one more step.

"Yes, sir."

"Oh, polite now. It won't save you."

"No, sir."

"Go."

I walked to the door and headed downstairs. I normally only called him 'sir' when I submitted; when I wore my collar. But I occasionally did it at other times; it added to the mood. And one implement? I knew what that was going to be.

A new one; a whip. After the play party, we'd decided to move up a notch. We'd bought one recommended for beginners. A short grip followed by a leather braid about eighteen inches long ending in three thin leather strips. We'd experimented a few times; lightly. Getting a feel for it. It was awesome. It produced a nice sound, and the effect was stinging rather than pain, like our favourite light cane.

So far, he'd not used it with any real force. I suspected tonight might be different; I hoped it would. I went through the bedroom, shed my dress, and headed to the playroom. Taking the whip from its hook, I knelt on the rug in the centre of the room and laid the coiled whip on the floor. And waited.

And waited. He would come when it suited him. He'd been known to make me wait half an hour, to build the anticipation. I had nothing to do but think about what was to come. All sorts of possibilities went through my mind.

Today it was imagining him using the whip on me in earnest. Imagining the sensations of those leather strips snapping against my skin. I knew they would sting. But I loved the feel of the whippy cane; it could bring me close to orgasm. How would this compare?

Perhaps it would actually make me come. I didn't understand how it worked. How could pain lead to a climax? I'd searched some BDSM sites, and I wasn't alone. Many people, male and female, reported coming from pain alone. But there were no explanations as to how. Perhaps I was thinking too hard. If it happened, just let it. Don't try to explain; just enjoy it.

I was brought abruptly back to the present as the door opened and Marcus walked in. He looked at me and closed the door behind him. I watched him as he turned the lights down a notch or two and put some music on. Philip Glass; it was perfect for what was to come. Gentle and slow, with a very repetitive rhythm. Ideal to measure the strokes.

He came to stand in front of me. The boxers and tee he was wearing were definitely good for me. I'd have to get him some other things. He loved me dressing up, why shouldn't I enjoy him doing the same?

But I was naked now. He bent over and put his finger under my chin. As my head lifted, he kissed me.

"The whip?"

His voice was soft; he rarely raised his voice when we were playing.

"Yes, sir."

"Up."

I rose to my feet.

"Pick it up."

I bent and lifted the whip off the floor and handed it to him. He took it and holding the handle, let it fall free.

"Good choice."

He hung it around his neck and led me a few feet to where we had a bar suspended from the ceiling on a winch. The bar had cuffs swinging from it.

"Hold it."

I raised my hands and closed my fingers around the bar. He snapped the cuffs onto my wrists and raised the bar until my body was gently stretched, my feet just touching the floor. He stepped away, and behind my back, cracked the whip a few times through the air. I heard the swish, followed by a small crack as the end rushed to catch up. I sensed him close behind me.

"Now, let's both get warmed up, shall we?"

He moved away again, and I felt the whip's touch for the first time. And it was only a touch. He was gently swinging the whip, letting it wrap harmlessly around my body. Starting across my chest and slowly moving all the way to my ankles. The swinging stopped and I waited for the first real stroke.

He always won this little game. I couldn't see him. I knew it would come; my body tensed in anticipation. But it could only hold still for so long. I tried; he waited. Only when I had to relax would he strike. I'd never found a way to counter it. Tonight proved no exception. I had to let out a breath and my body relaxed slightly. And the first stroke came.

The body of the whip wrapped around my side and I let out a sharp hiss as the ends came across my breasts. Only a gentle sting, but enough for my senses to awaken. They would go into overdrive before this was finished, feeling every touch of the leather. Amplifying it as it raced to my brain. That was the rush.

He continued at the same intensity. Swinging the whip around me; moving as he did so. The strips landing in a different place each time. My breasts, my tummy, my back. One stroke caught a nipple and I hissed. He stopped and cupped my breast, stroking the nipple.

24

"Okay?"

"Yes, sir."

He resumed his work. Except it wasn't work. I could see the glint in his eye. It was pure pleasure. I gave myself to him for this; he took my gift.

"Open your legs."

I did as I was told; as far as I could. The bar meant I couldn't open them far and keep my footing. But it was enough for the whip end to occasionally land between them and strike the insides of my thighs. I realised he'd increased the force a little. The sting was stronger now; particularly when it hit higher up the thigh. But he was precise. It never seemed to be in the same place twice.

Each strike was a mix of sensations. The sound of the leather hitting my body. Not a crack; he wasn't using much force. Just leather on skin. Followed a moment later by a flash of pain; gone almost before I felt it. Then the heat. It made me wince; made me shiver. Made me arch my body to try and meet the next stroke.

They were coming faster now. In time to the monotony of the music. I cleared my mind, concentrating on two things. The music, and the impact of the whip. He was timing it to perfection. I don't know how long this lasted, but I closed my eyes and lost myself in sound and touch. He'd noticed my state and went with it. The music beating time to his strokes. Still wandering all over me, still increasing in intensity. So slowly, I hardly noticed.

Until the track stopped and the next track began on a different tempo. I opened my eyes, and my body suddenly awoke; released from my torpor. I felt little points of heat all over my body. I'd never experienced anything quite like it. It didn't hurt, but it was almost overwhelming; my body unsure what to make of the sensations.

Marcus appeared in front of me. He kissed me.

"Okay?"

I took a long breath in and slowly released it, letting my body relax.

"Oh, yes; thank you."

He raised an eyebrow.

"Sir," I added with a giggle.

He walked over to the curtain and pulled it back, revealing the mirror. I gasped as I saw my body, suspended from the bar. I was covered in little red marks, mostly short lines. Breasts, tummy, thighs. I was amazed. It looked far worse than it felt. I felt wonderful; a warmth I couldn't describe. It stung; it stung all over. Like I'd got out of a hot bath. No pain; just a burning. A delicious burning.

As I looked at myself, I realised how turned on I was. But it was a deep need, not a frantic urge. I looked at Marcus, standing there with a smile on his face. We looked into each other's eyes. Nothing was said. It wasn't needed. Sometimes love works best in silence.

He came and stood by me; gave me a kiss. And slowly ran his fingers over my belly and between my legs. I gasped as they ran over my clit, slid down, and gently opened my pussy. It was then I realised how aroused I was. His touch had made me squirm, and I pushed forward to meet his hand.

It never worked. He chuckled and pulled away slightly. Looking into my eyes, he brought his hand up between us. His four fingers shiny with moisture. He put two in his mouth and sucked them. Then offered me two; I greedily licked them clean.

"Now," he said quietly. "Let's have a look at you."

I watched in the mirror as he walked slowly around me. Running his hands over my body, gently examining the marks he'd made.

"It's quite impressive," he said, standing behind me. "But there's one area still untouched."

He let his hand slide to my bum. I had noticed; he hadn't touched it with the whip at all.

"Strange that, isn't it?" he asked. I met his eyes in the mirror.

"Did you miss, sir?"

He laughed at my cheek.

"No, Sally. I've saved the best 'til last."

He lowered the bar a little; I knew why.

"Now; you hang on the bar and stick this gorgeous bum out."

"Yes, sir."

"And we'll see what this little whip can really do."

I let the bar take the weight of my upper body as I moved my feet back so I could push my bottom out. I looked in the mirror; I couldn't see him anymore, he was out of view. He enjoyed that; I was left feeling vulnerable again. Not knowing where the first strike was coming from until it was too late to prepare for it.

As I was thinking this, it came. Across my bum. I gasped. Before I'd caught my breath, another stroke, and another. They were as hard as any he'd landed on my body. Several followed; firm and quick. My body squirming under the onslaught. He stopped.

"Okay, Sally?"

"Yes, sir."

He appeared in the mirror again, standing behind me. His hand stroked my bum, his fingers creeping between my legs, and I groaned as he slid two into me, another carrying on to reach my clit. I pushed back, needing the probing, the rubbing. Needing to come.

"Not yet," he said.

I let my body slump; frustrated. He watched me in the mirror.

"You're going to earn it."

"How, sir?"

"We're going to see how much of this little whip you can take." I wanted to find out as well. "But you must promise to stop me when you need to."

"You know I will, sir."

"Bum out."

I stuck it out as far as I could. And waited. Again.

But not for long. I gasped as the whip struck my bum harder than any of the previous strokes. My body was still tense from that first stroke when the second landed. Harder than the first. I gave a little cry. No third stroke followed. I relaxed; then it came. He wasn't sticking to a rhythm this time. The strokes came intermittently; sometimes I was ready for them; sometimes I wasn't.

There was more pain than the earlier ones, but it was the tingling that slowly built. He was putting real force behind it now. The leather producing a searing spasm every time it bit my skin. My breathing was ragged; a sharp gasp coming with each stroke.

The gasps became little cries. They got louder. I recognised a familiar feeling; I was near orgasm. Not one part of me wanted it to stop. My brain was becoming overloaded; I could hardly feel the pain anymore. My hands left the bar; I was being held up by the wrist cuffs. He stopped.

"GO ON …!" It came out as a scream.

He resumed the thrashing. More rhythmic; regular strokes. Hard; biting. My body was tensing, the stinging was reaching every part of my body; my bum was burning. I cried out at every stroke. Then shrieked as my orgasm ripped through me. My body jumping; my feet doing little dances on the floor. I felt faint, hardly able to focus on the mirror in front of me. But that passed almost as quickly as it came.

I was panting now, taking great gulps of air to clear the fuzz in my head. I was aware of being lowered. When my knees touched the floor, Marcus came and undid the wrist cuffs, and knelt beside me. I flopped onto him, his arms coming around me.

"Okay?" he whispered.

"Yes. Oh, yes."

I don't know how long we sat like that; I wasn't really there. I was on a high and it took me a while to come down. He held me and stroked my hair, occasionally kissing my forehead. I held him tight. I cried a little. Releasing the remaining tension; we were used to that now. And my brain began to make sense of all the sensations it was getting; my body began to burn. Especially my bum. Finally, I lifted my head from his shoulder and kissed him. Hard and with real passion.

"God, I love you," I said.

"I know. Are you okay?"

"I'm beginning to feel all these marks. Towards the end, I wasn't feeling the impact at all."

"You seemed in a bit of a trance."

"Mmm. It was a bit like my special place."

"Was it too much?"

"No. I'd do that again tomorrow."

"Perhaps we'd better let you recover first."

"Okay. The day after. What was it like for you?" I knew he'd have a touch of doubt, and before he answered, I jumped in again. "And be honest."

"It was fabulous. Horny as fuck."

"Sorry, we didn't get that far, did we? I feel selfish now."

"Don't. Watching that was amazing. Did your orgasm feel the same?"

"No. It wasn't centred anywhere. It didn't come from between my legs. It was more in my brain. Were you trying to make that happen?"

"No, I had further plans for you."

"Sorry."

"Sally, don't keep apologising. These things have a life of their own."

"What were you going to do?"

"I'll save it for another time."

"Give me a little time to recover, and we'll carry on."

"We'll see."

"All right; save it. But after what we've done here, I'm sure as hell giving you a special thank you. Going to turn that down?"

"Probably not."

"Good. Now let me have a look at my bum."

We went through to the bedroom; the marks over most of my body had already dulled slightly. My bum, though, was covered in red marks. Vivid red. It still stung, but the memory was so good, it didn't matter. Marcus checked me carefully for any nicks, but there weren't any. I let him; I knew he always had that slight twinge of guilt after impact play.

He got me on the bed and started to gently rub moisturiser into the marks. As there were so many, this took some time. He took off his top and boxers partway through. By the time he'd finished, the attention he'd played to my body, watching his achingly hard cock and the memories of our earlier experience had me worked up again.

I got him to lie down and delivered my promised reward. I rode him until I'd had a couple of more conventional orgasms, then spent twenty minutes giving him one of my special oral experiences. His eventual climax was intense. All in all, it had been a rather special day.

Chapter 4 – Lucy

"How's your mum?" Sally asked.

"Oh, wonderful. She switches from prostrate with grief to just being miserable."

"God," Marcus said. "That sounds like my dear late mother."

"It's so wearing. I mean, I understand she's lost her husband. But she knows full well his death doesn't mean much to me. Why's she dragging me into it?"

"Perhaps she does that with anyone who'll listen at the moment," Sal said.

"Yea, I guess you're right. But it's getting me down and I'm not having that."

"You're still meeting her?"

"Yes. I need to work this through. If we can get some peaceful understanding, I'll accept that. But we'll see."

I was having dinner with Sal and Marcus. One of the points of contentment in my life. I always looked forward to it.

"Have you decided what to do about *your* father yet, Sal?" I asked.

"Not really. It's not gnawing away at me. There's no urgency, so it won't matter if I leave it a while. I'd love to find out more, but I'm wondering if it might be better to drop it."

"Yea?"

"Well, even if I find out he did have another family, what am I going to do? Knock on the door and say 'hello, I'm your father's daughter with another wife'?"

"It won't achieve anything, will it?"

"No. Although Marcus did come up with a good point."

"What was that?"

"Well," he replied. "What happened when Tony Crowther was killed? His family, and you, Lucy, sorted everything out. Dealt with the estate, arranged the funeral, finalised everything. But if he had another family, they wouldn't have known about any of that. He would have just disappeared, never to be seen again."

"They'd have been in limbo."

"Possibly still are."

"You think Sal should pursue it?"

"I'm not saying that. It's not Sal's job to sort out her father's chaotic life or give closure to this other hypothetical family. But it's an added complication."

"I see what you mean. Besides, Sal; you don't want it to affect you."

"I know, Luce. We're very aware of that. Life's too good."

After dinner, we settled for the evening. Sal and I generally drank too much on these occasions. Marcus was always amused, though I think he benefitted from Sal's lost inhibitions when they got to bed.

"Are you going to dress up for Rocky Horror?" Sal asked me.

"I don't think I'd dare. I haven't got anything suitable, anyway."

"That's no excuse. You can borrow something of mine."

"Are you two dressing up?" I asked.

"Yup. Wait until you see Marcus."

Sally grinned at him and he rolled his eyes.

"What are you wearing?" I asked Sal.

"Come on, I'll show you. We can look for something for you as well."

We went downstairs and she showed me what she intended to wear.

"You're going out in that?" I said. "It's very revealing."

"Yes, but lots of the audience will be in similar things. What do you fancy wearing?"

"God, Sal. I'm not used to anything like this even under clothes; let alone without any."

"Okay, where can we start?"

She took out a load of things to show me, and we laid them on the bed. Some I definitely wouldn't wear; others? Well, I might after a drink or two.

31

In the end, I tried a few things on. Some didn't fit well, as I was bigger than Sal, and tended to overflow. Not a good look. But a couple of things fitted well, and I had to admit to liking what I saw in the mirror.

"They both look great," Sal said. "If you're not comfortable, buy a short skirt to put over it. It's your choice."

"I'll think about it. I bet Mary's not dressing up."

"She is. She told me it's not revealing, but she's doing something. Won't tell me what."

"You've got a hell of a lot of underwear, Sal."

"Oh, this is just a part."

We were in the dressing room off their bedroom. It was quite large with wardrobes and drawers around three walls. She'd opened one door to get out the things she'd shown me. She now opened two more.

"These are all special things."

"Special?"

"Well, things I don't necessarily wear every day."

"Can I have a look?"

"Of course."

I looked at the things hanging up. Teddies, basques, short dresses, tight dresses. A few costumes.

"Is this all just for fun?"

"Yup."

"You must have a lot of fun."

"We have our moments. If you'd like me to wear something when I stay over, you've only got to say."

"I don't know. This is all new to me; dressing up. I'm not sure about it."

Sally raised an eyebrow.

"I don't mean there's anything wrong with it," I said. "I'm not sure it does anything for me."

"Perhaps I'll bring something over next week. You can tell me if it works for you or not."

"No harm in trying. I can always rip it off you."

We returned upstairs, and as we sat down, I had a thought.

"Does Marcus dress up as well?"

"Well," she replied. "He hasn't until recently. But I've got him a few things which seem to work. Don't they, darling?"

"Mmm. They're all right."

By the time we went to bed, Sal and I were quite merry. The episode on Boxing Day had been a one-off. I went to my room, and they went to theirs. I was happy with that; I was a guest in their home, after all. I listened to their nocturnal activities, accompanied by my vibe. They knew I was listening. Whether they got off on that, I didn't know.

***

"Hello, Mum. Come in. Hi, Tim."

"Hi, Lucy. I'll pick Ruth up at three."

"Okay."

And with that, my mother came into my home. I hadn't looked forward to it. But if we were going to make any sort of connection after all these years, we had to try to understand one another. So here I was, entertaining my mother for two hours on a Sunday afternoon. It was going to be an effort.

"Can I get you anything? Tea? Coffee?"

"Tea would be nice. Thank you."

I went through to the kitchen and made a pot of tea. I hadn't made a pot since ... God knows; I couldn't remember. And I'd picked up some cakes. Angry with myself at the attempt to fit in with what I thought she'd expect. Returning to the living room, Mum was sitting on the sofa, looking around the room. I put the tea things on the table and poured two cups.

"Help yourself to a cake."

"Thank you, Lucy. This room is lovely and bright."

"That's one of the things which sold it to me. It's great for drawing and painting."

"I didn't know you were an artist."

I bit my lip.

"There's a lot we don't know about each other, Mum."

An awkward silence descended for a minute or two.

"What sort of thing do you paint?" she asked.

I pointed to a few of my pictures on the walls. I'd done a thorough appraisal the day before and replaced a couple of things which might cause awkward moments. She looked from one to the other.

"I'm afraid I don't know much about art. It was always frowned upon when I was growing up, and your father held the same view."

"I know, Mum."

She looked at me. Another awkward pause followed. She finally looked back at the pictures.

"Do you teach painting?"

"No. I teach the history of art. The artwork is for fun mostly, although I do sell a few things."

"Really?"

"Yes. I put a few into a local gallery every so often and get the odd commission."

"Commission for what?"

I doubted she caught the look which crossed my face as I thought of the pictures for Sally and Marcus.

"Oh, portraits mainly."

"You're quite good then."

"People seem to like my work."

"But you teach art history?"

I tried to explain my role to her. Why it fascinated me. Why I fell in love with it. Why other people wanted to study it. She listened, but I got the feeling she didn't understand. I tried to put myself into her position, a life where art was deliberately excluded. But it proved impossible; I couldn't imagine a life without art, it would be so empty.

Apart from my family home, I'd never been in a house without at least a few pictures on the walls. They may have been awful; they may have been cliched. But they were there. I couldn't hope to explain a lifetime's passion to someone who hadn't been exposed to art at all. When I'd finished, she smiled for the first time.

"I don't really understand it, but I can see you enjoy it."

"I do, Mum. It's my passion."

We fell into awkward silence again.

"How are you getting on, Mum?"

She sighed theatrically.

"I'm a bit lost. I miss your father. My life seems empty. I'm managing okay day to day. Tim and Annie have sorted things out for me, so I'm coping with the house and stuff. But I get up in the morning wondering how I'm going to fill my day."

"What about friends?"

She looked at me with a face suffused with sadness.

"I don't have any. There's the church. At least, there was. But I haven't been since your father died. No, since before that. We didn't have any friends outside."

"What do you do?"

"I've started going for walks. I'd never done that before. It gets me out of the house, and it helps me to sleep."

"Do you have any hobbies?"

"No. I looked after the house; your father did everything else."

"Isn't there anything you've always wanted to try?"

"Not really, Lucy. I'm beginning to realise how little I know of the world around me. I don't even know what I'm missing."

This was hard work. I struggled with where to go next. She was right; it was difficult to encourage someone to try something when they don't know what there is to try.

"Have you thought about moving?"

She looked up sharply.

"Why would I move?"

"I don't know. Perhaps to a different area, make new friends. It might prove difficult where you are."

She thought for a moment.

"I don't think I could. Too many memories in the house."

"But are they all good memories?"

That was a step too far; I realised it as soon as I said it. It might be the way you'd talk to a close friend. It might be how Sally and I would talk to each other. But not to a mother you hadn't been involved with for fifteen years. She started crying. I didn't know what to do. I fetched a box of tissues, put them on the table in front of her, and sat beside her. She took a tissue and dried her eyes. Her tears had stopped.

"I'm sorry, Mum," I said. "That was insensitive of me."

"It's okay. I do sometimes look around the house and wonder if it's more a prison than a home."

"I think you need to find a way to meet new people. Didn't Tim and Annie invite you to go along to their church?"

"Yes, they have, but I'm not sure. It will be very different. Your father hated the Church of England."

"I know. But you're not him, Mum. It's time you found a way of being yourself, not somebody's daughter or wife."

"That's what scares me."

"It must be hard, but it'll be worth it in the end. Then you'll be able to live your life for you."

Whether she believed it or not, she seemed to brighten up after that. I wasn't sure she would do anything to change. She'd spent sixty years being an adjunct to someone else. First her parents, then her husband. To me, it seemed a waste of a life. But that was probably harsh.

We returned to safer subjects, although still with some awkwardness. I asked about Sarah & Nathan. I got the impression she wanted to get closer to them but didn't know how. They were at an age when a funky granny would have been a godsend, an antidote to bossy parents. But Mum was far from a funky granny. Looking at her, I felt sorry for her. Her whole perceived purpose in life, being a loving wife, had disappeared. I wasn't confident she'd find another.

***

I had no idea what Sally was doing. She had arrived after work, we'd shared a passionate kiss, and she'd said 'give me a few minutes' before disappearing into the bedroom. That must have been ten minutes ago at least.

I'd known the woman for over fifteen years and thought I knew everything about her. We'd shared most of our secrets over that time. But in the last eighteen months, she had constantly surprised me. I blamed Marcus. She'd changed since she'd met him. Not in a bad way, though. She oozed confidence now. Confidence to finally be the woman she was. And I was benefitting from that in a wholly unexpected way.

I heard the bedroom door open and the sound of heels on the hallway floor. I strained some pasta into the sink and put it on the draining board. When I turned around, she was standing in the doorway. Leaning against one side, with her arm raised, a hand against the other side. Her hair loose, with the tightest dress I'd ever seen.

Black latex; it clung to her like a second skin. Black heels. But all I could see was the dress. As I stared, I realised it was transparent. I could see her breasts clearly; her nipples pushing through the material. My eyes dropped, and I could make out her little bush.

I looked up to her face; a seductive smile playing across her lips. She blew me a kiss and turned around slowly. Her bum was clearly visible; the shadow between her cheeks drawing my eye. She bent forward slowly; that dress was short. Imagination didn't come into it. She was hiding nothing.

She slowly straightened and faced me.

"Well?" she said. "Still not interested in dressing up?"

"Wow, Sal. That's … amazing."

She walked over to me and threw her arms over my shoulders.

"Like it?"

"You look good enough to eat."

"I'll hold you to that later."

I wasn't going to argue.

"It doesn't leave much to the imagination," I said.

"No; but just enough. You can see it, but you can't reach it. That's what it's all about."

"You're not going to tell me you'd wear that in public?"

"Probably not. It's a bit more transparent than I expected it to be. I'll need to get one that's more opaque."

"But it's so tight. Where would you wear it?"

Over dinner, she told me about the fetish group she and Marcus had found. About the social events, and about the play party they'd attended. I listened enthralled. I'd heard about groups like this but wondered if they were a myth. Now my best friend was telling me she was part of one. At times I was slightly distracted by her nipples exposed under her dress. I had to tell myself there'd be plenty of time to deal with those later.

"What sort of people go?" I asked.

"Oh, all sorts. All ages, all shapes. All really friendly."

"All straight?"

"God, no. A good proportion were gay; I'd guess about a third. And no idea how many were bi. Everyone's accepted for who they are."

"Is it one big orgy?"

She laughed.

"No. Nothing like that. It's not really about sex. Most people dress up and anything goes. Some interesting get-ups. There's a big area for socialising; a place to talk and meet people. Then there's a play area where they have demonstrations and things."

"Demonstrations?"

"Yea. People with skills pass them on to anyone interested."

"What sort of skills?"

She told me about the events she and Marcus had watched.

"A woman whipped two naked men in front of you?"

I could hardly believe it.

"Yea. She was good."

"And the men?"

She chuckled.

"They were good too. Two very fit lads. They seemed to enjoy it."

I sat back in my chair.

"God, Sal. I'm no innocent. But compared to you, I find I'm a nun."

"I seem to remember there were a couple of girls dressed as nuns. But I don't remember many nuns in such revealing habits."

She was teasing me now, but I was intrigued.

"Is there swinging and stuff."

"No. I mean, some people probably do hook up, but that's not the main aim."

"Well, that's good to know. I had visions of you taking on all comers."

She gave a wicked grin.

"There are private rooms, though. You can use them to do what you want. They seemed popular."

I looked at her. She was challenging me to ask.

"Did you …"

"No. It was our first time. We didn't have the nerve, to be honest. We waited until we got home."

"Is it all about whipping people, then?"

"Oh, no. Fetish covers just about anything you can imagine."

"And some I can't."

"One chap we spoke to has a thing for jelly."

"Jelly?"

"Yea, jelly."

"But what does he do with it?"

"We didn't ask. But I'm sure he'd have been happy to tell us. Everyone's really open. It's a safe environment; nobody judges anyone else."

"Are you going again?"

"Yes. We're going on Sunday."

"Do you dress up?"

"The first time, I wasn't sure. Marcus had bought me a beautiful basque for my birthday and some lush silk stockings. I wore them under a dress. But after an hour, I took it off."

"And paraded around in your underwear."

"Yup."

"What are you wearing on Sunday? You're not wearing that dress?"

"No. If it was less transparent I might. At the first one, we met a gorgeous girl wearing a pink version of this. Slightly less see-through. But she looked wonderful. You'd have liked her."

"Thanks."

"It's what prompted me to get this. But I'll wear something else this time."

"And Marcus. Does he dress up?"

"He's going to this time. I've got him some good stuff."

"Whose idea was all this? You or Marcus?"

She thought for a moment.

"We're doing it together. To be honest, neither of us would have the courage to go on our own. But together, we feel confident enough to do it."

"Well, I know one thing. I couldn't do it."

"But would you like to?"

I knew her expression. She wanted to know if it would interest me.

"I'm intrigued, I won't deny it."

We cleared the table and tidied up. Every time she came into my vision, I couldn't help looking. She drew my eyes to her body. Those gorgeous curves visible yet out of reach. I realised there was more to this dressing up than I'd considered. I opened another bottle of wine, and we settled on the sofa.

For the first time, I understood how she teased Marcus. Because she was teasing me. Even when we were chatting about banalities, she would sit in a particular position, move her legs. Making sure I had a good view of what she wanted me to see. When she deliberately stood up and bent forward to pour some wine, the dress rode up far enough for me to get a wonderful view. I burst out laughing. She turned around with that look of fake innocence.

"What?"

"If I were Marcus, I'd have pulled you over my knee by now."

"Whatever for?"

"To give you a damned good spanking."

She bent and gave me a lingering kiss.

"And what's to stop *you* giving me a damned good spanking?"

I thought for a moment and broke into a smile. And pulled her over my lap.

Chapter 5 – Marcus

Peter sent me a contract. It appeared to be standard stuff. It didn't commit me to anything, except to pay him handsomely if I signed a publishing deal as a result of his efforts. He rang me to say Eva had read one of the books I'd sent her and was going through the other. She'd be in touch.

Eva and I hadn't clicked, so I was surprised when I got a call inviting me to her office. As I waited in the reception area a week later, I wondered if I wanted to tie myself to a publishing contract.

I knew no publisher would welcome my variety of styles and genres. If you were successful with one book, and it was a big if, they'd want another just the same. Could I do that? I loved being able to write whatever I wanted. I'd been honest with Eva when I said I didn't need the money, but I wanted to know if my writing would be successful on the bigger stage, with a publisher's muscle behind it.

"Mr Foxton?" The voice dragged me from my musings. "I'm Miss Cassini's secretary. Would you come with me?"

The lift whizzed up the building, while we made small talk about the weather and the journey. I hated small talk. I followed her along a corridor to an open door which she tapped before introducing me. Eva sat behind a desk on one side of the room.

"Ah, Marcus," she said, offering her hand. "Come in. Please, sit down. Good journey?"

"No, terrible. I got chased by a crocodile."

She gave me a puzzled look.

"I'm sorry, Eva, but I don't do small talk."

"Okay. Let's get to business."

She did, and I realised she was in the right job after all. She took one book at a time and gave a considered critique of each one. Itemising the good, the mediocre and the bad. Largely, I had to admit, in line with my own feelings.

"Do you use an editor?"

"No. I have a couple of critique partners for different genres, and a range of beta readers."

"An editor would make a real difference."

"If you say so."

"I do, Marcus. I'll admit you have a spare style. There's not much waffle or padding. They're the bane of my life. New authors who are proud to have written a hundred and fifty thousand words when they could have told the story in half that. There's not a lot to remove, but an editor could tighten these up. Certainly with Shadows of Gold. I liked the story. It's original, which is rare these days. I'm less certain about Spewn Words."

"It has a limited audience, I suspect."

"Yes. I'm not even sure how to categorise it. The title isn't exactly appealing, either."

"No, but it's an accurate description of the contents."

"True.

Spewn Words was one of what Sally called my stream of consciousness works. A collection of themed short stories which I wrote as they came to me. No trying to make logical sense. Sometimes no linear plot and as little editing and changing as possible. I'd published a lot of these stories in magazines and online. They'd proved popular with a certain audience, but I wasn't sure a collection of them would be commercially viable.

"Right," she said. "As you want to get to the point. What I'd like to do is pass Shadows of Gold to one of my editors. Let them work on it and see what the result is. It'll take a couple of weeks. Is that agreeable?"

"Yes. Ever since I've been writing, I've been hearing how important editors are. I'll be interested to see if they're worth all the hype."

"You're a cynic, Marcus."

"I prefer to think of it as being realistic."

"Perhaps that's no bad thing for a writer. Meanwhile, I'll sit on Spewn Words and think about what I could do with it."

"Only polite options, I trust?"

"If you insist."

At least I'd found out she did have a sense of humour. At our first meeting, I hadn't been sure.

"I have to warn you," she said. "If we decided to take Shadows of Gold, we wouldn't be offering any sort of advance."

"I didn't expect one. I believe they're as rare as hen's teeth, these days."

"Something like that. Besides, if I remember rightly, you said you didn't need the money."

"True. I found myself a rich woman."

"Lucky you."

***

We were far more relaxed as we drove to our second play party. We arrived early again, but not from nervousness this time. We intended to stay longer but still leave ourselves time to get home and have some fun on our own. I parked the car and we walked down the side of the building to the open door.

"Hi, Dave."

"Hello. Welcome. Sally, isn't it? Sorry, I can't remember …"

"Marcus. Don't worry, Sally's a lot more memorable than me."

"Depends what you're looking for, darling."

We made our way to the changing rooms. I didn't need to change. I'd worn the wet-look jeans and top Sally had bought me, and she didn't waste any time either, whipping her dress off and putting it in our locker.

"Well?"

She hadn't let me see what she was wearing before we left home, but I could see it now. A deep blue lace-skirted basque and black hold-ups. Very high heels. The basque was laced up the front and gave her a lovely cleavage. The skirt was shorter at the front, getting longer as it went around the back. But not very long. She turned away from me and bent forward; more than a hint of bare cheeks appeared. She stood up and smiled.

"Just to tempt you."

She walked over and gave me a kiss. I went to grab her bum, but she moved away.

"Shall we?"

I followed her through the hallway, and we entered the main area, putting our food and drink on the appropriate tables. We soon found several people we'd encountered last time, and one or two from the munch who we hadn't seen here. We felt at home straight away, and this time, we both got the odd compliment about our attire. Unsurprisingly, Sal got a lot more admiring looks than I did.

We went to look at the timetable and noted a couple of things of interest. As we returned to the social area, Sally nudged me.

"Wow," she said. "She's impressive."

I knew who she was talking about. A woman talking to Matt. Statuesque, elegant, with a mass of red hair woven into a long, loose braid. She was wearing a cinched, heavily embroidered corset, and a long leather skirt. With platform heels. She towered over Matt. Even from ten metres away, she radiated authority.

"I don't think she'll be taking orders from anyone," I said.

"Like to try?"

"I'd come off the loser."

We were happier about introducing ourselves now, and we spent time deliberately seeking out people we'd not met before. Not all the introductions were successful. Some people tended to stick to their friends or those who shared their interests. They weren't rude, but after the introductions, they tended to tactfully move on. Matt had told us it would happen. Some of the attendees travelled long distances to these events and they wanted to make the most of it on their terms.

"Hello, you two."

We turned to find Yas at our side.

"Hi, Yas. How are you?"

"Great thanks. You're looking good again, Sally. Great you've made an effort too, Marcus. I like the wet-look."

"Thanks."

"I had to push him," Sal said. "But I think it suits him."

"Me too. I love Matt dressing up. Mind you, he doesn't need an excuse; he's a bit of a tart."

"He's your master, Yas."

"Indeed he is. Doesn't mean I can't tease him."

"Mmm. You never know where it'll lead."

"Exactly."

"Yas, who's the striking redhead?"

She followed Sally's gaze.

"Oh, that's Helen. I hadn't spotted her. She hasn't put in an appearance for a while. She was one of the founders of the group, but she doesn't show up much these days. Really nice; a little other-worldly."

"Other-worldly?"

"Yea. I mean, lots of people here live double lives. Their normal everyday selves; work, children, families. Then they have this side to them. Helen doesn't separate the two. If you saw her in town, she could be dressed as she is today. Possibly with lower heels. Most of us aren't afraid to be different, but Helen doesn't mind being *seen* to be different."

"Sounds fascinating."

"Talk to her. She'll always chat. But she'll learn more about you than you do about her."

Yas went off to mingle and we grabbed a drink and something to eat.

"Nearly time for the first demo. Coming?"

I followed Sally through to the play area and we found a seat. We were waiting for a demonstration about suspension. We had the equipment at home. We'd used it, but not for full suspension. Sally wanted to be hung upside down, and we needed to know how to do it safely. The following half-hour filled in the gaps better than all the reading and YouTube videos ever could.

"Well, darling," Sal asked. "Got all that?"

"I think so."

"Good. I fancy trying it."

"You'll be completely helpless."

She looked at me, mischief in her eyes.

"Yea," she chuckled. "I know."

"Hi, Sally. Hi, Marcus."

"Hello, Penny," Sal replied. "How are you?"

"Good thanks. Find that interesting?"

"Yes. We needed to see how to do it safely."

"Unfortunately, you need to find the equipment."

"We've got it already."

"Really?"

45

"Yea. Our very own playroom."

"Wow. You are taking this seriously."

While Penny and Sally were talking, I couldn't help studying Penny. This time, dressed in a tight halter top and a short skaters skirt, with PVC boots coming above the knee. And a change of neckwear.

"Different collar today, Penny."

She touched it with a finger.

"Well spotted, Marcus. This is my true collar."

"Why the difference?" Sal asked.

"I wear this one if I'm out with my mistress."

"She's here today?"

"Yes. I'll see if I can introduce you later. Right now, I'd better go and see if I'm needed."

We kept our places through a couple of demos we weren't interested in. Sal leaned against me, and I put my arm around her, letting it drop until I found her skirt. Pushing it aside, I found her bare cheek and began stroking it. I heard her purr. She shifted slightly and crossed her legs to allow me better access. I edged my fingers between her cheeks, and she gave a little whimper as I ran it under her thong and across her ass, rubbing it gently. Then slowly moved my finger forward. She looked up at me, a dreamy look in her eyes.

"No," she whispered, making no attempt to stop me.

I carried on, feeling moisture as I reached the edge of her pussy. She tensed as I gently stroked her, hardly moving my fingers. Not going further, just sliding my finger between her pussy and her ass, stimulating that sweet spot. She gently rested her hand on my cock. Didn't move it; it would have been too obvious. But no-one could see my hand. They probably guessed what I was doing, though. She was breathing more heavily now. I could feel her gently rising and falling with each breath.

"No," she hissed again, her expression saying exactly the opposite.

"You just relax," I whispered in her ear. "Look around you. I can see at least three couples doing exactly what we're doing. Who do you reckon's going to come first?"

She gave me a panicky look.

"No. I can't. You know how loud I can be."

"You do feel horny?"

"God, yes."

"So, you're going to come."

"Marcus, no."

She was squirming gently on my fingers.

"Yes. Here, or we go to a room."

She glanced up at me.

"Not here."

I retrieved my hand and put her skirt back in place. She stood up and grabbed my hand. Walking as casually as we could, we made our way to the corridor of private rooms. Most doors were closed. One was open but occupied, a small group watching what was going on. We found a free room and Sally pulled me in and shut the door.

She kissed me hard, her hands scrabbling to undo the button and zip on my trousers. She pushed them down and dropped to her knees, her mouth engulfing my cock. She started to suck it hard, her hands going around my bum, pulling me towards her.

But I didn't want that. I bunched her hair in my hand and gently pulled it, bringing her back to her feet. My other hand went straight between her legs, roughly rubbing her pussy. She groaned. She was staring at me with those lust-filled green eyes.

"On all fours."

She jumped onto the bed on her hands and knees, and waited, looking back at me. I pulled my trousers off and climbed up behind her. Pushing the skirt over her back, I gave her bum a few hard slaps. She wiggled her hips, chuckling. I pulled her thong to one side and slid into her firmly. She gasped as I buried myself in her. No finesse; no gentle teasing. I fucked her. We both wanted it; needed it.

I held her hips and drove hard. She didn't last long. My finger had done its job earlier. Within a couple of minutes, she was grunting as her orgasm came. Her hips bucking; her cheeks wobbling as her body convulsed. I gave them a few more hard slaps and carried on. I wasn't changing position. I wanted to come too; exactly like this.

As she dropped from the peak, I resumed my actions. Reaching up, bunching her hair, and twisting it around my hand, I gently pulled it as I fucked her. I hadn't allowed her to recover. If I timed it right, I could keep her in a near orgasmic state. I timed it right. She was chuntering now. Random words; a flurry of moans and groans. Demands for me to fuck her harder. Little squeaks and giggles.

Then it stopped, replaced by a rising groan as her orgasm built. Mine did too. Suddenly she let out a series of little shrieks, and dropped to her elbows, her back arching as she came. I felt her spasm around my cock and that did it for me. I groaned as I came as well, pulling her back onto me with each contraction of my balls. By the time I'd stopped, she had collapsed onto her shoulders and was making little murmuring sounds.

We collapsed onto the bed, and I held her as she recovered. Finally, she turned around to face me.

"I needed that," she said.

"I couldn't tell."

She punched my arm and kissed me. We had a quick cuddle and cleaned up. First ourselves, then the sheeting and the room. There was cleaning stuff in every room, and it was up to you to leave it as you'd found it. When we'd finished, we went to the door.

"Ready?" I asked.

"This is the worst part. Who might see us coming out."

"Does it matter?"

"I suppose not."

With that, I opened the door and we both stepped out; right in front of Adrian and Guy coming out of the room opposite, with a third man.

"Marcus, Sally. Hello."

"Hi, Adrian. Hi, Guy."

They saw our embarrassment.

"Oh, don't be bashful. We all need to get rid of the tension sometimes. This is Zac, by the way."

We accompanied them back to the play area. No-one even looked in our direction as we entered.

"I need something to eat, and a drink," I said.

"Me too, but I need the loo first. I'll meet you by the buffet."

As I made my way through to the social area, I realised I was exchanging nods or a brief 'hi' to several people along the way. When I got to the food, I picked a couple of items and looked around as I munched on them. This event was better attended than the last. Busy, but not crowded. Plenty of room for people to meet and chat without feeling crushed. I saw Sal come in through the door. As I watched her walk over, she was smiling and nodding to a few people as well. We were beginning to belong.

"That's better," she said, as she rejoined me. "There was still rather a lot of you in there."

"Can't help that. It's your fault for being too damned sexy."

"You old smoothie. I need something to drink."

We grabbed a drink and a few more bits to eat and sat on two nearby chairs. People were standing and sitting around in casual groups. Some sticking with likeminded souls, others happily mingling with all sorts. A few people in civvies, but not many.

"We must have stood out at the first one," I said.

"I guess we did, but I didn't feel different."

"You weren't, remember? First opportunity and you ripped your kit off."

"Oh, yes. So I did. Glad I got you something to wear now?"

"Yea. It does feel good. Although seeing some of the men here, I'm positively boring."

"There are some interesting things, aren't there?"

There were. Leather, lace, rubber, PVC. From completely covered, to barely there. Even as a straight guy, I had to admire some of the men's outfits. Really fit bodies encased in tight material. There were also those more like me; doing our best with what we had.

But it was still the women who excelled, though. Some of the outfits were wonderful. In this safe environment, it didn't seem to matter about looks or size or shape. Some of the best-dressed were women who you probably wouldn't notice on the street. But they looked good. Happy with themselves, and happy with their style.

When we'd finished eating and drinking, we made our way towards the play area again. We were about to go through the partition when a voice made us pause.

"Marcus? Sally?"

We turned to find Penny standing in front of us. With the striking redhead by her side.

"Hi, Penny," Sal replied.

"I'd like you to meet Helen. Helen, Marcus and Sally."

I looked up at Helen. I had to; she towered above my six feet by a good five or six inches.

"Hello, Helen. Pleased to meet you."

"Likewise, Marcus. And you Sally. I gather you're new to all this."

She swung her arm languidly around the room as she spoke.

"Yes," Sal said. "I gather you were one of the founders of this group."

"Strange what you hear, isn't it? I may have had a minor role years ago."

She was totally self-assured. One of those people who fascinate you from the moment you meet them. She had a real presence. I saw immediately what Yas had meant by 'other-worldly'. I found myself looking at Helen's corset. It was incredibly intricate. Beautifully made, with embroidery on almost every surface. Sumptuous would probably be the right word.

I wondered how many hours of work had gone into it. It fitted her frame perfectly. She was well-built; her shape complimenting her height, and the corset gave her a discreet but prominent cleavage. I suddenly realised she was watching me.

"Sorry, Helen," I said. "I didn't mean to stare."

She gave me a slightly mocking look.

"That depends what you were staring at, Marcus."

I was about to reply, but stopped myself, as her mouth took on a wry smile.

"Neither answer will be right, will it?" I said.

She laughed for the first time.

"Correct. I shall feign shock if you were looking at my breasts, and disappointment if you were not."

"Then I will risk your disappointment, Helen. I was admiring your corset. If I remember rightly something Penny said, could it be one of your own creations?"

Helen smiled indulgently at Penny.

"You are quite right. Although there are a few more hours in this one than in most I make."

"It's beautiful, Helen," Sally said. "Do you do everything yourself?"

"Everything except the embroidery. I have a couple of wonderful women who do that for me."

Sally looked at Penny.

"No," Helen said. "It's not Penny. She has many skills…" Penny blushed, beautifully, "… but embroidery is not one of them."

"Are you open to new clients, Helen?" Sally asked.

"Provided they value my work. And can afford it."

Sally looked at me.

"Fancy me in something like this, darling?"

"Definitely. What do you think?"

Sally looked back at Helen's outfit.

"I'm not sure I could carry it off as well as Helen does, though."

I watched as Helen looked Sally up and down a few times; slowly. Her face softened as she took in Sally's shape.

"We could try," Helen said finally. "It would involve several fittings."

"As long as I get her back in between," I said, jokingly.

Helen gave me a sharp look.

"Oh, Marcus. Don't be such a spoilsport."

She took a card out of a concealed pocket and handed it to Sally.

"Get in touch if you're interested. Good to have met you both."

And with that, Helen swept away, Penny following in her wake. I watched them briefly and turned to Sal. She was still looking at them. A few seconds later, she turned and gave a slightly startled look when she saw I was watching her.

"What?" she asked.

"Don't tell me. You were imagining those two together."

She flushed slightly.

"Don't worry," I continued. "So was I."

By the time we left, we'd met a few more people, and realised as the day progressed, the demonstrations evolved into performances. We would have to arrive later at some point and see what went on nearer the end.

As I was retrieving our stuff from our locker in the changing room, Sal went to the loo. Adrian, Guy and Zac came in.

"Hi, Marcus. Lost Sally?"

"In the loos."

"Ah. Leaving?"

"Yes. Although I think we might arrive later next time. Not sure if we're missing anything towards the end."

Guy laughed.

"Well, it does sometimes liven up. No orgies, though, if that's what you're looking for."

"What was that about an orgy?" Sal asked as she came out of the loos.

"There aren't any," Adrian said.

"Ah well, better go home and start our own."

"Exactly what we're doing," Guy replied. "Have fun, you two."

Sally slipped her outer dress over the basque, and we walked out to the car. Throwing our stuff in the boot, I opened the door for her, and she climbed in. As I went to shut it, she stopped me.

"Wait, darling."

She bent forward to the storage compartment. Opening it, she lifted out a velvet bag, loosened the pull string and lifted out the sapphire collar. She stepped out of the car again and leaned against it. Kissing me, she offered me the collar.

"I'm yours tonight."

I took the collar from her and gently kissed her, then laid it around her neck and clipped the clasp into place.

"Comfortable?"

"Yes, sir. Thank you."

"Good. You can start by taking that dress off."

She lifted the hem and slipped it over her head. Now I understood the choice of basque. Its blue colour matched the sapphire. She looked stunning; and incredibly sexy.

"Let's get home," I said. "The journey will give me time to decide what I'm going to do with you tonight."

"Anything you wish, sir," she said, giving me her best demure smile, which she knew drove me crazy.

Chapter 6 – Sally

"Will she do anything?" I asked.

"I don't know," Lucy replied. "I think she wants to, but she's too scared. She has been to church with Tim and Annie, though."

"It's a start."

"But even that could be another place to hide."

"She might make some friends."

"I don't think she knows how."

"You make her sound like a lost cause."

Lucy came to the table, put two bowls down, and sat on the seat next to me.

"She's such hard work. I find myself censoring everything I say, and it gets tiring."

"I can imagine. Someone like you. All fuck this and fuck that."

She elbowed my arm.

"If only it were that simple. But I avoid anything about my relationships, or about the split. Then try and steer away from anything I think might upset her."

"Doesn't leave much to talk about."

"Exactly."

We were quiet for a few minutes while we ate.

"Perhaps you need to stop all that," I said. "Just be you. If she doesn't like it, it makes the decision for you."

"I was thinking about that. I'm working on it with Jenny."

"Come on, Luce. It seems to me you're doing this more from duty than need. Why put yourself through the mill? Even if she accepts the person she sees, it won't be you. You're trying to be the person you think she needs you to be."

"Maybe."

"I know it's easy for me to say, but you need to show her the real you. You know, all the fuck this and fuck that."

She laughed.

"I know, you're right. I don't want to pretend, but I can't help it."

We fell silent again, food now finished. Leaning back, each holding a glass of red.

"What about you?" Lucy finally said. "Going to follow up your dad's stuff?"

"Marcus and I have been talking about it. We've made a decision; sort of."

"Sort of?"

"Marcus eventually told me his thoughts. He thinks we should at least find out a bit more, without necessarily contacting the other family, if that's what they are."

"How?"

"Well, he asked what we'd do if all this had happened fifty miles away."

"And?"

"We've got an address, and two names. We've also got a couple of business cards from the same area; one with an address in Nice, and one from Monte Carlo. If they were closer, wouldn't we take a look?"

"Ooh, have a snoop."

"Yes."

"But they're not fifty miles away."

"No. We're thinking about going over for a holiday. Staying somewhere near and looking around."

"Sherlock Foxton and Indiana Fletcher."

"Something like that."

"I didn't think Marcus was well enough to go abroad?"

"Since the op, he's been much better. He's got more energy. It's great."

"I'll bet."

I laughed.

"Want to come with us?"

Her head jerked around to look at me.

"What?"

"Why not?"

"The three of us on holiday together? That could get awkward, couldn't it?"

"It wasn't a problem at Christmas if I remember rightly." Lucy grinned. "We'll sort something out if you're interested. Your choice."

Lucy went to say something, but I jumped in.

"And yes, Marcus has already agreed."

"Okay," she said. "If the dates are right, I'd love to. Holidays with you seem to be so interesting these days."

We both went quiet, thinking about our last holiday, and its consequences. Lucy was the first to return to the present.

"Talking of that, fancy a massage?"

"Why not? Got any gelato?"

***

"I'm still not sure about the heels," Marcus said. "I have a new admiration for women who wear them."

He was finishing dressing. I was ready and had been helping him. We'd been getting ready for over an hour now, and there had been a lot of giggles. For me, wearing this sort of gear was perfectly normal. But Marcus?

When he finally slipped into the heels, he stood up and went to look in the mirror. A red basque, fishnet stockings, a full pair of briefs and modest heels. A feather boa completed the look. I watched his reaction. He stood facing the mirror, turned to look at the sides, then requested a hand mirror to check the back.

"Well?" I asked.

"I don't look as good as Tim Curry. But it's not bad."

The doorbell rang.

"That'll be Lucy," I said, and went upstairs to answer the door.

"Hi, Sal," she said. "I'm not sure about this."

"You'll be fine. Come downstairs, we need to finish our make-up."

When we got to the bedroom, Lucy saw Marcus posing with one foot on the bed and burst out laughing.

"Thanks a lot, Luce," Marcus said.

"Sorry," she replied. "You look … wow … you look great. I was … surprised."

"What have you gone with, Luce?" I asked.

She hesitated, looking a bit sheepish. Then she shrugged and took her coat off. Revealing an outfit similar to mine; well, it was mine. An opaque wired teddy, with stockings and a full pair of briefs. She looked fabulous.

"How do I look? I'm not used to wearing all this. And I've never worn anything like this in public."

"Marcus?" I turned to him. I'd given him a good excuse to take a long look at my lover in her underwear.

"You look ravishing, Lucy. Perfect."

"Thanks. Sal?"

I gave her a quick hug.

"Luce, you look great. I'm keeping my actual thoughts to myself. They might get me into trouble, and we haven't got time."

I heard Marcus laugh.

"Right," I said. "Makeup."

Lucy and I squeezed onto the stool and did ours at the same time. It was a strange feeling. Both of us in underwear, pressed together, knowing Marcus was behind us; no doubt watching us. We went for an over the top effect, appropriate for the occasion, slapping it on heavily. Then I set to work on Marcus. To my knowledge, this was the first time he'd worn make-up and he watched closely as I layered it on.

The doorbell rang again.

"I expect that's Mary. I'll go."

Sure enough, Mary was waiting at the door. She'd been right; she had made an effort. Nothing as revealing as our get-ups. She was dressed as one of the guests. A man's black suit with a bright red bow tie and cummerbund. Her hair frizzed up and a party hat in her hand.

"We're nearly ready; just a few minutes."

"Okay, darling. Take your time."

Returning downstairs, Marcus and Lucy were making the finishing touches.

"Ready, you two? We need to eat something before we go."

"Yup. Ready as I'll ever be."

"Ah," Mary said as we entered the living room. "That brings back some memories."

"Really, Mary?" Marcus asked. "Another glimpse of your scandalous past?"

"I went to several performances when I was younger. Dressed pretty much as you are."

"I hope you looked better than I do," Marcus said.

We sat at the table and shared some food we'd prepared. We'd decided we weren't going for a pre-theatre meal dressed as we were.

"I'm going to wear my coat," Lucy said.

I made clucking noises, and she threw a crisp at me.

"I'll try the car park by the theatre," Marcus said. "We won't have to walk far. I'm putting a coat in the car in case we have to park further away."

I made more clucking noises. He went to say something but remembered Mary was there and narrowed his eyes at me. I poked my tongue out in return.

"Well," I said. "I'm going as I am. There will be loads of people milling around like this. I don't think we'll feel out of place."

We didn't. There were lots of similarly dressed patrons making their way to the theatre and Marcus and Lucy decided they didn't need their coats after all as we joined the throng. The crowd were happy and friendly; everyone looking at everyone else. Lots of compliments about outfits. People we didn't know from Adam telling us we looked great. Lucy gradually got more confident about her first public outing in her underwear.

"Do you see what I see?" Marcus said to me quietly.

I followed his gaze and couldn't miss the shock of red hair standing out above the heads of those around it.

"There can't be another; let's head that way."

We made our way towards the landmark, finally reaching a little open space which seemed to appear miraculously in front of her as she walked. She was dressed in a similar fashion as at the play party. An elegant corset; tight-fitting and perfectly shaped. But tonight, the skirt was different. Leather again, but open at the front, all the way to the waist. Suspenders from the corset holding up stockings. But they were nearly covered by soft boots which came above the knee.

The heels appeared unwearable, even to me, but seemed so natural to her. Her hair was loose; cascading over her shoulders, falling a long way down her back. A sudden image of Merida appeared in my head. She seemed oblivious to the interest she sparked in those around her. She spotted us.

"Marcus. Sally. What a pleasant surprise."

"Good evening, Helen."

Helen looked us up and down. Her visual appraisal gave you some anxiety. It was as if you needed her approval.

"You're both looking good," was the final judgement.

She saw Lucy and Mary, and we made the introductions. Helen was gracious in her greeting; as gracious as such an imposing figure could be.

"Are you a fan?" I asked Helen.

She gave me a look which sent shivers through me.

"I was in an all-female production once. Many years ago."

"Frank'n'furter?"

She smiled. A deep, infectious smile. The first time I'd seen it.

"We called her Frank'n'pussy."

Lucy laughed.

"I hope I haven't caused offence?" Helen said, looking at Mary with a little concern.

"Oh, no, my dear," Mary said. "I've been many times dressed as you all are. I may be the senior here now, but I think I might like to have seen that performance."

Helen gave Mary a gentle nod in appreciation as Penny appeared by her side. She looked fabulous, dressed in a red corset with matching knickers and stockings. With her was a striking young man with a shock of blond hair, dressed as Rocky.

Well, if you could call it dressed. He was wearing a pair of tight gold shorts, and gold boots. His body was worth a second look; not overly muscular, but I noted the sculpted shapes across his stomach. Particularly as he was oiled. His body glistened, even in the dim light outside the theatre.

Introductions were made. Rocky's real name was Ben and he shook hands with us all. Mary was the last to be introduced, and she held Ben's hand for a time, looking at him.

"Well, Ben," she said. "Where were you when I was younger?"

He wasn't fazed at all.

"Waiting for you, Mary," he replied. "Can I escort you in?"

She laughed but didn't say no. We were in a different area to Helen's party and we separated in the foyer. As we wended our way to our seat, I looked around. In the stalls, most people were dressed up. A few of the costumes were spectacular; a couple of Frank'n'furters were accurate to the smallest detail.

"Feeling okay now?" I asked Lucy.

"Fine; I didn't realise how seriously people took this. It's fantastic."

The next two hours were glorious. The production was good. The cast were all excellent; the audience sang along, joined in, and called out in all the right places. People got up and danced; at their seats, in the aisles. By the end, we were all exhausted.

As we were slowly filing out, Marcus turned to me.

"Shall we find somewhere for a drink?"

"Be nice, but everywhere's going to be packed."

"What about Shad's?"

"That's a thought."

Shad's was a small bar tucked away in a side street a couple of corners away. Locals would know it, but people came from miles around for Rocky Horror. They'd all head to the first bar they found. By the time we reached the foyer, Mary and Lucy had agreed. Then we bumped into Helen again, Penny and Ben trailing behind her.

"Fate seems to be throwing us together tonight," she said. I still wasn't sure how to take her. Was she being facetious? Or was this how she was? Was she happy to see us again? Or annoyed?

"Indeed, Helen," Marcus replied. "We're going to try and get a drink. Fancy joining us?"

She looked at him for a few seconds, as if trying to read his thoughts.

"It won't be easy to find anywhere, Marcus."

"We're going to try Shad's."

"Not a bad idea. Thank you, Marcus. We'll join you."

We finally found ourselves outside the theatre, and Helen and Marcus strode off; the rest of us trying to keep up. Ben was keeping Mary company again, and Penny, Lucy and I followed on. It was a little difficult to know what to talk about. Mary didn't know how we knew Helen, and we didn't know who Ben was. We stuck to discussing the performance we'd seen.

As we walked, I couldn't help studying Ben's bum a few feet in front of me. It was beautiful; tight and firm. Every movement was visible in those clinging shorts. My mind wandered a little.

"Nice, isn't it?"

"Sorry?" I turned to see Penny smiling at me, Lucy grinning behind her.

"Ben's bum," Penny said. "Nice, isn't it?"

I burst out laughing.

"You caught me. Yes, it is."

"Don't worry. I think so too. Lucy?"

"Well, I guess it's all right. But I'm not an expert on male bums. I prefer a nice female one."

I noticed the glint in Lucy's eyes as she offered the flirtation. She found Penny as attractive as Marcus and I did.

"Oh, I see," Penny said. "There were quite a few around tonight."

"Come on, Penny," I said. "You've got the finest bum I've seen tonight ..." she went to say something, but I continued, "… and you know it."

Even in the darkening light, I saw Penny look down. Perhaps she blushed.

"I'd say the juiciest," Lucy added.

"Pert. Definitely pert."

Lucy and I looked at each other and winked. Penny turned to us each in turn and smiled shyly, unsure how to respond.

"I'm sorry, Penny," I said. "You'll have to forgive us."

"Oh, it's okay. I'm just a bit embarrassed. But, thank you."

"Is Ben your boyfriend?" Lucy asked. I winced as I realised this could get awkward. Penny looked at me.

"Does Lucy know …?"

"Not exactly," I replied. "Although she does know about the play parties."

Penny turned to Lucy.

"Do you know what being collared means?"

"That's part of a BDSM relationship, right?"

"Yea, I'm collared to Helen. She's my mistress."

"Oh, I see."

She turned back to me.

"And so is Ben, but only part-time."
Helen seemed to get more and more interesting.

When we got to Shad's, Marcus and Helen checked they'd be happy with our attire. They were, and when we went in there were a couple of tables with other audience members. Even so, we caused a silence to descend before people resumed their conversations. Luckily, there was one long table free apart from a couple on one end. We commandeered it, and Marcus and Ben went to buy the drinks.

We were all slightly on our guard because of Mary's presence. She wasn't stupid and would probably have accepted the situation. But I wasn't ready to explain all this to her. So, we talked about the show. Mary was soon regaling us with tales of her visits, years ago. She was particularly impressed with Helen's clothes.

"Where did you get that corset, Helen? It's quite something."

"I make them, Mary. I'm a corsetiere."

They got into a discussion about various forms of underwear. I spent a few minutes surreptitiously watching Helen. I was trying to place her age. From a distance, she easily passed for mid-thirties. But when you looked closely, her face showed signs of either age or a hard life.

I realised she was cleverly made-up. Not covered, but a skilled application. I ended up deciding she was probably somewhere between forty-five and fifty. If I looked anything like that at that age, I'd be more than happy.

Ben offered to go and get another round of drinks. When he was at the bar, I noticed four lads standing by him. Late teens, early twenties. I could see they were cocky, and one of them was clearly making a few remarks about Ben, and about us. He was ignoring it. The lad nudged Ben's arm. He didn't take the bait. Helen and Marcus had noticed, and Marcus went to get up and help Ben, but Helen put her hand on his arm.

"I'll handle this, Marcus."

The leader looked over at us, and Helen beckoned the lad over. He did that laddish thing of shrugging his leather jacket on his shoulders and wandered over, a smug look on his face. He got to the table and stood over Helen. Ben followed with the tray of drinks. I noticed he had a grin on his face. I looked at Penny; she was smiling, too. I realised this could get interesting. The lad's mates were watching with leers on their faces.

Helen put on a friendly smile. She turned in her chair, and with infinite slowness, stood up. The smirk on his face drained away as she rose a good foot above him. He had to look up to meet her gaze. He suddenly appeared very small.

"What's the problem?" she asked in a friendly way.

"No ... problem," the lad said.

"Then why hassle my friend?"

He looked over at his mates for support; they were less certain now.

"Just a bit of fun, that's all."

"Fancy him, do you?"

Ben stifled a laugh.

"No, no. I'm not ..."

"Prefer me?"

The lad was unsure of himself now. But his mates were watching, and he couldn't back down. He drew on all his remaining confidence and straightened up.

"Well, more my type."

Helen spat a mocking laugh in his face and bent towards him.

"Listen, boy." The 'boy' came out like a silenced bullet. "An hour with me and you'd be a quivering wreck. I'd flay you alive. Your balls would be as shrivelled as a walnut, and the skin would be hanging off your back. You wouldn't walk for a week."

He was shrinking away from her; terrified.

"Now apologise, and we can all get on with our evening."

He should have walked away, but youthful bravado stopped him. He looked around, gaining a little confidence in this public place. A slight smirk reappeared on his face.

"What are you going to do if I don't?" he asked.

Helen had had enough. I watched in puzzlement as she bunched the lapels of his jacket in her fingers. Then in astonishment, as she lifted him a foot off the floor with one hand, his face now level with hers. The look on his face will stay with me for a long time.

"Okay ... Okay," he stammered. "I'm sorry. I'm sorry, all right?"

She held him there for a few seconds and let him go. He was too stunned to find his footing and fell in a heap on the floor. Helen calmly sat again and turned back towards us, a look of deep satisfaction on her face.

I watched the end of the table; I couldn't see the floor and wondered where the lad was.

I finally saw him a few feet away; frantically scrambling to his feet and heading towards the door. His mates were rushing to join him. As they left, I realised we weren't the only ones who had been watching events. The two tables with Rocky guests gave a cheer and a whistle. Some of the other guests were smiling. Helen excused herself and went to the loos.

"That was interesting," I said to Penny.

"Helen's not normally like that. But if you're a friend, she'll support you all the way. She can be a bit intimidating sometimes; if she wants to be."

Helen came back and sat down. The conversation resumed, and the incident was forgotten, for now. Helen finally decided it was time to go.

"We'll walk back with you," Marcus said.

"Very chivalrous of you, Marcus. But you saw I can look after myself."

"I was thinking you can save me if I get into trouble."

She laughed. A genuine laugh. I realised that was rare from Helen. Curious. We walked back to the car park and split up. We gave Mary a lift home and made sure she got indoors safely before dropping Lucy off. I didn't go in. I didn't want to start what I couldn't finish, and I wanted to get home. I'd been enjoying watching Marcus in his basque and stockings. There was something I wanted to do while he was dressed like that.

Chapter 7 – Sally

"How are your feet?" I asked Marcus, as we entered the flat from the garage.

"I didn't think about them until we walked from the theatre to Shad's. They were aching a bit by the time we arrived."

"You'll soon get used to it."

"Soon? I'm not sure I'm going to make a habit of it."

I stopped him in the passageway and pushed him against the wall.

"Perhaps you can wear them at home."

"You like me in this?"

His face showed me he was interested in my reply.

"It's rather intriguing," I said.

"It could be all the sexy people you've seen tonight."

"Could be."

"Or Ben's bum?"

"Did you hear that?"

"Bits of it."

"I guess that means Helen did, as well."

"Probably."

I was running my hands over his body. It was strange. He was usually dressed or naked. Tonight, my hands ran over material and skin alternately. I began to see what was so appealing to him when I dressed up. His hands were cupping my bum, and I felt his fingers move around my thighs, heading between my legs.

"Ah, ah," I said. "I've got plans for you. Wait for me in the bedroom."

Going into the playroom, I picked up the double-headed dildo and clipped it into a harness. I slid a little lube into me and along one end of the dildo, lifted my leg onto a chair and eased it in. When it was comfortable, I tied the harness on. I was ready.

He was lying on the bed waiting for me. When he saw me, he smiled.

"I guess you're in charge?" he said.

"For now. Come here."

He crawled across the bed to me, and I bent and kissed him.

"Stand up."

He stood on the bed, his groin at just the right height. I put my fingers in his knickers and peeled them down. I couldn't resist grinning as his hard cock was released. He kicked the briefs off, and his cock bounced around in front of me. I reached out and cupped his balls. Squeezing them, the skin tightened, and his cock steadied. I moved forward and took it between my lips.

He shivered at the touch. I slid my mouth onto it, closing my eyes as I enjoyed the taste and the heat. I ran my hands up and down his thighs, crossing his stocking tops several times. It was a new sensation for me.

A wobble from Marcus reminded me he was standing on the bed; not a stable platform for anything. I released his cock and beckoned him to kneel in front of me.

"I like you in this," I said.

"Do you?"

"Mmm. Brings out the bitch in me."

"Really?"

"Yea. I'm going to fuck you. Any questions?"

"Just one."

"What's that?"

"How would you like me?"

"On your hands and knees."

He turned on the bed and moved to the centre, grabbing a couple of pillows to rest on, and made himself comfortable. His bum was in the air, his cock jutting between his legs. I moved behind him and pulled it back towards me. Bending, I took it in my mouth and fiercely sucked it.

His body tensed at the action. I gave his bum a couple of slaps and ran my fingers between his cheeks, letting them linger along his perineum. He pushed his hips back to meet my touch. I opened the lube, and dribbled it onto his ass, letting it run over his balls.

Using one finger, I gently pushed at his hole. Moans told me he was enjoying this. My other hand was caressing his balls, occasionally stroking his cock. But the finger remained steadily massaging his ass. Then it went in; a tiny gasp as it cleared that first resistance. I continuously changed the angle, pressing all around his ring of muscle.

Then I introduced a second finger; his body tensing as it forced its way in to join the first. Both were soon searching for his prostate. A sharp groan told me I was in the right place, but I didn't want to give him all the pleasure here. Not yet.

My fingers still in his ass, I used the other hand to dribble more lube on the dildo and spread it around. I got up on my knees, and slowly withdrew my fingers. I shuffled behind him and put the end to his ass. He held still as I slowly pushed at his tight ring and twitched as it finally entered him, sliding in and out gently, going further with each stroke until it was deep in his ass. I dribbled some more lube over everything and started to speed up. He gave a little shudder at the deepest point of each stroke.

I looked down at him. The man I loved; dressed in a basque and stockings, while I fucked his ass. It was a huge thrill. And the other end of the dildo was doing its job too, pushing deep into me with each stroke. I grabbed his cock, giving it a hard tug every time I drove into him. I knew my orgasm was near. I let his cock go and steadied myself on his hips.

I was fucking him hard, driven by my own need. I needed to come. My body pushing against him. The dildo deep in his ass, causing the one in me to go deep as well. The feeling; the view; the sense of control. I stiffened, pushing the final few millimetres into both of us. Then groaned as an orgasm flowed through me.

I vaguely heard him grunt as my spasms reverberated inside him; transmitted through the dildo. I collapsed over him, running my hands up his back, and locking them over his shoulders. I stayed like that for a while, recovering. When I'd got some breath back, I dropped one hand and grabbed his cock.

"Desperate?" I asked.

"No. Not now."

"Were you?"

"I was close before you came."

"Sorry."

"I'll get you back."

"Now?"

"Why not?"

I knelt up, and gently withdrew the dildo from his ass. I watched as it slowly closed. I slapped his bum, and he turned around. We put our arms around each other and kissed. Long, slow kisses this time. He watched me unhook the harness and slip it out and off.

"Two can play at that game," he said.

He got off the bed and disappeared through the door to the playroom. When he came back a couple of minutes later, I gasped. He was wearing the harness I'd bought for his birthday. His hard cock sticking through the hole. We'd tried it a few times with a small dildo on the socket. But this time, he'd attached a large dildo, as big as he was. He had a wicked look on his face.

"On your knees."

I didn't hesitate. I didn't know if I could take both, but I wanted them. I jumped up and bent over, pushing my bum towards him. He climbed onto the bed and laid his cock and the dildo between my cheeks. He put three pillows under me, and I went to lay on them, but he pulled me back up and bent over me.

"Not yet. They're ready for when you can't hold yourself up anymore."

There was an edge to his voice. I was grinning like an idiot as he leaned to my ear.

"I'm going to fuck you hard," he whispered. "I'm not going to stop unless you need me to. Understand?"

"Mmm."

"Good."

I felt him lift off me and flinched as he poured lube between my cheeks. His finger pushed smoothly into my ass, quickly followed by another. I gasped as another pushed its way in, and he started to fuck it. I pushed back to meet his force. Then it stopped; his fingers slipped out. I braced myself for the real thing. I tried to relax. I wanted this. A part of me was tense, but there was no time.

My mouth fell open in a silent cry as the dildo caused a flash of pain pushing its way into my ass, while his cock slid into my pussy. No rocking it in and out. He pushed firmly until both cocks were embedded all the way in. The feeling was intense. I let out a long, loud moan. I heard a chuckle.

He slid out, then drove into me again. Without giving me time to catch my breath, he held my hips and started to fuck me. Almost immediately, my body responded. My pussy was tingling; my ass burning. My whole groin was a mass of conflicting sensations. I just let them happen. I was beginning to feel spaced out as he drove two cocks into me. He slapped my ass a few times, and I came.

A hard, sharp orgasm. An intense few seconds of mind-blowing confusion; my head thrown backwards and forwards. It calmed almost as quickly as it came. But he carried on. I was losing track of events now. I didn't care. I felt that rare sensation in my ass. I couldn't cope anymore and let my body drop. It hit the pillows under my hips.

Marcus followed. Now I didn't have to hold myself up, I lay there. I wasn't needed here; I could let this happen to me. He was doing the work. My body moving rhythmically as he pounded me. I vaguely heard his breathing; heavy and loud as he fucked me. I knew what was coming, a double orgasm.

Excitement and fear surged through me in unison. My body began to tense; pressure building like a coiled spring. Heat filled my groin. Suddenly a heavy throb went down both legs, making them twitch. The feelings were overwhelming. Then it hit me. Like someone smacking me in the face. My vision went first; light, stars, flashing. I lost my hearing; I heard nothing around me. Except for a long scream; a weird mix of high-pitched calls and a deep reverberating groan. Then a distant deep cry, as the regular movement of my body gave way to a row of irregular jerks and spasms. Then nothing.

I opened my eyes. I could hear a faint pounding in my ears. I could hear breathing. Mine? His? I studied it for a moment. His. I gradually became aware of his weight laying on top of me. I could see my hand on the bed next to me, his fingers entwined with mine. I was slowly aware of the pressure between my legs. I wriggled. Both cocks were still in place.

"Are you okay?"

"Mmm?"

"Are you okay?" His voice, faintly in my ear.

"Mmm. Did I pass out?"

"I think you may have for a few seconds."

"Wow."

"Hold still."

"Mmm."

I wasn't going anywhere. His weight lifted and I held my hips still as he gently withdrew the dildo from my ass. I heard him undo the harness and drop gently onto me again; half his weight now resting on the bed. He enclosed me in his arms. I was so sleepy; I didn't want to talk. He knew.

I felt him undo my suspenders and roll my stockings off, then unhook my basque and roll me over to remove it. He lifted me gently to remove the pillows. I curled up, and after he'd taken his lingerie off, he cuddled in behind me, holding me. Tears ran down my face as I fell asleep in his arms.

Chapter 8 – Marcus

I was used to occasional extreme reactions from Sally after some of our play. The tears we accepted now. They were a release. Of tension? Of pleasure? Of emotion? We didn't know; she couldn't explain it herself. She always said they were tears of love; that was how she felt when it happened. I wasn't going to argue. They only appeared after an intense experience. But I wasn't sure about the passing out.

"I think you ought to get checked out; just in case."

"Oh, I don't think it's anything to worry about," she replied.

"Probably not. But I've never seen it before."

"It's never happened to me before you."

"Is that three times, now?"

"Yea."

"Get it checked out."

"Mmm."

"Promise?"

She poked her tongue out.

"Promise?"

"All right."

***

Eva sent me my manuscript after her editor had worked on it. I spent a day or two going through it. Some of it annoyed me, but I had to admit most of the comments and amendments were logical. Perhaps editors were useful after all. I was still undecided. But I had another meeting booked with Eva the following week; I'd wait and see what happened.

When I arrived at her office, the editor, Eleanor, was waiting with her. We spent an hour going over some of the suggestions. She was a little pedantic; the purpose of an editor, I guess. I put my foot down in a few areas but agreed to make many of the other changes and re-submit it. Eleanor left us, and I went to leave as well.

"Marcus, a couple of other things."

I sat down again.

"I'm thinking of taking Shadows of Gold. Eleanor likes it …"

"Could have fooled me."

"… she likes it and feels it has commercial potential. I do as well. When you've edited it, and we've re-read it, I'll confirm that."

"Okay. Thanks, Eva. I'm on holiday in a week. I won't be able to start the editing for at least three weeks."

"That's fine. The other thing is Spewn Words."

"Oh, yes."

"I showed it to someone I know. He runs a sister imprint and is quite taken with it."

"Is he as mad as me?"

"Quite possibly. But he wants to show it to a couple of his team. For now, he'll come through me. If he wants to take it further, I'll let you know."

I came away feeling quite good. Eva was interested in one book and had found someone who might be interested in another. Things were looking up.

***

We flew into Nice airport on Wednesday afternoon. We'd managed to come away for twelve days; it had been difficult for Sally to get time off. Lucy was going to join us on the fourth day. After we landed, we picked up our hire car and headed towards the villa.

After some debate, we'd decided not to stay in a hotel. A villa would give us more freedom, and when Lucy arrived, it would be easier all around given our slightly unusual situation. No nosey hotel staff to pass judgement. Once we'd made the decision, Sally had insisted on something a bit special. I didn't argue, and when we arrived, I was glad I hadn't.

The road followed the side of a hill about a half a mile from the sea. Dotted along it were several villas, well-spaced and private from each other. All with views along the coast. When we found ours, I turned into the gateway, and large metal gates swung open. The villa was set back from the road. An austere front, with a typical Mediterranean front garden. Waiting at the door was a middle-aged woman, in a coat and headscarf. The temperature was at least twenty-eight Celsius.

She greeted us in clear English and gave us a quick tour. She would be up to clean every other day at ten in the morning. If we needed anything, we just needed to ask. With that, she was gone. We went through the villa to the back. The front may have been austere, but this was where the action was.

It opened out onto a terrace the width of the building, split into three areas, a couple of steps up or down from each other. The area nearest to the house was covered with a trellis supporting flowering climbers. The next area was open to the sun, and the final one was the pool. Not huge, but big enough for some gentle exercise, or just cooling off. Chairs, tables, and sunbeds were on each level.

"How many people does this usually accommodate?" Sally asked.

"God knows. There are enough chairs for about twenty."

But the real bonus was the view. From each level, all you could see was a brief strip of countryside, the thin ribbon of the coast road, then the sea and coastline. Miles in each direction; the sun reflecting off the water, even from this distance.

"This is some place," she said, hugging me.

"Not bad is it?"

"Let's get our things in, then we can relax."

We found there were five bedrooms. Three were simple and plain, but the best two were at the back, either side of the main living area. Both opened out directly onto the terrace. They were beautiful; simply furnished, but elegant with soft, homely touches. We chose one and unpacked.

"Let's see what the welcome pack contains."

We went into the kitchen; it was surprisingly well-equipped. Sally looked through the fridge and the box on the centre table.

"There's more than enough here for today," she said. "We can do some shopping tomorrow."

"Good. I want to chill out for the rest of today."

"I fancy a swim."

"Great idea. I need the loo first."

In the bedroom, I changed into some swim shorts and walked out to the pool. Sally laughed when she saw me. I spotted her clothes in a pile on the terrace.

"What do you need those for? There's no-one to see us."

She rolled onto her back as I got to the pool, to show me her naked form. I pulled my shorts off and jumped into the water. Our holiday had begun.

Except it wasn't all holiday. We'd come here with a purpose. To visit Beaulieu-sur-Mer to see the house, and visit the addresses we had in Nice and Monte Carlo. Whether any of these would lead anywhere, we didn't know.

"What shall we do today?" Sally asked as we had breakfast the next morning.

"Well, we need some shopping. Beaulieu isn't far away. Let's not put it off. Why don't we go and look around? We're bound to be able to pick up supplies."

Beaulieu proved to be a pretty town. Quite affluent, with two spacious marinas. We drove around before parking and exploring on foot. It had a classic Mediterranean feel. The pace of life was leisurely, the people friendly. Even this early in the season, there were a lot of tourists.

We found a lively market and bought lots of fresh fish, fruit, and veg. We found a baker, a cheese shop, and stocked up with some local wine. By lunchtime, we were hungry and went towards the Marina to find a restaurant. We ended up in the African Queen, where lunch was excellent and the views wonderful. It wasn't too hot yet, a gentle breeze coming in off the sea.

We strolled back to the car arm in arm. We came to a square and paused to get our bearings. I looked around at the roads leading off it.

"Look. That's the street."

The house was there.

"Shall we?" I asked.

Sally looked at me.

"Yes. Let's walk by."

"What number was it?"

"Twenty-three."

We turned into the street and studied the house numbers. As so often in France, they weren't very logical. But we soon worked out it would be on the opposite side. As we walked, Sally gripped my arm harder. I knew she was in two minds about all this. Then it appeared. Number twenty-three.

A large detached house, different from its neighbours. They were clearly built after the war, but this one was older, nineteenth century, if not earlier. Simple but ornate, with an air of faded grandeur. Set far enough back to allow a small front garden, consisting mainly of grass and a couple of ubiquitous palms. A parking space for two cars, currently empty.

We stood for a few minutes; I let Sally take her time. If Martin was right, her father had spent time in that house. Possibly with a wife and at least one child, who would be Sally's half-brother. I could only guess how that felt. Eventually, she turned to me.

"What now?" she asked.

"Let's move on. We know where it is. There have been no rivers of fire or brimstone. No clues, either."

We returned to the car. When we were ready to go, I turned to her.

"Okay?"

She looked at me.

"Yes. I expected to feel something. But I don't."

"I don't think you will from a house. It's people who tend to have that effect."

We returned to the villa and stowed our shopping. After a rest and a swim, we headed towards Nice and spent the evening along the seafront. More seeing than being seen, but it was fun, nonetheless. A good meal followed, before heading home.

The bedroom was a perfect setting for soft, gentle sex. With all the doors open to the terrace, the air circulated over our naked bodies. The heat of the day was passing, and the gentle breeze and calm sounds soon lulled us into slumber.

We woke the next morning with the doors still open, the breeze still drifting into the room. Holidays seemed to stimulate Sally, and she slowly rode me to our mutual pleasure. The villa played to her exhibitionist streak. She didn't wear anything when we were there. Stripping off as soon as we got home. I did the same; it did feel liberating. It was also tiring, as it led to frequent episodes of physical activity.

"What shall we do today?" she asked as we lay on the bed.

"Well, we ought to get the investigating done. Then when Lucy arrives, we can do holiday things."

"I guess it's either Nice or Monte Carlo."

"Yup. You choose."

"Monte Carlo. It's further away."

We set out an hour later, with the business card from the safety deposit box. A name, an address, and a phone number. Nothing else. No clue as to who this person was or what they did. The name itself, Adnan Moranghi, gave little clue to his origins. We'd googled the name; not much had come back.

When we arrived, we found a place to park and set off on foot. Wandering around the famous streets, doing the tourist bit first. It was quite a place for people-watching. We stopped for coffee in an outdoor café.

"This place certainly lives up to its reputation," I said.

"Yea. It's a bit … up itself."

"And you can almost smell the money."

"I know. We're well off by most people's standards," she said. "But this place makes me feel like a pauper."

"Well, we don't have to stay long. Shall we see what we can find?"

We headed for the address on the card. It turned out to be an anonymous office block, with a long list of company registration plates by the doors.

"Looks like this was an accommodation address," I said. "I'm not sure we'll find much here. But let's see if there's a reception desk or something."

There was; in the lobby. We showed the receptionist the card, but the name meant nothing to her. She was in her twenties, so this card going back perhaps twenty years or more was a long shot. She assured us there was no-one of that name currently in the building.

"Let's try one last thing," I suggested. "There's something like a public records office by the station. Perhaps it might mean something there."

We climbed the hill and reached a building housing several government offices. We eventually found the right department and went in. A couple of elderly men sat behind one large desk and looked up as we entered. We showed them the card and asked if they'd ever heard of the man. They looked slowly at each other.

"Of course. Where did you get this?"

We told them the minimum we thought safe to impart.

"Well, your father must have moved in interesting circles."

"Who was Adnan Moranghi?" Sally finally asked. We were both getting a little impatient.

"That wasn't his real name. Probably an alias. He was resident here for many years in the eighties and nineties. Respected businessman. Ran several companies in various fields and gave to local organisations and charities."

"You say it wasn't his real name?"

"No. But no-one's sure now who he was. In the late nineties, he disappeared. Ninety-seven or ninety-eight, I think it was. It turned out his companies were mostly shells. No real business, but lots of money flowing through them. He's not been heard of since."

It was the first documented proof we had that Sally's father had at least one dodgy contact. We thanked the two gentlemen and walked back to the entrance. Sally was quiet.

"Surprised?" I asked.

"Hardly. We know there's something dodgy about him. It's hardly surprising he had contact with other dodgy people."

"I'm not sure there's anything else we can do here. This place is famous for its secrecy. Even if we find the right people to ask, I suspect they won't give us any answers."

We drove out of Monaco, and meandered along the coast road, stopping at Villefranche for lunch.

"Look," Sally said. "This morning we got a bit of information, but not much. Nice is just up the road. Why don't we visit that address this afternoon?"

"Get them both over in one day?"

"Yes. If it produces as little information as Monaco, we're probably done."

The card we had wasn't much more helpful than the Monte Carlo one. Except this one wasn't for a person. 'Le Sphinx' was all it said. With an address and a phone number. The number seventy-six was elaborately printed in red on the reverse side.

When we found the building, it appeared to be a typical nineteenth-century French townhouse. A large double doorway, through which we could see a courtyard filled with flowers. There was no sign of any business activity. It appeared to be a residential block.

"Perhaps there's a concierge," I said.

We crossed the road and went through the open door. As expected, there was a smaller doorway just inside, and I knocked. Moments later, a woman of indeterminate age appeared.

"Oui?"

"Bonjour, madame. Parlez-vous anglaise?"

"Yes. Though not often, these days."

"Excuse the intrusion, but does this mean anything to you?"

Sally showed her the card. She looked at it, turned it over, and looked at us. A blank expression on her face.

"Where did you get this?"

"It was in my father's effects."

The concierge nodded.

"You may not want to know."

"I know my father wasn't a saint. Tell me."

She studied us for a few seconds and made a decision.

"Come in."

We followed her into her home. One room was a living room and kitchen, with presumably a small bedroom and a bathroom at the back. Typical accommodation of its type. We sat, and she poured us two small cups of coffee, then went over to a cupboard and searched amongst piles of papers for a few minutes. Finally coming back, she threw several cards onto the table. All identical to the one Sally held. We looked at each other, and back at our host.

"What are these?" Sal asked.

"I haven't seen another one of these for over ten years. This wasn't always a block of apartments; it was once a house of pleasure."

"A brothel?" Sally asked.

"If you like. But a select one. Very expensive; very exclusive. One only got in by personal recommendation. These cards are membership cards. Never more than one hundred at a time."

We looked at the cards. There were about a dozen on the table.

"Only a hundred customers?"

"No. If you were a member you could bring guests or lend your card to someone you trusted. But you were responsible for their behaviour."

"You were … familiar with …"

"I worked here, yes. But I wasn't one of the girls. I wasn't beautiful or sophisticated enough. I didn't have the skills some of them offered. I was one of the maids. I looked after the girls."

"It closed?" Sally asked.

"Yes. In two thousand and three. It was all very sudden. The owner arrived one evening as we were about to open, and gave the staff notice. It never opened again. I was lucky; the block was sold and turned into apartments. The new owners gave me this job."

Sally opened her bag and looked at me. I nodded. She took a photo out and showed it to the concierge. Her face broke into a smile.

"Ah, let me see … Mr … Mahoney, yes? You are his daughter?"

"Yes."

"He was a real gentleman."

"He visited often?"

"I seem to remember he came and went. Sometimes here often, then not for weeks. I think he had a favourite, but I can't remember now."

She leaned forward and put her hand on Sally's.

"I'm sorry, you may not want to hear all this."

"It's fine. I wouldn't have come if I didn't want to know."

The concierge reminisced about the place, but it soon became clear she couldn't tell us any more about Sally's father. We stayed until it was polite to make our excuses and leave. As we walked down the street, Sally suddenly stopped and burst out laughing.

"We've discovered my father was acquainted with a dodgy businessman in Monaco who used a made-up name, and now he was a regular visitor to an up-market brothel in Nice. What's next?"

"God knows. He's the present that keeps on giving."

She kissed me.

"Come on. That's enough for today. Let's find somewhere to eat, I'm hungry. Then back to the villa and see if we can think of anything to do this evening."

"I've got one or two ideas."

"Me too. Care to discuss them while we eat?"

Chapter 9 – Lucy

The warmth of the Mediterranean air hit me as I stepped out of the plane door onto the gantry. I stopped for a moment and took a deep breath; a smile crossing my face as I exhaled. It wasn't a big airport, and it didn't take long to retrieve my luggage and head for the exit. I saw Sally as I came into the arrivals area.

"Hello, you," she said, giving me a bear hug, followed by a surprisingly passionate kiss.

"Hi, Sal. A bit late, I'm afraid."

"Oh, it's only an hour. I went and had a coffee. Let me carry something."

I gave her my carry-on and trailing my case, followed her towards the car parks.

"No Marcus?"

"No. I left him at the villa."

"Is it far?"

"Only about fifteen or twenty minutes."

We threw my stuff into the car.

"Well, we're on holiday again," Sal said, looking at me.

"Yes. I keep thinking of last time."

"Me too."

"Different this time, though."

"It'll still be fun."

As we left the airport and hit the coast road, I thought about that. During our holiday in Italy, we'd become lovers. But we'd been on our own. This time, Marcus was here as well. It made me feel uncomfortable.

Not about Marcus. I liked him, and we got on well. He shared the same sense of humour as Sal and me, and he was happy with the relationship I had with her. But to spend a week under the same roof? There was plenty of room for embarrassment; or worse. But Sally didn't seem to see any problems, so I had convinced myself it would be fine.

I looked out over the water as we drove along the promenade and headed east. Sally had been right; after less than fifteen minutes, she turned onto a road into the hills, and a few minutes later drove through automatic gates into a circular driveway. We took my stuff in through the front door.

"Dump it all here and I'll show you around."

The hallway opened out into a large living area, with the kitchen off to one side. There was a row of open doors at the back, all covered with billowing voile drapes. She led me out onto the terrace, where we found Marcus. He rose from a sun-lounger and gave me a big hug. Sally leaned over and gave him a kiss.

"I was getting worried," he said to me. "I was afraid you hadn't got my SOS."

I looked at Sal; she looked as baffled as me.

"What SOS?" I asked.

"I need help, Luce."

I knew he was joking, but I hadn't worked out what the joke was.

"Help?"

"Yes." He leaned close to my ear. "You remember we said Sal would need to work twice as hard to keep us both satisfied?"

"Yes."

"And how we wondered if she'd manage it?"

"Yea."

"Well, she has. Thank God you're here, Luce." He was hamming it up; his voice taking on a melodramatic tone. "I can't cope on my own. She's draining my lifeblood away." He dropped to his knees in front of me, raising his clasped hands. Sally was frowning and I was trying not to giggle. I'd never seen Marcus in such a playful mood. "Save me, Lucy. Save me, I beg you. Save me from this sex-crazed hussy."

Sally finally picked up a cushion from one of the chairs and started bashing him about the shoulders. He continued his act, dropping to the floor.

"You see. You see what she's like. She beats me if I don't do what she says."

Sally threw the cushion at him. He smiled, and she offered him her hand and pulled him up. She kissed him.

"Idiot. I'm not that bad. Besides, I haven't heard you complain."

"Who said I was complaining?"

"I'm going to show Lucy her room and help her unpack. You get some rest. Apparently, you need it."

He slapped her bum as she walked by; she winked at me. I was beginning to feel in a relaxed holiday mood already. We retrieved my bags from the hall, and she led me back into the living area.

"That's our room; this is yours. They're both the same."

Going through the door, I entered a large welcoming bedroom, with a shower room off it. One wall was a row of glazed doors opening onto the terrace. I threw my case on the bed, and Sally put the bag next to it.

"I think I'll take a shower first," I said. "I'm all sweaty after travelling."

Sally closed the door and looked at me.

"Like someone to scrub you down?"

"But … Marcus …?"

"Marcus …" she called in a strong voice.

"Yes?" wafted in from the terrace.

"What time's dinner?"

"Whenever you two have finished. You're cooking."

She raised an eyebrow; I had to laugh. Perhaps this was going to be easier than I'd feared.

I was in full holiday mode as Sally and I prepared dinner. It normally took me a while to unwind when I went away, but it was different this time. An hour with Sal had worked out all the tensions and knots. We put together a simple meal; pasta, a tomato and cheese sauce and some bread. When we took it out onto the terrace, Marcus had cleared a table and opened a couple of bottles of wine. We sat down and started a leisurely meal.

"Lucy was wondering how we're going to work this, darling," Sal said.

I winced, but it still bothered me.

"How would you like it to work?" he asked me.

"I … I'm not sure. I feel like the other woman."

"Well, I suggest a couple of rules. First, we all wear something around the villa."

"Ooohh," Sally whined.

I looked at her and Marcus laughed.

"It's okay, Luce. She's been parading around naked since we arrived."

"As have you, darling."

"Yes, but I'm pretty sure Lucy doesn't want to be put off her dinner by seeing me naked, or the other way around."

"You'd be put off your dinner by seeing Lucy naked?"

"You know what I mean. I'd certainly be distracted, and we don't want anyone feeling uncomfortable. It's all right for you; we've both seen everything you've got."

Sally grinned at him, then at me.

"Secondly," he continued. "Whatever two of us might be doing, don't embarrass the person not involved."

"You don't want to watch Lucy and me?"

Sally was loving this.

"Behave, you. Lucy won't want to see us, and she won't want me seeing you two. Whatever you might want."

She stuck her tongue out at him. He looked at me and shrugged.

"Basically, Luce. That's your room, and that's mine. Where this little minx sleeps is up to her."

Sally's face took on a serious air and she looked at him.

"Really?" she asked.

"Of course."

I was a bit embarrassed.

"No," I said. "That doesn't sound right."

"Luce, we're on holiday. Normal rules can go hang. If Sal wants to sleep with you one night and me the next, I'm fine with that."

Sally laid her hand on Marcus's arm.

"I do love you," she said and gave him a kiss. As she turned to me, smiling, Marcus continued.

"Mind you, I'll expect you to make up for it the following day."

"I think I can manage that."

She poured some more wine. I felt more comfortable having discussed my doubts openly. I still couldn't believe how accepting Marcus was of me; or at least, my relationship with Sally. The fact his partner was openly sleeping with someone else didn't seem to bother him. Indeed, he had encouraged it. I wasn't prudish at all, but I wondered if I could have been as understanding.

"Darling?" Sal asked.

"Mmm."

"About the dress code …"

He frowned at her.

"… would topless be all right? I mean, most of the beaches around here are topless."

He shook his head in resignation.

"Luce," he said. "Don't let this wicked witch lead you into bad habits."

"I think it might be me who's led her into sin."

"Then you're as bad as one another. Which means I must be the resident saint."

Sally laughed.

"If you're a saint now I cannot wait until you become a sinner."

I asked how they'd got on with their investigations and they brought me up to date.

"Wow. Disappearing conmen and brothels. What's next?"

"We're not sure," Sal said. "We're at a bit of a dead-end. The only option would be knocking on the door of the house in Beaulieu, and we're not sure that's a good idea."

I understood their position. If the other family lived in that house, it would come as a hell of a shock to them to find out the truth.

"Probably better to leave them in ignorance."

"Yes," Sally said. "I'm not sure it would achieve anything."

She cleared the table and took the dishes inside.

"Luce," Marcus said in her absence. "While we're here, do whatever you want. But if anything makes you feel uncomfortable, please say. You two won't have a problem, but I don't want to do anything to embarrass you."

"Thanks, Marcus. It'll be fine. Anyway, I'm not sure you could embarrass me; I've seen a few photos, remember?"

He blushed slightly; the first time I'd seen it.

"Oh, yes. I'd forgotten that."

When Sally came back, Marcus sighed and rolled his eyes. She'd already adopted the new rules. Dressed now in just her bikini bottoms, she brought a couple of plates of fruit to the table. She noticed us both looking at her.

"What?" she said, with that alluring look on her face which was both brazen and innocent.

By the time we had finished dinner, the air had cooled, and Sally and I moved out onto the unshaded section of the terrace. Lying on adjoining sun-loungers, we let the food settle. I had removed my wrap but kept both halves of my bikini on. As I lay there, I wondered why.

It was Marcus's presence that made me hesitate. I smiled to myself when I thought about it. Hanging on the wall of their playroom was one of my paintings. Of me playing with myself. I finally decided to go with the flow. Sally watched as I removed my top half. I was happy with my body. If Marcus wanted to look, I wasn't going to stop him, and I was quite sure Sally wouldn't either. I laid back and closed my eyes.

The next thing I knew, Sally was gently rubbing my arm.

"Fancy a swim?" she said.

Marcus was slowly sculling about in the pool. A moment's hesitation as I debated putting my top back on, but Sally was already on her feet waiting for me. I got up and followed her. As we approached the pool, Marcus turned to us; he saw my naked breasts and smiled. I was surprised to find myself comfortable with his gaze and smiled back.

"She won, Marcus."

"She usually does," he replied.

We walked down the steps into the water and floated around. I'd never had a whole pool to myself; well, apart from my companions. No-one to bother us, no shouting louts, no screaming kids. Just friends, sunshine, and peace. After a while, Marcus got out and went to the covered area, returning with our glasses and a fresh bottle of wine. Sitting on the edge, he filled them, and we floated towards him. Resting one arm on the side, we slowly sipped our wine.

"Beautiful view, isn't it?" Sally asked.

I looked behind me to take in the vista of the green slope leading to the blue sea.

"It is. This is a perfect spot."

"Mmm. Which view are you looking at, darling?"

I turned to Sally. She had a wicked grin on her face, as she looked at Marcus.

"Well, I'm spoilt for choice," he replied, a soft smile on his face. "I have a wonderful view over the Mediterranean; clear, peaceful and calming. But I also have two beautiful women almost naked in front of me. I'll enjoy both if nobody minds."

"I don't. How about you, Luce?"

I saw the humour in the situation and laughed. They looked at me quizzically.

"Oh, come on. You two are lovers; as are you and I," I said, looking at Sal. "I've painted your cock in all its glory, Marcus, from some explicit photos, and you've got a painting on your wall of me spread wide open. Let's scrap the rules."

I undid my bikini bottoms and pulled them away, dropping them on the side of the pool. Almost before I'd finished, Sally had done the same. We both looked at Marcus. For the first time, he looked unsure.

"Come on, darling," Sal said. "Get 'em off."

He looked at me, a mild frown on his face.

"Don't blame me if it wakes up, with you two walking around like that."

"Don't worry, Marcus," I said. "I might learn something."

He shrugged, stood up, and slid his shorts off.

We lounged about in the pool or on the steps for some time. It was liberating. I couldn't remember ever swimming naked; possibly a long time ago in the sea, but this was so natural. We were easy together. We looked at each other; we made no attempt to hide that. We were enjoying our time together, our friendship and more, and admiring each other.

I thought about how I felt when Marcus looked at me and was surprised I was quite enjoying it. I hadn't sought men's interest for years. Dealing with pests was commonplace, but all women had to cope with that. As a gay woman, I hadn't spent any time thinking about how a man would view me. The wine gave me the confidence to ask.

"Marcus …" I said.

"Mmm."

"Do you see me any differently, knowing I'm gay?"

He looked puzzled.

"No. I don't think so. Why would I?"

"I just wondered."

"Do you mean because he can't have you?" Sally asked.

"Possibly."

"That's irrelevant," he said. "If I saw you, I wouldn't know you were gay. I'd see what I've always seen, a beautiful woman with a beautiful body. What's not to like?"

I smiled at the compliments; genuinely meant, freely given.

"Now you see the attraction for me," Sally said to him, putting her arm around me.

"Oh, I've always seen the attraction," he replied. "I'm just seeing a lot more detail."

Sally laughed.

"Careful, Luce. He can be an old smoothie when he wants to be. It's getting a bit cool. Let's have a quick shower to wash the pool water off, then we can put something on and get drunk on the terrace."

She wrapped her arms around me and gave me a lingering kiss, looking at Marcus as she did so, then headed for the steps. I joined her, and we walked out of the water and across the terrace towards the doors. Marcus followed a few paces behind, and I could almost feel his gaze focussed on our nakedness.

By the time we went to bed, Sally and I had indeed drunk too much. Marcus generously told us to sober up together, and Sally spent the night with me. We weren't too drunk to enjoy ourselves, though. When my eyes opened the next morning, Sally's head was on the pillow beside me. She was watching me.

"Good morning," she said softly.

"Hello."

"Sleep well?"

I rolled onto my back and went through that first wonderful stretch of the day.

"Mmm. Yea."

Her hand slid across my tummy. I closed my eyes at its touch. Before I knew it, she'd rolled on top of me, her thighs straddling my hips. She started kissing me; soft, gentle, teasing. Ah, well; it was still early. No hurry to get up.

As we lay recovering from our mutual pleasure, she turned to me, a glint in her eye. She gave me a kiss.

"I think I'll see if Marcus is awake."

"And if he isn't?"

"I'll find a way to wake him."

She slid out of bed and disappeared through the open doors onto the terrace. This was turning into some holiday. In the space of twenty-four hours, I'd gone from worrying about how it could work with the three of us, to a point where I was happily wandering around naked in front of Marcus, with Sally bed-hopping between us. I was learning more about myself all the time.

"There's breakfast out here if you want some."

Sally was standing by the door leading onto the terrace, holding back a drape with her arm. She was wearing a thin wrap.

"I'll be there."

I popped to the loo and grabbed a beach dress. Going onto the terrace, Sally and Marcus were sitting at the table, with a variety of things laid out.

"I see we've found some clothes this morning," I said after a few mouthfuls.

"We discovered it's best to cover anything too tender when eating," Marcus replied.

"You 'discovered'?"

"Yes," Sal said. "On our second night, he dropped a piece of sardine."

"Oh …"

"Mmm. Stung a bit, didn't it darling?"

"Fell right between my thigh and my balls. Could have scarred me for life."

"Now we wear something when we're eating; just in case."

"Good idea. I suppose you had to kiss it better, Sal?"

She looked at me, then Marcus.

"No, I didn't. Missed a trick there, darling."

We took a leisurely breakfast. Even with all our activity, it was still early.

"What are we doing today?" Sally asked.

Marcus turned to me.

"We've got a few things we wouldn't mind doing around here. Anything you've got in mind, Luce?"

We compared lists; they mostly overlapped.

"Okay," Marcus said. "We've got over a week, so we don't need to rush. I guess we might also want a couple of days lounging around here?"

Sal and I both nodded our agreement.

"How about Nice today? It's nearest, and the only place which needs a whole day."

"Sounds good," I replied. "There are a couple of museums I'd like to visit. I'll go on my own if you're not interested."

They shared a look.

"Matisse and Chagall?"

I might have guessed they'd have done their homework.

It was a long day. We visited the two museums. It was an interesting experience, both in its own right and for what I learned about Marcus. I loved talking about art; even though neither artists were my forte. I'd been to museums and galleries with Sal; she was always keen to learn.

He turned out to be the same. Asking questions about style, technique, influences. The more time I spent with him, the more I understood why Sally found him appealing. After we'd toured the Matisse museum, we sat down for coffee.

"I hope we haven't pestered you too much, Luce. If you want some time to wander around on your own …"

"No thanks, Marcus. There's much more to art than just looking. I love talking about it; I don't usually have any willing accomplices. You're not getting away that easily."

We had lunch in a small café near the cathedral, before moving on to the Chagall museum. Then spent the afternoon wandering around the city. We finished up by the beach, taking time to stroll along the Promenade des Anglais; being tourists. We found a beachside restaurant and spent three hours over a leisurely meal.

By the time we arrived at the villa, we were all shattered and agreed to plan our days more carefully. I went to my bed, and they went to theirs. The next few days were wonderful. The weather was perfect; sunny and hot, but not sweltering.

Lucy

One evening, we were laying on loungers, when the sky darkened in a matter of minutes. Almost without warning, a spectacular thunderstorm engulfed us. Lightning flashing across the sky, thunder rumbling all around us. Rain coming down; warm and heavy. Sal and I made a move to go under cover, but Marcus went to the pool and jumped in. I looked at her and we burst out laughing. We both ran across the terrace and joined him.

It was surreal. Three naked people in a pool, while thunder and lightning reverberated around us. Rain falling heavily onto the water; onto our heads. Sally went over to Marcus and threw herself at him, hugging him and calling him a mad fool. She called me over, and I joined the hug. Our bodies embraced under the torrent. And we laughed; laughed until it hurt.

Then it stopped. One enormous flash; one deafening roar. Then nothing. Silence. No noise, no flashes, no rain. It had gone as quickly as it had appeared. I was suddenly conscious of our closeness. Our mutual embrace. We looked at each other; our embrace held firm. Sal gave Marcus a passionate kiss, then turned to me and did the same. She looked at us. Part of me wanted something to happen; wanted to see where this might lead.

But it wasn't to be. Marcus released his hold on Sally and me and drifted away towards the steps. As he climbed out, I briefly saw his cock. Fully awake this time. I turned to Sal; she had seen it too. There was a strange look on her face, a mixture of puzzlement and disappointment.

Before we could do anything else, Marcus returned, wrapped in a towel, holding two others. The storm had lowered the temperature, and I had goose-bumps on the skin exposed above the water.

We went to the steps, and as we left the water, he threw a towel over our shoulders. I noticed his cock pushing the towel out. Sal would be sleeping with him tonight. We returned to the house, dried off and put some clothes on. The momentary awkwardness forgotten.

When I went to bed later, I thought about what had happened. The closeness we'd felt in the pool had been exciting; strangely erotic as the storm spent itself around us. They'd both had their arms around me; mine around both of them. Nothing had happened, but as I lay there, I began to wish it had. I was glad I'd brought my vibe with me. That night, I needed it.

The next morning, we decided to spend the day lazing around the villa. It had been a busy few days, and we deserved a rest. We set ourselves up on a row of loungers, with everything we needed on tables in front of us. We each had books we dipped in and out of; we chatted about nothing and took the occasional swim. I'd once again feared a little awkwardness after the events of the previous evening, but realised it was all in my head. Everything was fine.

A few times, I found myself looking at Marcus. Looking at his cock, docile once again. Watching it move as he walked; glancing over at it when he was lying on the lounger. I blushed as Sally caught my gaze on more than one occasion. She raised her eyebrows and smiled but said nothing.

I suspected while he was happy to share her with me, she would be equally happy to share him as well. I spent some time thinking about that eventuality.

Marcus went in to make some lunch and returned with a tray of food.

"It's all cold stuff. All right if I bring it down here?"

We agreed and shared a meal naked. It seemed natural, but I still found it amusing. Suddenly, I burst out laughing. Marcus and Sally looked at one another, then at me.

"Care to share?" Sally asked.

I tried to control my laughter, which had caught me by surprise.

"Sorry," I spluttered. "I suddenly had a vision."

"Of?"

"Of my father seeing me now. Lazing in the south of France by a pool, eating and drinking alongside my lover and her other lover, all naked. If he hadn't already had a stroke, this would probably have given him one."

I could see they weren't sure whether to laugh or not, but I was still giggling.

"Oh, you can laugh. It's too funny."

They joined my amusement.

"What about your mum?" Sal asked.

"Oh, she wouldn't approve of it either. And she wouldn't begin to understand the connections between us. I'm not sure she knows what gay people actually do."

"Seriously?" Marcus asked.

"Too ignorant. Probably never even thought about it. And I'm not telling my own mother what I do in bed."

I was still chuckling after several minutes. Even I wasn't sure it was that funny, but it kept me amused. Sally went to get some more wine.

"We need some more red; these are the last two bottles. We can go after lunch."

"You stay here," Marcus said. "I'll pop into Beaulieu. I can't stay in the sun all day anyway. You two can work on your tans."

She bent and kissed him.

"If you're sure."

"Of course. Is there anything else we need?"

An hour later, he set off with a shopping list. Sally poured some more wine, and we went back to our books. A little while later, she put hers down and rolled onto her front. I let my eyes settle on her bum.

"Marcus thinks I should apologise," she said.

"What for?" I asked, though I suspected I knew. I knew him well enough to know how conscious he was of other people's feelings.

"For last night in the pool. He thinks I might have made you feel uncomfortable."

"No, Sal. No apology necessary."

We fell silent.

"It was interesting, though," I said.

"Interesting?"

"Mmm."

"In what way?"

Chapter 10 – Marcus

I smiled as I looked at the list we'd eventually compiled. It had been wine we needed; now I was looking for about twenty items, mostly from different shops. But Beaulieu was quiet. Sensible people were sheltering from the sun. I made my way from shop to shop, getting everything we needed, and a few others I saw along the way.

This was the first holiday I'd had for years; abroad, anyway. My health hadn't been up to it, but the operation had changed things and I was better than I had been for a long time. I knew it wouldn't last, not if past experience was anything to go by, but I was determined to make the most of it. I decided we'd have at least one more good break this year.

Sally and Lucy would want to go away as well. I was happy with that. They were good for each other. I'd never been one for friends. It sounded odd, put as bleakly as that, but I'd never had a male best friend. My best friends had always been women. Perhaps I was simply weird.

As I was driving out of the centre, I came to the square, and on a whim, decided to drive past the house again. There was a car parked there this time. A swanky AMG Mercedes. There were no signs of life in the house itself, but the car meant there was someone there. As I drove back to the villa, I wondered what Sally wanted to do. The only option was to turn up and knock on the door. It was risky, and the consequences worried me, but we'd have to make a decision.

I carried the provisions into the kitchen when I got back. There was no sound coming from the terrace; they were probably asleep. I worked quietly to put the things away and went into the bedroom and slipped off my clothes. Going to the doors onto the terrace, I pushed a drape aside and looked out.

Straight into Lucy's eyes, looking back at me, her head buried between Sally's open legs. She didn't move. I did. I did one of those things you only ever see in the movies. Without stopping, I turned in a small circle and went back into the bedroom. I stood still, replaying the scene. I was a little embarrassed, yes. But that wasn't in the forefront of my mind. The image was. An image I'd imagined many times.

"Darling …"

Sally's voice calling.

"Yes?"

"You can come out."

I quickly pulled some shorts on, took a deep breath, and pushed through the drapes. Sally's head was turned looking at me, and her arm was outstretched towards me. But her feet were still on the floor either side of the lounger, her legs spread. Lucy was still lying between them, her head resting on Sal's thigh. She was watching me with no sign of embarrassment. I walked over and took Sal's hand. She looked up and smiled.

"You can take those off," she said. "We all know what's in there."

I shrugged and slid the shorts off. I could already feel the blood pumping in my groin.

"Why don't you sit down?"

She nudged me onto the lounger next to her, and I gave in, making myself comfortable. If they wanted to carry on, I wasn't going to object. Sally gave me a sultry wink and turned to Lucy.

"Now. Where were we?"

She laid back on the cushions, and Lucy lifted her head, lowering her mouth over Sally's open pussy. Sally groaned. I'd obviously interrupted them in the later stages. I couldn't take my eyes off them.

Lucy rested her arms on Sally's thighs and was gently massaging her outer lips with her fingers, leaving the most sensitive areas for her tongue. She licked along the entire length; slowly, deliberately. From bottom to top. Sally twitched at the top of each stroke, as Lucy's tongue flicked over her clit.

My cock was stiff now; I made no attempt to hide it. Sally looked at me, and down at my erection. I tensed my muscles to make it jiggle and she laughed. Lucy looked over in response to Sally's amusement and rolled her eyes.

"Huh. Men."

She dropped back onto Sal, who gasped as Lucy covered her clit with her mouth and sucked hard. Sally was moaning. Lucy lifted slightly, and I could see her tongue lapping at Sal's bud. Regularly and firmly, pressing it up and down. Sally responded with each movement. Lucy moved a hand and slid two fingers into Sal, who responded by tensing her bum, lifting her hips to meet Lucy's touch.

Lucy seemed oblivious to me. She was watching Sally, altering her movements to Sal's response. She paused for a moment, then looked at me, and I smiled as she dropped and started nibbling Sal's clit as she rubbed her fingers inside. I knew Sal's sounds.

She turned to me, with that wonderful expression just before her release. She held out her hand and I took it. She gripped tightly, almost pulling me towards her, and I watched, mesmerised, as Lucy brought Sally to orgasm. Sal pressing Lucy's head onto her, as she came. Her grip tightened with each spasm.

Lucy lifted her head and kissed the skin around Sally's pussy, slowly withdrawing her fingers. Looking at me, she licked one clean, then held the other in my direction. I leaned over and took her finger in my mouth. Holding her gaze, I licked it clean. It was one of the most erotic things I'd ever experienced.

My cock was straining between my legs; it wanted some of the action. Sal's hand stroked my thigh and she gave me a languid smile. I leaned towards her, and we shared a lingering kiss, her breathing still not settled. I pulled away and sat back on the lounger.

"Doesn't Lucy get a kiss?" Sally said.

I looked at Lucy, still stroking Sally's thigh.

"Does Lucy want one?"

"She missed out last night."

"Did she?"

"Yes. You could at least make up for that now."

I squatted and leaned over Sal's open legs. Lucy came up to meet me. I placed my lips on hers; I could taste Sally on them. We held each other's gaze as we kissed. A gentle, delicious kiss. I pulled away, and she rested her head on Sal's tummy again, smiling. I sat down, and realised I was the only one who wasn't sure what was going on here.

"It's dangerous leaving you two alone," I said.

"Not dangerous, darling," Sally replied. "Interesting, perhaps."

She looked at Lucy and beckoned her with a finger. Lucy slowly slid up Sal's body until they were able to kiss, Sally's hands roaming all over her. They exchanged a whisper I didn't make out, and Lucy lifted herself up. Sally slid out from under her, kissing me as she passed, and running one hand gently over my balls and along my cock. The touch made me groan.

When I looked back, Lucy was lying on her back, and Sal climbed on top of her. For the next ten minutes, I watched as Sal kissed just about every pore of Lucy's body. She spent some time licking and sucking her breasts and nipples. I was free to examine them now. They were beautiful. Larger than Sally's, with large pale aureoles and nipples. They were sensitive too, judging by her response to Sal's mouth.

Sal worked her way down Lucy's tummy. She spread Lucy's legs and made herself comfortable between them, then started to slowly open her with her tongue, pushing to one side, then the other.

Sal had been right about Lucy's anatomy; she was very neat. Normally nothing visible but a gentle curve and a dark valley. Everything else hidden. Now Sally slowly exposed it. Gradually stretching her, revealing those glorious folds, their rich colour contrasting with the pale skin hiding them. Lucy was laying back and enjoying the attention.

Sally hadn't told me much about her activities with Lucy. We'd agreed that at the beginning. But she had said they were different. Sally was multi-orgasmic; certainly when she was in the mood. Lucy wasn't. She enjoyed sex as much as Sally, but orgasm wasn't her only goal. She loved the activity itself almost as much.

I was seeing the truth of this. Watching her, I could see her responses to Sally's touch. Her body moving and twisting; her face going through a myriad of expressions and movements. One moment a smile, the next a surprised grimace, then an open-mouthed gasp.

Occasionally, Sally looked at me and held my gaze. I knew her face; she was enjoying what she was doing almost as much as Lucy. If she enjoyed giving oral sex to Lucy as much as she did to me, she was in heaven. I saw her look at my cock, staring at it as she licked Lucy. She lifted away and held out her hand. I hesitated. She pointed at the ground by Lucy's foot. I got onto my knees, my cock hovering above Lucy's thigh. I moaned as she cupped my balls in her fingers. Lucy looked down, her eyes lingering on my cock.

Sally propped herself up, leaned over and took the head of my cock between her lips. It made me cry out and I dropped my hand to steady myself, right onto Lucy's hip. I looked at her to see if it was okay; she smiled. Sally was teasing my cock, sucking it into her mouth. I dropped my gaze from Lucy's face to her breasts.

Lifting my hand off her hip, I let it hover over them. Lucy's eyes assented, and I let it fall gently onto them. As Sal continued to suck me, I gently stroked Lucy's breasts. Warm, soft, supple. Squeezing her nipples between my fingers, eliciting my first moans from her.

Sally released my cock as she went back between Lucy's legs. I turned slightly, and bent over Lucy, lowering my mouth over the nearest nipple, hard between my lips. Sucking on it, stretching it. Her hand rested on my head, playing with my hair. I used my hand to play with the other breast, stroking the aureole.

I wasn't sure whether it was me or Sally, but Lucy was louder now, moaning almost continuously. I lifted my head and looked down. Sally was working hard now, and I could see she had a hand under Lucy. I knew Lucy had a sensitive ass and guessed Sal was playing with it.

Lucy's hand pulled my head back in her direction. She puckered her lips. I lowered mine onto them and we shared a long, soft kiss. I could feel her moans as vibrations. A strong groan made her move her head away, and I turned to Sal. She was lifting Lucy's feet onto the lounger.

She held out her hand, and taking mine, she placed it under Lucy's bum. I cupped her cheek in my hand, watching Sal lick and suck Lucy's flesh. Moving my hand slowly, I slid my fingers towards Lucy's ass, and she jumped as I touched it. I now had one hand caressing her breast, the other gently circling her ass. She was breathing heavily, lifting her hips.

I accepted the invitation and pressed at her asshole. She groaned, and I pressed harder. My finger burst through, and she gasped. Only the tip was in, but my movements were working. She was panting now. I went no further, simply repeating what I was doing. Even I could see she was close.

Her head suddenly went back, and she let out a long deep groan. Her body went rigid, and her hand gripped my arm. After the initial stillness, her body relaxed onto the lounger, and she went through several strong spasms. The groan still loud and strong.

Eventually, the groan petered out, and Sally gently pulled my hand, my finger slipping out of Lucy's ass. Sal held up her hand, telling me to pause. Lucy was still breathing heavily but had a huge grin on her face; her eyes still closed. After a couple of minutes, they opened, and she looked from me to Sally and back again.

"I could get used to that," she whispered.

Sally gently stroked her thigh and gave her pussy one more kiss. Even at that, Lucy jumped. Sal looked at me again.

"Lucy's very sensitive for a couple of minutes, aren't you?"

"Yes. Sorry."

"Why be sorry?"

She shrugged.

"What happens if we don't stop?" I asked.

"It can get painful. It did years ago, anyway. I haven't tried it recently."

"Really?"

She narrowed her eyes at me.

"Don't go getting ideas. She's the one who's into pain," she said, looking at Sal.

"Talking of pain, darling," Sally said, looking at my rigid cock. "Would you like to do something with that?"

"God, yes. Indoors?"

Sally looked at Lucy, who laughed.

"No, stay here. My turn to watch."

"Lie down," Sally ordered.

I did. She got up and came over to my lounger. She knelt between my legs and went down on me. No gentle teasing; firm, long strokes. Her lips clamped hard. She was making me groan. I saw her look over to Lucy and recognised a change of plan. She moved up my body and straddled me, watching me as she eased herself onto my cock.

That made me groan louder. I grabbed her bum and pulled her to me. She started to grind. I knew she needed another orgasm and let her use me first. She held out her hand to Lucy, who swung her legs off her lounger, and knelt beside us. Sal leaned over and they shared a passionate kiss, Lucy's hands caressing Sal's body. I wanted some of that. I placed my hand on Lucy's bum and started to stroke it. She turned to me with a smile on her face. Leaning towards me she kissed me and stuck her bum out.

I could reach both cheeks now, and as I stretched my hand over one, I met Sally's hand caressing the other. I looked up at her and the same thought hit us at the same time. We lifted our hands away, and brought them down hard, slapping Lucy's bum in unison. She giggled and pushed a breast into my face. I grabbed it and started to suck her nipple.

Sally reached her climax, grunting several times as she bucked on my cock. As she came down, I gently bit the nipple in my mouth, making Lucy gasp.

"If you want something to eat," Sal said. "You might have a choice now."

I looked from one to the other and gently let my hand slip between Lucy's legs, touching her pussy for the first time. She widened her stance and wriggled backwards onto my fingers. I gently ran them over her soft folds.

"I might like that," I said. "But not right now."

Sally laughed.

"Need to come, darling?"

"Yes. Right now."

She started to ride me, hard and fast. I wasn't going to last long. I just let it happen. I cried out as that first spasm went through my groin. She was an expert. Falling hard on me at the first release, then rising and falling in time with my pulses. Milking me. I came hard, feeling my cum surging through my cock. Sal even squealed as she felt the first shot deep inside her. My body jerked with each release. I let my head fall back on the cushion. As the spasms ended, my body relaxed, and I just laid there. Lucy was stroking my chest, and Sal was leaning back, stroking my thighs.

After a few minutes, Sally leaned over and gave me some gentle kisses. She reached back for Lucy, who leaned over as well, kissing both of us.

"I think we've broken most of the rules," I said. "Are there any left?"

"Let's see," Sal replied. "No nudity. Nope. Broke that the first night. Sex in private." She grinned. "I think we may have broken that one, too."

"Broken?" Lucy said. "Shattered, more like."

Chapter 11 – Sally

I was glowing for the rest of the day. I'd wanted the three of us to get together for months. And it had finally happened; well, something had happened. While Marcus was shopping, Lucy had told me how she was feeling. She was enjoying the freedom between us. Her relationship with me, and Marcus's acceptance of it. Their friendship.

But it was more than that. She was enjoying the simple fact of our openness. We were able to talk freely about our unusual set-up, with no embarrassment or jealousy. She'd had her fair share of jealous partners. To joke about it and openly flirt with each other. She sometimes wanted to flirt with Marcus, but always stopped herself.

It had surprised her. She hesitantly told me about her recent forays online, looking at straight sex. Apparently spurred on by what we told her of our activities and the photos we'd given her for the playroom art. I listened with interest; my heartbeat increasing as I considered the possibilities.

"Lucy Halstead. Have you been getting off on straight porn?"

"Yes and no."

I raised an eyebrow.

"Well, a lot of it's horrible," she continued.

"True."

"Some of it's interesting, yes …"

"But?"

She looked bashful and turned her gaze away. I waited.

"I have used the photos of you and Marcus once or twice."

I laughed.

"Never thought of myself as a porn star."

"That's the point; you're not. You're people I know, who I'm … familiar with."

"Very familiar in my case."

"You know what I mean."

"Yes."

"I've found myself watching Marcus."

"I'd noticed."

"Sorry."

"God, don't apologise. I watch him all the time. Especially here, where we're all naked. If I'm not watching you, that is."

She smiled.

"After the thunderstorm," she said. "When we hugged in the pool?"

"Mmm."

"I was impressed he didn't try to take advantage."

"I tried too hard there. Sorry."

She waved my apology away.

"When he got out and I saw him erect, I was almost disappointed nothing had happened."

"Do you want him?" I asked.

She held my gaze for some time before answering.

"I don't know, Sal. I'm gay. I haven't been interested in a man for years. But I am interested in your man; at least, in the two of you. I'm sorry; that sounds terrible."

I swung off my lounger and sat on the edge of hers. I bent and kissed her.

"No, it doesn't. I'd love you and Marcus to get it on."

She laughed; she knew.

"I'd love to watch him fuck you," I said. "Or you fuck him."

Her face took on a strange expression.

"So, you're pimping him, now?"

"Marcus and I are living a great life. We have each other; I also have you. I'd be very happy if you two had each other as well."

"Would Marcus …"

"Oh, yes, Luce."

"He's told you?"

"No. But he'd jump at the chance if you wanted it. Come on, think about how he looks at you; what he's said."

"He never makes me feel uncomfortable."

"He won't. He's not like that. That's part of his appeal. Fabulous friend and lover, but far from a typical man."

"Yea. I'm realising that."

"If you want to join in, I can safely say we'd both welcome you. But at your own pace, on your terms. It's your choice."

"Thanks, Sal."

She put her arms around me and gave me a lingering kiss. I responded, and we started to caress each other. It was working for me. Her hands over my body; my mind thinking about what we'd discussed. Life could be about to get a lot more interesting.

"Sal …"

"Mmm."

"What would happen if Marcus came home and found us …"

I looked at her. She'd ended the internal debate; her fingers were stroking my bush.

"Let's find out."

Now we had, I was relieved we were all relaxed about it. After the event, we'd been the same as we had before. We didn't discuss what had happened or what might happen. I knew, and Lucy trusted, that Marcus wouldn't push. Over the rest of the day, I noticed she touched him occasionally; friendly touches on the arm or shoulder. And one smack on his bum. He appeared to relish it but didn't respond. I wanted him to, but I knew patience was needed.

***

"Why don't you two have a girly day?"

"Doing what?"

"I don't know. You're both big girls now; you can make your own decisions."

"Fancy it, Luce?"

"It's not fair on you," Lucy said to Marcus.

"Oh, I don't know. I need to recover from all these unnatural acts. Find a beach somewhere or drive along the coast. Bring me back something nice."

I smiled at him. His thoughtfulness was one of his big attractions.

"Right, Luce. By the car in ten minutes."

We both jumped from the table and changed into something suitable for sightseeing and shoved a few things in a bag for the beach if we needed them. Returning to the terrace, I gave Marcus a kiss and was unduly pleased when Lucy did the same. She lingered longer than I had.

"What about driving along the coast?" I said. "Italy's only just up the road."

"Great," Lucy replied. "We can stop off when we feel like it."

We had a glorious day. The weather was perfect, the views were stunning, and there were plenty of small towns and resorts along the way. We stopped for coffee and did a bit of shopping. Lunch was in Italy and we did a bit more shopping. We decided to turn for home and find a beach to laze on along the way. As we drove through the last Italian resort before the border, Lucy shrieked.

"Stop. Pull over."

I found a safe place to stop.

"What's wrong?"

She was grinning from ear to ear. I was baffled. She leaned across me and pointed to the other side of the road. I burst out laughing. Gelato. We had to get one. I found a proper parking space and we went to the shop. Right on the seafront. We sat and ate on the wall overlooking the sea. It was hot, the sky clear, the water an intense azure. I was sitting with my best friend and lover, eating gelato.

We recalled our escapade the previous year and descended into fits of giggles. People were looking at us, but we didn't care. At one point, I did feel a pang of regret Marcus wasn't with us, but it soon faded. We'd all have gelato together another day.

When we got back to the villa, Marcus was in the pool, lounging against the side. He watched us strip off before joining him. I floated over and wound myself around his body. Lucy gave him a brief kiss and leaned on the side close to us.

"Good day?" he asked.

"Yea. We did some shopping; we ate and drank, and we had gelato."

"Ah …"

Lucy grinned; I'd told him about that particular adventure.

"And we've spent the last two hours on a nudist beach," I said.

"Didn't you find anyone nice to bring home?"

"We didn't see anyone we fancied more than each other, did we, Luce?"

I saw her blush slightly at my words.

"I hadn't thought of it like that," she replied, leaning over and giving me a kiss. "But you're absolutely right."

"What are we doing for dinner?" I said.

"Have you used all your energy or are you up for going out?" Marcus asked.

"Luce?"

"I'm fine. Where are we going?"

"Have you two brought anything to dress up in?" he asked.

"I'm sure we can find something. Why?"

"How about going into Cannes, finding somewhere for dinner, and on to a casino?"

Lucy and I were out of the pool and heading indoors before anything else was said. This wasn't a dressing up holiday, but it would be fun for one night. Luckily, we'd both packed one dress each which proved formal enough, and our shopping trip earlier came in handy too. An hour later, with Marcus in a casual linen suit and tie, we set off for Cannes.

"Do you know where we're going?" I asked.

"Might do."

"You've booked somewhere, haven't you?"

"Possibly. I have had all day."

"What if we'd been knackered?" Lucy asked.

"I'd have cancelled."

"Don't you love him, Luce?"

"Mmm."

He drove along the promenade looking for somewhere, but Lucy and I couldn't help. We didn't know where we were going. Eventually finding what he was looking for, he parked the car and led us across the road to La Palme d'Or. We were shown to a table on the terrace.

The setting was fabulous, the food excellent, the service discreet and professional. It was a perfect evening. Cannes came alive at night. Lights ran along the promenade, people strolled up and down, and cars cruised around slowly. There were the wealthy, those pretending to be and those just watching.

"Why did you choose to come here, darling?" I asked.

"I fancied somewhere where we'd all feel comfortable. Monte Carlo was too stuck up. Let's face it, we didn't show any special skills when we went to the casino at home."

"Where's Mary when you need her?" Lucy asked.

"She did do well, didn't she? She was the only one who came out with more than she took in."

"Where did she learn that?"

"Something about a boyfriend who was a croupier."

"Mary's been a model of propriety ever since I've known her," Lucy said. "Was she a bit of a girl when she was younger?"

"I don't know, Luce. She's always been open about sex. She was with us when I went through puberty, and she always told me anything I wanted to know. She wasn't afraid of those discussions. But I didn't know her well when Mum was alive. Mum never seemed to trust her, so there may have been something."

"I reckon she went through men like a scythe through a meadow," Marcus said.

Lucy spluttered.

"Really, Marcus," I said. "How could you say such a thing about my maiden aunt."

"Who dressed up several times in Rocky Horror gear ..."

"Doesn't mean anything."

He put his hand gently on my wrist.

"... and had a fling with her brother-in-law."

I chuckled.

"Perhaps I should have a talk with her sometime, I might learn something."

"God," Lucy said. "If she could teach you anything, she must have had a very colourful life."

Marcus let out a loud laugh. I pouted and stuck my tongue out at Lucy.

"Don't know what you mean."

"Yes, you do," Marcus said. "And we both love you for it."

That phrase made me pause. I turned to Lucy who was looking at Marcus with an odd expression on her face. She'd picked up on it too. The waiter interrupted our thoughts. Dessert time. Lucy and I looked at the menus and ordered, and the waiter turned to Marcus.

"Monsieur?"

"The mango and pineapple gelato, please."

Lucy and I exchanged a glance and burst out laughing.

"Well," he said. "There's obviously something about gelato. I need to find out what it is."

We watched passers-by watching us. The light had gone now, replaced by rows of streetlights and brightly lit hotels and restaurants. It was still warm, though. Comfortable. As we ate our desserts we talked about the holiday. At one point, I noticed Marcus staring into the distance.

"What are you thinking?"

He gave a little start.

"Mmm?"

"You were miles away."

"Oh, nothing."

"Tell."

"Just admiring a vision, that's all."

"Of?"

He looked from me to Lucy and back again, clearly looking at our bodies rather than our eyes. He waved the gelato spoon.

"Of you two, naked, covered in this stuff. I was quite enjoying it."

"Stick to eating it. It gets you in an awful mess, doesn't it, Luce."

"Yea. But it was good fun. What the hotel staff must have thought when they saw those towels …"

We ordered coffee and liqueurs.

"Sal," Marcus said, a serious look on his face. "I hate to bring the evening down, but I need you to do something."

"I know. I need to make a decision."

"Yea. We've got three days left. If you want to visit the house, we shouldn't leave it to the last day. Let's get it over with."

"Okay, I'll decide overnight. If we're going, we'll do it tomorrow."

He put his hand on mine.

"Thank you. Then we can enjoy what time's left."

At the end of the meal, we walked past two or three impressive hotels, before going into a huge, brightly lit, wedding cake of a building. Turning left, Marcus led us into the casino. We had to sign up as members; ID and ten euros each was all it took.

"Right, you two," I said. "We've got a thousand euros each."

"What!" Lucy said. I gave her one of my looks and she smiled guiltily. "Okay, okay. Sorry."

"I can think of a way you can pay me back if you like."

She gave me a kiss.

"You don't have to pay for that."

We wandered around getting our bearings; finding out what there was to play. We watched a few games as we passed. We recognised them, but we didn't have a clue what we were doing. We tried roulette, but it wasn't as simple as it seemed. Then blackjack, where Lucy had a short run of luck. She came away about fifty euros up. We spent some time on the slots.

"I can't see the attraction," Lucy said. "It's fun the first few times but it gets boring."

"Doesn't that apply to all gambling?" Marcus said. "It either appeals or it doesn't. But it's easy to see how people get hooked. These will take some big stakes."

He was right. You could put anything up to fifty euros a time. Even a thousand wouldn't last long at that rate. Marcus and I watched as Lucy yet again started winning.

"Somebody's feeling lucky tonight," he said.

I stood behind her and gave her bum a quick squeeze.

"I wonder what her luck will bring?"

She gave me a gorgeous smile; I couldn't resist giving her a kiss. Then she started losing but had the willpower to cut her losses and stop.

"I think we should play at being grown-up," Marcus said. "I fancy another go at the roulette table."

"Okay," I replied. "Mind if we split up? Fancy trying the blackjack again, Luce?"

We went our separate ways. Lucy seemed to know what she was doing. Over half an hour, she won another three hundred. I'd lost the same amount. She also knew when to quit, walking away with her profit. We wandered back to the roulette table and I spotted Marcus perched on a chair.

"He thinks he's James Bond," I said to Lucy.

"Why don't we help the illusion?"

We went to the bar and ordered cocktails and wandered up behind him, each laying a hand on one of his shoulders. He looked up and smiled. I noticed several people look at Lucy and me and then at Marcus. It may have been our little joke, but we caused a bit of a stir.

"Hello, darling. How are you doing?"

"Not bad. I think I'm getting the hang of it."

I watched several spins. I knew it depended on the ball and the wheel; that bit was simple, but the gambling options still baffled me. Marcus seemed to understand it; I couldn't work out what he was doing. But he had a large pile of chips in front of him. I had no idea how much. After about fifteen minutes, he leaned back.

"Had enough?" he asked.

"We can stay if you want."

"No, I'm done here."

He stood and threw a few chips to the croupier, gathering up the rest and we went to the desk to cash them in.

"Have you made a profit?" Lucy asked.

"Well," Marcus said. "I started with a thousand euros. Now I have …" he looked at the printout, "… four thousand three hundred and seventy-five."

"Wow. That's incredible."

"How about you two?" he asked.

I pouted.

"I've got five hundred and twenty-five."

"Too bad." He kissed me. "You don't need the money."

"I've got just over seventeen hundred," Lucy said.

"Luck was with you tonight."

He gave Lucy a kiss too.

"I hate you both," I said.

Lucy went to give me the money. I gave her a look and she frowned.

"Keep it, Luce. Please."

She put it in her clutch, but I knew that wasn't the end of it.

Leaving the casino, we strolled along the promenade, alongside many others doing the same. Marcus was in the middle with Lucy on one arm and me on the other. It was getting late, past midnight.

"Shall we go home?" he asked.

"I think so, otherwise it'll wipe out tomorrow."

Returning to the car, we headed back to the villa.

"Was it my imagination?" Lucy asked. "Or did we attract a lot of looks?"

"It wasn't your imagination, Luce," Marcus said. "This place is full of famous people. They were trying to work out who I was."

"Why?" I asked.

"Because they wanted to know how the hell I managed to end up with the two most beautiful women in Cannes."

Lucy and I both laughed, but we basked in the compliment.

"Smooth-talking can get you into trouble," Lucy said. I noticed the playfulness in her voice. He turned back briefly to look at her.

"I certainly hope so, Lucy."

Chapter 12 – Sally

When we arrived at the villa, we weren't ready for bed. I grabbed a couple of bottles of wine and went out onto the terrace. Marcus went to take his suit off and appeared in his shorts. It was still warm.

"Luce, we haven't shown Marcus what we bought today."

"Shall we?"

He gave us a quizzical look. We both stood up and wriggled out of our dresses. In one of the shops, we'd found some underwear we both liked. Beautiful soft silk; pale blue and dusky pink. We'd both bought the same bra, and I'd bought a pair of shorts, while Lucy had gone for a high cut brief. Marcus looked and I saw the smile on his face grow. We did a twirl.

"Well?"

"They're gorgeous. Sit down before I do myself an injury."

Lucy and I smiled at each other and sat down. We lazed around for a while, and I made my decision.

"I want to go to the house," I said.

Marcus looked at me.

"How do you plan to do it?"

"Ask for Genevieve or Jacques Mahoney and take it from there."

"Okay. Tomorrow morning?"

"Yes."

He leaned over, took my hand, and kissed it.

"Proud of you."

I was nervous but making the decision had taken a weight off. At least we'd find out one way or another. It made me feel better.

"What are you going to do with your winnings, Luce?" Marcus asked.

I didn't know if he said it to deliberately raise the issue, but I knew what her answer would be.

"Well, I don't think they're mine."

"Luce …"

"Sal, I know. But this is different. At least take the thousand back."

"You'll keep the seven hundred if I do?"

She nodded.

"Deal," I said. "Darling, remind me to buy something for Lucy, will you? Something around a thousand euros?"

He grinned as Lucy threw a cushion at me.

"What about you, Marcus?" Lucy asked.

"I'm not sure. I might buy something special for my two favourite people."

I looked at Luce.

"Ooh."

"But," he continued, "I'll probably end up spending it on you two, instead."

The cushion found itself hitting him; several times.

We chilled and drank wine. Marcus being his usual abstemious self. Alcohol didn't agree with him in anything other than small quantities, but Lucy and I had had some epic sessions over the years. They'd declined as we got older, but we found ourselves still able to consume a fair amount without much drama. As we relaxed, we started to get bolder.

"Come on, Luce," I said. "Tell us about you and boys."

"I don't remember much, to be honest. None stand out in my memory."

"Was your first time with a boy?" Marcus asked.

"Sort of. I'd messed around with a couple of girls, but nothing you'd call sex. If I remember rightly, the first guy was the one all the girls were after."

"And you got him first?"

"Not sure I was the first, but if I wasn't, he hadn't learnt anything from his previous experiences."

"Not good?"

"I seem to remember it was all over before I'd even got started."

"First times are often like that."

"So I gather, where men are involved."

"Oh, come on. You must have had some dud girls, too."

"Yea. A few, I guess. But the impulse is different, isn't it?"

"I know what you mean. But you need to find the right man, like you need to find the right woman."

"Think I've found her," she said.

I flushed and Marcus laughed.

"Either you were fishing for compliments or you walked into that one, Sal."

"I walked into it, I think. What I mean is … well, take you, darling. You're not all out for yourself, are you? You've got the patience of Job."

"Not always. I seem to remember using you a few times …"

"Yes, but …"

"Bending you over and fucking you …"

Lucy was grinning; swirling wine around her glass while she watched him wind me up. He turned in his chair to face Lucy.

"Mind you, Luce. You must have seen how demanding she can be."

"I know, Marcus. She comes in, expecting me to satisfy all her urges."

"Exactly. She's the same with me. And what urges. Never seems to be satisfied. You saw how she'd almost worn me out by the time you arrived."

"All right, you two." I held my hands up. "We all love a good quickie now and again. What I was trying to say was, generally, you're a sharer rather than a taker."

"I guess so," he replied. "But we all have different needs."

"That's true," Lucy said. "I've never met anyone as orgasmic as Sal."

I felt myself flush again.

"I'm different," she continued. "I'm happy with one; sometimes two. I still enjoy carrying on, but it's more about the intimacy and giving pleasure after that."

The conversation continued, getting more and more intimate. It became quite flirty and I was beginning to feel horny. I'd had a fair bit of wine, we were sitting around in nothing much, and I was with my two lovers. I couldn't help it; I wanted to make love to them. Tonight.

"I fancy a swim," I said.

I stood up and as I walked away from them, I shed my bra and knickers. As I walked down the pool steps, I saw them following me, already naked. I watched as they approached. Lucy looking gorgeous. Her body always looked wonderful; curvy, sinuous. Marcus always turned me on; I knew the pleasure we could give each other. They came into the water and floated towards me.

"Are you two safe in the water?" Marcus asked.

I put my arms around his neck and wrapped my legs around him. My pussy nestled onto his cock; not yet hard. His hands moved around me and settled on my bum.

"We are," I replied. "Are you?"

I held out a hand to Lucy and she joined us. I put my arm around her and pulled her into us. She put an arm around me and the other around him. I kissed him, slowly and gently, then kissed Luce the same way. A warmth spread through me and his cock began to rise. She responded and another hand settled on my bum. They chuckled as they encountered each other's fingers.

"You know you said I'd have to work twice as hard to keep you both satisfied?"

"Mmm."

"How would it be if we satisfied each other?"

Marcus gave me a look; he thought I was pushing my luck. I looked at Lucy. She bent over and kissed Marcus, a long, lingering kiss.

"How about it, Marcus?" she said. "Can I join you?"

"Are you sure you want to?"

"Do you want me to?"

"Yes."

"So do I."

"I've promised Luce, darling. It's her choice, her pace, her terms."

"That's fine," he said softly. "Watching you two is heaven."

"Oh," Lucy said. "I hope you'll do more than watch."

We pulled closer; kissing, stroking. Hands exploring more intimate places now. But this wasn't going to work in the water.

"How about we dry off and go in?"

When we got inside, we all had a quick shower to wash the chlorine off and towelled down. I led them both back to the bedroom and brought them together.

"I want both of you tonight," I said between kisses. "How much you enjoy each other is up to you, Luce. Tell him what you want."

I pushed them gently back onto the bed. Lucy laid on her back and I climbed over her, spreading her legs with my knees. She sighed as I dropped onto her, our pussies nestled together. Marcus laid beside us, stroking my bum and back, moving his hand onto her thigh occasionally. I noticed the smile on her face. The one which said she was at peace, living in the moment.

I made my way down her neck, planting delicate kisses as I went. She ran her fingers through my hair and guided my mouth to her nipple. I moved to one and Marcus leaned over and took the other between his lips. We teased them together; stretching, licking, nibbling. Her response was to move one hand onto the back of his head and hold it there.

I left him to it and moved slowly over her tummy. As I settled between her legs, I could see Marcus's cock beside her hip. It sent a thrill through me, going down on Lucy with him inches away. I shook my head to ensure it wasn't a dream, but when it settled, they were both still there.

As I ran my tongue along Lucy's tight slit, she opened her legs wider, inviting me in. She was already wet; I knew she was finding this situation a turn-on. I lapped at her wetness, inducing some gentle moans. Marcus was leaning over her, using his mouth on one breast, and stroking the other with his hand. Occasionally going up and kissing her; she wasn't being passive. Her response was to pull him onto her mouth.

One of her hands came and playfully stroked the side of my face as I explored her with my tongue. The other started to run over Marcus. Up his leg, over his tummy and chest. I slowed my licking to watch it slide back down his tummy and encounter his cock for the first time. It touched it and hesitated.

Not for long. Her fingers carried on over his balls, before surrounding his cock. It was in her grip; she started slowly stroking it. I heard him groan. He looked down, taking in her hand and me at the same time. He left his hand on her breast but slowly moved his mouth nearer me. I raised my head and kissed him; my lips covered in Lucy's wetness.

He gave me a final kiss and lowered his mouth onto her. I could see her watching him; still smiling. A little groan as his larger mouth enclosed her and drew her into him. Her hand was now cupping his balls, weighing them. His occasional twitches showing his enjoyment.

He lifted his head and kissed me again.

"Change places," he whispered.

I climbed over Lucy's thigh and he laid full length between her legs, his head over her groin. I'd learnt quickly with her that no man was as good as a woman at eating another woman. But he was good. He could give me intense orgasms that way. I laid half-over Lucy and watched him.

She was watching him too, a warm smile on her face. She pulled me to her and we gently kissed, our hands caressing each other. My hand settling on her breasts, stroking them more firmly now; she liked that as she built. Her hand slid between my legs and I shifted position so she could reach. Her fingers rubbing along my pussy; wet now. Responding to her touch.

She was moving gently; her body slowly writhing under our touch. I leaned up and kissed her. At one point, Marcus hit a soft spot; her head bent back, and she let out a low whimper. As her head relaxed again, she stuck her tongue out and wiggled it, a pleading look in her eyes.

I knelt by her shoulders. Turning, I straddled her and lowered myself over her face. Her arms went around my thighs, her hands resting on my bum and she pulled me down. I jumped as her tongue found me. She wasn't playing; she'd gone straight for my clit. Her tongue flicking it, pressing it, licking it.

I saw Marcus watching us. His mouth and fingers still working on Lucy, but his eyes were firmly focussed between my legs, watching Lucy lick and suck me. That was enough. I put my hands on Lucy's breasts. She tightened her arms around my thighs, and I felt her mouth surround my bud. She sucked it in and my orgasm came. A deep, gentle wave of pleasure running through my body.

As I came down, I realised Lucy had stopped and I heard her breathing rise over mine. She was whimpering now; Marcus was bringing her to climax as well. I dropped over her, and my head landed just in front of his. He stared into my eyes as Lucy began to twitch. I heard that familiar groan begin. A deep echoing rumble as her orgasm hit her.

The arms still around my thighs squeezed me tight. I could feel her breath on my pussy. Irregular blasts of warmth hitting my moist flesh. A couple of long cries partly muffled by my pussy so close to her mouth, her legs twitching and swaying in the air. He carried on until her volume began to reduce. I placed a hand on his cheek and gave a gentle push. He understood and lifted his head. I bent forward and kissed him, tasting Lucy all over him.

Lucy's body was still quivering under me. We stayed quiet for a couple of minutes as she stilled. I swung off her and laid by her side. She had come down and was lying back with a contented smile on her face. I kissed her.

"Okay?"

"Mmm."

She chuckled, then stretched. She always did after an orgasm. I don't think she knew she did it, but she did. Marcus was still between her legs, gently stroking her thighs.

"Thank you," she said.

"No thanks needed. I love watching a woman come."

She patted the bed by her, and he climbed alongside. Bending over her he kissed her, and she pulled him in and gave him a breath-taking kiss lasting a very long time. I think she'd enjoyed her first demonstration of what my other lover could do.

Chapter 13 – Lucy

I was buzzing. Lying with Sally on my left and Marcus on my right. Both of them gently caressing my body; my legs still almost obscenely spread. It was a whole new experience. My orgasm hadn't completely left me yet. Tiny tremors were running down my thighs, my pussy still hot. God, that had been good. I suddenly giggled; it surprised me.

"What?" Sal said.

"I've just realised why it seemed different."

"Why?"

"Stubble."

She gave me a quizzical look.

"When Marcus started, I realised it felt different, but I couldn't work out why. I was enjoying it too much. But it's his stubble. I'm not used to it."

"What?" he said. "Sal shaves closer than me?"

She stuck her tongue out at him and slapped his arm. He pulled her to him and kissed her. They were above me, and her breasts swung invitingly. I raised my head and managed to capture a nipple between my lips. She lowered herself to make it easier. I took it between my teeth and nipped it; she let out a little shriek and went to pull up, but he held her there.

"I'm beginning to wonder if getting you two together was a good idea," she said.

Marcus looked at me and winked. He rolled onto his back, pulling Sally with him. She shrieked as she ended up laying over me, her face close to his hard cock. She didn't need another hint. Moving one hand over his balls, she slid the other around his cock. She looked back at me to ensure I could see and started to lick the shaft. I moved my hand onto her bum and stroked it. I watched her run her tongue up and down, nibbling the head with her lips. Occasionally placing them over the head and eliciting a groan from him.

I studied his cock. Just like the photo, except now it was two feet from me, being sucked by a woman lying over my body. I hadn't thought about cocks much, but it was beautiful in its way. Swollen, almost angry, with veins running over it. I watched as she slowly rose and fell on it, sometimes coming off and taking a ball into her mouth.

I was lost in my study until Sal moaned. I realised I had my fingers in her; deep in her. She rose to her knees, clearly enjoying my attention, wanting more. As she continued to suck Marcus, I started to fuck her with my hand. She was giving a little grunt with each penetration.

Then she stopped and in one move, climbed over me and straddled Marcus. Holding his cock, she dropped herself onto him, both of them groaning as he filled her. I rolled onto my side, leaning against Marcus, and running my hand over his chest. Sal was grinding herself on his groin. I looked down and watched her using his cock. She was enjoying herself. Her neck and chest flushed, a gorgeous smile on her face.

"The drawer …" she said.

I turned around, opened the bedside cabinet, and laughed. I'd brought one vibe with me. They'd brought a bit more. Quite a few toys stared at me and I grabbed a lovely curved vibe and turned back to them. She held out her hand and pulled me over Marcus. I straddled his abdomen, facing her and went to use the vibe between her legs. But she took it from me and pulled me towards her. We kissed and I put my arms around her shoulders. I jumped as the vibe touched my perineum; she'd passed it to him.

"Move back," he said softly, and I shuffled my knees up his chest. I was bent forwards, my bum sticking out. Sal was kneading my breasts as he used the vibe between my legs. I felt the vibrations move along my pussy, reaching my clit, then moving back. Gently pressing into me. Then he ran it over my ass. I gasped; Sal chuckled.

"I think you've found the spot, darling."

He had. He placed the end firmly over my hole, while his fingers played softly between my legs. I was in heaven. All the sensations, and the view of Sal riding his cock. It was so hot. She was building now; her breathing heavier. We leaned together, almost holding each other up. It was surreal. We were both getting off, but neither of us was the source. Marcus was the source of both our pleasure.

We kissed; fiercely now, as Sal moved towards her climax. My own body was beginning its long build too. He was pushing the vibe hard against my ass, stretching it. I wondered if he'd push it through; I needed him to.

"Yes," I said in a loud whisper.

He took some moisture from between my legs and rubbed it on my ass. The vibe returned, hitting me with a new wave of pleasure and I cried out as it pushed into me. He left it there; not moving it. Letting it do its job. He'd turned it low and the feeling was intense.

At the same moment, Sally hugged me tight and came. Pushing forward hard on his cock and grunting as each wave of orgasm went through her. Then slowly releasing her hold on me as it passed. She grinned and kissed me through heavy breaths. The vibe slipped gently out of my ass, but the vibrations had spread through my groin and I made my decision.

I looked from Sal's face to her pussy impaled on his cock, and back again. She knew what I wanted; her face told me. My mouth said the words, but with no volume.

"Can ... I ..."

She leaned forward and kissed me.

"You sure can."

She gently lifted off him, eliciting a groan, and moved to the side. I dismounted the opposite side. Marcus watched as I straddled him, and Sal held his cock. I opened myself and let my entrance drop onto the head. Looking into his eyes, I pushed gently, and let it slip inside. I took a couple of breaths and pushed down adjusting my hips. It was stretching me; I was making little noises as I slid slowly down.

They were both smiling, watching me. I suddenly felt self-conscious, but I didn't care. Marcus and I both groaned as I finally dropped onto him, my pussy impaled on his cock. I relaxed as much as I could. I was used to dildos, but this was different. Sally was right; it felt hot, real, alive.

She put her arms around me and kissed me.

"It's all yours. Use it."

I wriggled to get comfortable and leaned forward slightly. My clit hit his bone. That was it. My body took over and started to grind on him. His cock moving inside me, filling every bit of space, my clit rubbing his skin. I gasped as the vibe touched my ass. Sally didn't mess about but firmly pushed it into me, making me cry out.

She left it there and her hands started to caress me. Over my breasts, my back, and my bum. It was too much; I knew I was going to come. I concentrated on my breathing, wanting this orgasm. Needing it. I looked at Marcus, a slight grimace on his face. I wondered if he was all right, but Sal kissed me.

"Keep going."

I did. My orgasm crept up on me. It began somewhere around my ass. My groan started as it moved between my legs and gradually spread through my body. Finally, it took over. I pushed myself onto him hard. I heard him cry out and his cock jerked inside me. My body responded by rocking harder. His hips bucked under me as I felt his cum hit me.

A feeling I wasn't used to, but my body seemed to know. I wailed as my climax reached a peak and started to drop away. I slowed and felt the vibe slip out. Sal put her arms around me and held me. I relaxed onto her, closing my eyes. Marcus's cock throbbed two or three more times in me before stillness took over.

At some point, Sally started to kiss my face. I opened my eyes slowly, looking at Marcus, a soft warmth now radiating from his face. He looked exactly how I felt. I dropped onto him and kissed him fiercely; he responded after his initial surprise. His hands gripped my bum and squeezed it hard. Sally lay beside us; her face suffused with a winning smile. My body had relaxed now, and his cock was moving inside me as it shrank.

"I'm going to …"

Too late; I gave a little gasp as it fell out. Sal grabbed some tissues and stuffed them between us. I went to get up, but she stopped me.

"It's only cum. Stay there."

I relaxed again and they both stroked and caressed me. I suddenly laughed.

"What?" Sally asked.

"I don't know. This is so strange."

Marcus frowned.

"Are you okay?" he asked.

"Oh, God, yes. That was incredible. This is incredible. I feel … fucked. It's not supposed to be this good."

"Does it matter?" he asked.

I looked at him, then at Sally.

"No. It doesn't matter one bit."

It was late now; very late.

"We should get some sleep," Marcus said.

When we returned from the bathroom, I hovered by the bed, unsure what to do.

"Come on," she said, holding out her hand. "The bed's big enough for three. Besides, I might want you in the morning."

I climbed on and after a lot of laughter and swapping around, we found an arrangement comfortable for all of us. Tucked up together, our arms around each other. Contented.

As they fell asleep, we moved apart to find a good position. I found myself lying on my back. I was tired, but my mind was racing. I still had a smile on my face. I'd loved it. But I was confused. Joining these two had been on my mind for a while. I'd dismissed it at first. It was a whim, a hypothetical fantasy.

But fantasies work for a reason; because they turn you on. Why would thoughts of sex with a man turn me on? They hadn't for most of my life. Why now? I fell asleep still wondering.

I was woken from an interesting dream the next morning by Sally. Cuddled into me, her hand between my legs. I was surprised by my need. She kissed me, her kisses immediately passionate and strong. I responded. As she rolled on top of me, I saw Marcus watching us. He smiled; I grinned back. Sally quickly disappeared under the covers and between my legs. He pulled the sheets off in one go.

The next twenty minutes were better than breakfast. Sally and I made love; assertively but gently. Marcus didn't join in; just watched, but his cock proved he was enjoying it. After we'd finished, I lay on top of her as she recovered from her second orgasm of the day. Finally, she kissed me and turned to Marcus.

"Enjoy that, darling?"

"I know it's a cliché; man gets off watching two girls. But God, you two were beautiful."

"Seems to have worked," she said, looking at his cock.

"Are you surprised?"

"What can we do to help?"

"Anything you damn well like."

"Well, how about something special?"

She pushed him onto his back, crawled over and laid between his legs. I lay on my front, my head near his thigh. I guessed what she was going to do, and I was curious. He reached over for my bum, but couldn't quite get there, so I shifted position to let him grab it. I watched for a quarter of an hour as she brought him to orgasm with her mouth. I had to admire her skill. I'd watched a few online but realised what she'd told me was right. They just looked good on camera. This was different.

She took her time, licking and teasing him. But always with her mouth; not her hand. That was reserved for his balls, thighs, and tummy. I joined in, letting my hand caress and stroke his balls.

As I watched I wondered what it was like. I loved going down on a woman. It turned me on and getting the response was powerful too. I could see this was the same. Marcus was completely in her power. What would it feel like? Having my mouth around a cock? I smiled to myself, realising I would have to find out.

By the time he came, he had been in what looked like ecstasy. His body moving gently; muscles twitching and flexing. His face in turn smiling, grimacing, and frowning. The noises he made were amusing. He wasn't quiet where sex was involved. The previous night I'd noticed he made nearly as much noise as Sally or me, and this morning his moans, groans, grunts, and whimpers were part of the eroticism of the moment.

His eventual orgasm was powerful. His whole body going through strong spasms as he came. I watched his balls jump as they emptied and the muscle under his cock contracted sharply as it drove his cum upwards. Sally didn't flinch. She stayed on him long after he'd finished.

The look on her face was gorgeous. I knew it was a mixture of her pleasure and the pleasure she'd given him. I'd seen it many times. She finally let his cock go and pulled me towards her. As my lips met hers, she opened them slightly and I felt her tongue enter my mouth. She gave me a lingering kiss and pulled away, a questioning look on her face. I closed my mouth. I could taste him; at least, I assumed that's what it was. I lapped my tongue a few times. Unusual, but not unpleasant.

I pulled her towards me for another try. She laughed and let my tongue push around her mouth this time. I recognised the taste now; searched for it. I knew one thing; it wouldn't put me off giving it a try.

Chapter 14 – Marcus

"I don't want to move," I said. "I want to stay here forever."

I was lying on my back, my arm around Sally on one side and Lucy on the other. I didn't believe in heaven but thought it might be like this if I did. Sally kissed me.

"It is rather special, isn't it?"

She leaned over and kissed Lucy.

"Are you happy?" she asked.

"Oh, yes," Lucy replied. "Some night. I'm not sure how we top this."

"Oh, we can. Believe me."

Lucy looked at us.

"You know … with you two, it wouldn't surprise me at all."

After a few moments of peace, Sally sat up.

"Right. I hate to spoil the mood, but we've got a job to do today."

I stroked her back.

"Sure you want to do it?"

"Yes. I'll regret it if we leave without finding out."

"Okay. How about a quick swim to wake us up? Then a shower and breakfast. Then we can face the day."

An hour later, we were sitting on the terrace. Awake, clean, and dressed, lazing over a leisurely breakfast. I knew Sally was anxious. I still wasn't sure it was the right decision but understood her reasoning.

"Shall I stay here?" Lucy asked.

"No, Luce. Come with us. I don't know how long this will take, but when it's finished, we'll still have the rest of the day."

As we drove into Beaulieu, we were quiet. No small talk. Nothing. I turned into the street. It was late morning. We'd discussed how to approach it several times, but that ended up with us trying to cover all eventualities. We gave up, knowing the one we hadn't considered would be what happened. We'd play it by ear.

I parked out of sight of the house. Leaving Lucy, we walked to it, the car was still there. At least there would be somebody in. Sal and I approached the front door. She had a couple of pictures of her father; the only ones she had, apart from the passports.

I squeezed her hand and went to press the bell but stopped myself. I looked at her and stepped away. She kissed me and pressed it herself. It seemed as if there would be no answer, but we heard a rattling and the door swung open. A woman in her thirties greeted us. That threw us for a start.

"Oui?"

Sally's French was better than mine, but still not good enough if we got into any delicate conversations. The woman recognised our difficulties.

"You are English?"

"Yes."

"I get my husband."

She disappeared and shortly afterwards a man of about the same age appeared. He looked friendly enough.

"Hello. How can I help you?"

"We're looking for someone. Well, two people. Genevieve or Jacques Mahoney."

He frowned briefly.

"Ah, Mahoney. Yes. They used to live here."

My heart sank.

"Oh," Sally whispered. "They don't live here now?"

"No. Only me and my wife. We bought the house from them about three years ago."

"Oh."

He could see how crestfallen Sally was.

"Come in, come in. I might still have a forwarding address; we had one after we moved in."

Sally looked at me. I could see she was on the verge of tears. I took her arm and guided her into the house after our host. He explained to his wife, and they went over to a large cupboard and took out a box. We watched as they pulled stuff out of it. After a few minutes, he gave a triumphant whoop and came over to us with a sheet of paper.

"Here. An address in Paris somewhere, we did forward a few things. There's also an email address, but I don't know if it still works."

"Can we copy them?"

"You can take it."

Sally took the document and he led us out to the front door. We thanked him profusely and walked towards the car. When we got to it, I opened her door, but she pushed it shut and threw herself on me. The tension came out; she burst into tears. I held her as she sobbed. Lucy got out of the car and came around to us, a questioning look on her face.

"Not there," I said. "They moved three years ago."

Lucy put an arm on Sally's shoulder. Passers-by looked at this strange tableau, but I didn't care. I was pleased Sal was letting it out. She soon recovered. Drawing away, she wiped her tears and sniffed.

"This has all been a waste of time," she said.

I looked at her, then at Lucy and back to Sally again.

"You didn't say that last night."

She whacked my arm.

"I don't mean that. You know what I mean."

"Yea. But we do have another lead."

"It's like following a ghost. Just when we get near, it reappears somewhere else."

"I think that's how your father worked, Sal."

"Mmm."

"Let's find somewhere for lunch," Lucy said. "And decide what to do."

Leaving the car where it was, we walked into the centre and stopped at the first restaurant we found. After eating something, and a couple of glasses of wine, Sally recovered her composure.

"We can't do anything else here. So, we've got the rest of today and tomorrow. Let's have fun."

"What do you want to do this afternoon?" I asked.

"Well," Lucy said. "I did want to do something. But I don't think you'll want to go."

"What?"

"I wanted to go to Monte Carlo, but you didn't like it."

I looked at Sally.

"How about giving it another try? It's only up the road."

"Fine by me."

We enjoyed our second visit more than the first. Perhaps it was because we were there with no purpose. Sally and Lucy dragged me into several shops. They proved us right about one thing. You needed money in Monte Carlo.

As soon as you entered, you were being appraised. Instant decisions were made about whether you were worth a nod, a spoken greeting or, presumably, an effusive welcome. We tended to get the formal 'Bonjour' in most, but the reception was often icy. We obviously didn't look wealthy enough.

The shops were mostly international brands. Gucci, Fendi, YSL. Some were the kind of shop with only a handful of items on display. But there were some friendlier places. Sal and Luce came across a few things they liked. Lucy blanched at the prices, but Sally ignored her and bought them anyway.

We were getting tired and decided to take all the shopping back to the car and drive to the marina. Sally suddenly stopped.

"Ooh, Luce. Look."

I followed her gaze; a lingerie shop. Lucy laughed.

"You've got so much, Sal."

That was true.

"A girl can never have too much underwear, Luce."

That was also true.

"Come on, let's have a look."

I went to follow them.

"Darling," Sal said. "How about you take all this to the car? We'll have a quick peek and follow you. The car park's just around the corner, isn't it?"

I knew when a request was really an order.

"Yes," I replied. "By the way ..."

"Mmm?"

"You've got three thousand three hundred and seventy-five euros to spend."

"Come on, Luce. Let's go shopping."

It was over an hour before they appeared, laden with bags, which they put in the boot. We drove around, at some points following the course of the annual grand prix. Passing the marina and the famous casino. It was all a bit touristy, but we agreed it was better than Sally and I had thought earlier in the holiday.

"What do you want to do for dinner tonight?" I asked.

"I would suggest finding somewhere here," Sally replied. "But I feel under-dressed and in need of a shower."

"We could go home and come back later."

"No. I've got an idea. Why don't we get dressed up and go into Cannes again? It had a nice feel to it. And Lucy and I have got some new clothes to show off. Fancy it, Luce?"

"Sounds good to me."

Back at the villa, I had a shower and got dressed. I only had the one suit with me, so had to wear it for a second night. The girls were both getting ready in the other bedroom while I waited on the terrace. They were in no hurry. The sound of laughter and conversation drifted through the open doors. Eventually, I heard heels on the floor and turned. My heart leapt. They were standing in the doorway.

"Will we do?"

I stood up. They looked fabulous. I could see why they'd taken so long. They'd gone the whole hog. Hair, make-up; all stunning. And new clothes. Sally in a wonderful teal calf-length dress; fitted but not tight. Lucy in a similar dress in a dusky pink. I couldn't help noticing they were both wearing stockings; a sheer almost nude colour, with the merest hint of sparkle. Hardly noticeable unless you looked; I always did.

"God," I said. "I feel shabby in comparison."

Sally made a show of looking me up and down.

"Mmm. You probably are. But we'll have to make do."

I went over and gave them both a kiss.

"You both look a million dollars."

"Thank you," they said together.

By the time we arrived at the restaurant, we were hungry. Our table was on the terrace overlooking the sea.

Dressing up had put the girls in a good mood; they were both on form. Sally, confident and sassy; her eyes sparkling and alive. The disappointment of the morning forgotten, or at least, well hidden. I'd realised Lucy wasn't as confident as Sal. She was independent and nobody's patsy, but there was a diffidence about her, at least in public.

"Are you still with us?"

Sally's question drew me back to the present.

"Sorry," I replied. "Yes, I'm still here."

"What were you thinking?"

"Oh, nothing."

Wrong answer.

"Go on, tell us. No secrets between us now."

"If you must know, I was watching you both, and thinking."

"What about?"

Her question had lost the challenge of the earlier ones. She was genuinely interested.

"It wasn't very gentlemanly …"

"Why? What did you see us doing?"

"No, it wasn't that."

"What, then?"

"I was thinking back to when we first met. How much you've changed."

She frowned slightly.

"Have I?"

I looked at Lucy.

"Luce, have you noticed any changes over the last year or so?"

"God, yes."

"What?" Sally said. "How? I don't feel any different."

"Really?"

"No. You've got me worried now."

Lucy looked at me shrewdly.

"Why were you watching me, Marcus?"

"Because when I first met Sally, she was similar to you now."

"In what way?"

"You were both independent, strong and self-willed. You still are."

"And now?" Sally asked suspiciously.

"Oh, you're still all of those things. But your confidence has grown. You like yourself more than you did then."

Lucy and I stayed silent as Sally thought about my words.

"And that shows?" she said.

"In everything you do, Sal," Lucy said. "It's gorgeous."

"You've noticed?"

"Of course. The change since you met Marcus has been wonderful to see."

"Oh," I said. "I'm not taking any credit for it. She's done it by herself."

Lucy looked at me.

"I don't think so."

She turned to Sally.

"Would you have gone to fetish parties without Marcus?"

Sally looked at me and broke into an alluring smile.

"No," she said softly.

"Would you and I be lovers now?"

"Probably not."

I was getting embarrassed now; I hadn't intended this to turn into a Marcus-fest.

"Built a dungeon?"

"Definitely not."

"But you have. All since you two got together. Coincidence?"

"But Lucy," I said. "I wouldn't have done any of it without Sally, either."

"I know. It makes me sick."

Sally turned to her but softened as she saw Lucy was grinning.

"You've benefitted too," Sal said.

"Too right I have."

She chuckled and looked at Sally.

"I was supposed to find a way of thanking him, wasn't I?"

"You found that the last two days, Luce," I said.

Lucy looked at me, smiling.

"I might still want to thank you some more."

"I'll look forward to that."

She swirled wine around her glass.

"What were you thinking about me?" she asked.

"I think you're where Sally was. I don't want to bring you down, but you're dealing with your family and you haven't found your soulmate. Life's good, but you want more."

"Go on …"

"Not sure there is much more. I can't read you as well as I can Sal."

Sally pouted and I blew her a kiss.

"I don't know what you want," I said.

Lucy laughed.

"After the last couple of days, I'm not sure I know myself. But I might have some fun finding out."

We raised our glasses and drank a toast to finding out. We'd chosen a tasting menu and as course followed course, we enjoyed the food, the wine, and the company. Especially the company. Sally and Lucy were enjoying the wine; they were completely relaxed, and the flirting increased. Sally was an expert flirter. She always said enough without being explicit. She knew that for me the look in her eye was as powerful as any words.

Lucy knew that; I suspected she found Sal's eyes as erotic as I did. But she was also giving as good as she got. Subtly suggestive to both of us. Asking Sally what it was like being spanked, tied up, flogged. Looking at me as Sal told her. Then quietly wondering whether she ought to try it. Sally offering my services to help her find out. They knew exactly what they were doing, and Sal knew exactly how it would affect me.

By the time we finished our meal, I was rather warm. I was sure they were too. But I offered them the chance to go to the casino again.

"I don't know. What do you think, Luce?"

"No. Let's get back and see if we can think of something to do."

We paid the bill and headed for the car. I opened the front door and Lucy let Sally get in. As I went to shut it, Sal held out her hand and pulled Lucy in as well. She sat on her lap. Probably illegal, but what the hell. I got in and drove off. The villa was only two or three miles away. Lucy was sitting between Sally's legs and they kissed for the whole journey, their arms around each other. Not a word was said.

When we arrived, I helped them out. They both gave me a lingering kiss as they got out. Indoors, Sally grabbed a couple of bottles of wine and led me over to one of the sofas. She whispered something to Lucy, who looked over at me and laughed.

"You sit there, darling."

She pulled the coffee table to one side, creating a space between the sofas. She put some music on, and they stood in front of me, arms around each other kissing. Lucy slowly lifted Sal's dress, first revealing her stocking tops and suspenders, then her knickers, finally pulling it over her head. A lovely set of underwear in a soft turquoise, almost see-through.

Sally did the same for Lucy's dress. She was wearing an identical set but in soft pink. They cuddled, their hands roaming each other's bodies, sliding into knickers. Occasionally holding my gaze; teasing me. The whole thing was wildly erotic.

"He's overdressed," Sal said.

They came towards me and held out their hands. Pulling me to my feet, they proceeded to strip me, kissing me as they did so; occasionally kissing each other. When I was naked, my cock rigid, they pushed me onto the sofa again, kissed me and moved into the centre.

They slowly removed each other's underwear and Sally pushed Lucy onto the sofa. Then she disappeared into the bedroom, coming back with a shopping bag. Putting it by her, she got between Lucy's legs and I watched as she started to play with her. Lucy was already worked up; I wondered how Sally had got this far without needing an orgasm.

She soon solved that. Lucy was directly facing me, Sally on her knees between her legs. She knelt up; my view was her naked bum between her girlfriend's legs. She reached into the bag and as she continued eating Lucy, she brought a vibe between her own legs.

It didn't take long. She started to moan. Lucy held Sal's head as an orgasm went through her. I watched as she pushed the vibe deep into her pussy and came on it, her moans muffled between Lucy's legs. She dropped the vibe. Lucy stroked her head and searched in the bag.

I was surprised when she pulled out a flogger and offered it to me. I stood and crossed to take it. Kneeling by Sally's side, she turned her head to look at me, her fingers still stroking Lucy.

"Flog me."

A simple request. I bent and kissed her; her lips covered in Lucy's wetness. I nudged her aside briefly to kiss Lucy's pussy.

"It'll be a pleasure."

"I know."

"I'm going to flog you until Lucy comes."

"Mmm. I might not let her."

"Then I'm going to flog you all night."

Her eyes almost made me growl. I just wanted to get behind her and fuck her. But first things first.

132

"Bum up."

She adjusted her position, with her ass sticking out. I let the flogger trail over her back, falling between her cheeks. She twitched. I decided to get stuck in, no warm-up. She was warm enough. I started to flog her; not with my full power, but enough for her to feel it. Each stroke elicited a little sound; varying depending on how hard I struck and how much of Lucy she had in her mouth at the time.

I started to swing the flogger between her legs. This produced a lot more sound as the fronds hit her pussy. I occasionally let my hand wander over her bum, dropping between her legs. She tried to push herself onto my fingers; I didn't let her. Lucy was watching intently, but she was also building; her body gently writhing under Sally's tongue.

"Make her come, Sal."

I stood behind her and flogged her from there. The fronds coming vertically across her cheeks. Sometimes aiming directly between them, striking her asshole, making her jump. Lucy started that now-familiar groan. I lessened my strokes allowing Sally to concentrate. As Lucy's orgasm overtook her, I knelt and stroked Sal's bum; my hand roaming between her legs.

Lucy was coming down now, and I let my fingers go to work on Sally. She dropped the top of her body onto Lucy and let me take over. I slid three fingers into her and lay my thumb on her clit, rocking my whole hand. She didn't take long. I watched as the muscles in her bum cheeks tensed, then spasmed as she came on my fingers, her head still in Lucy's groin.

Luce was back with us by now, and stroked Sally's head and back while she came. I stopped and eased my fingers out; Sal's breathing was slowing. She grunted as I gave her bum a hard slap.

I leant over both; kissing Lucy and bending to kiss the still-recovering Sally.

"Sorry," Sally said suddenly. "Need a pee."

I moved to let her up and she wandered off. Lucy was looking at my cock. She put her hand around the base, her fingers resting on my balls and bent slowly. Her lips hesitantly went over the head and I groaned as she slid a long way down my shaft. She gently raised and lowered her head, her lips tightly clamped. I looked up and saw Sally watching us, a satisfied smile on her face. She blew me a kiss and came over to join us. Lucy lifted off me as she did but stayed in position.

"Well?" Sally asked.

"I could get used to this. It's so hot."

"It is, isn't it?"

"You'll have to give me lessons."

Sally looked at me.

"Happy for us to practice on you, darling?" I chuckled. "I think that's a yes."

For the next five minutes, I thought I was going into pleasure overload as they both licked, kissed, and sucked my cock. Kissing with it between their mouths. I was in heaven. Sally looked at me.

"Want to come like this?"

"No. I want to fuck you."

"Me or Lucy?"

"Both of you."

Her eyes widened; she thought for all of two seconds. Standing, she gently brought Lucy to her feet and led her to the opposite sofa. They both knelt in front of it and bent forward over the seat, then cuddled together and put an arm around each other. I'd never had a better invitation. Two beautiful naked women, bent over, asking to be fucked.

I knelt behind Lucy, and she spread her legs slightly. Sally kissed her as I slid my cock into her. She grunted as I filled her. I wasn't delicate; I was too aroused. I began to fuck her, holding her hips and pulling her back onto me with each stroke. I slapped Sally's ass a few times as I took her lover.

I switched to Sally; she was wet and welcoming. She groaned as I eased into her. Lucy looked back at me as I fucked Sal. I laid my hand on Lucy's bum and raised an eyebrow. She nodded and I gave her bum a few gentle slaps.

She let out little whimpers and pushed her bum up slightly, so I slapped her harder, which produced some deep chuckles. Sally was moaning; Lucy went back to giving her a long, passionate kiss. I put my fingers under Sally, and she came as soon as I touched her clit, pushing back onto me to draw out her orgasm.

As she came down, I switched again. I knew this would be the end for me. I started to fuck Lucy. Sally was recovered enough to put both arms around Lucy and kiss her. But I couldn't hold out any longer. I gave Lucy's bum a few hard smacks as I pushed, squeezing her between me and the sofa with every stroke.

I cried out as I came, my cock almost hurting as it expelled my cum. I heard Lucy grunt as my cock jerked inside her. The feeling was intense. The view was awesome. I thrust into her several times as my climax came to an end, and almost collapsed onto her, my body temporarily exhausted. Sally beamed at me. She kissed Lucy and put her arm around me. We lay still for a while.

"Did you enjoy that, darling?" Sal asked.

"Mmm."

"Giving my girlfriend a good fucking?"

"Mmm."

"And spanking her?"

"Mmm."

"Are you okay?" she asked Lucy.

Lucy chuckled.

"Worked for me."

I gently pulled out of Lucy and sat back on the floor. Sliding off the sofa, she turned around and kissed me, got up, and went off to the loo. Sally went over to the other sofa and picked up the vibe, lobbing it at me. When Lucy came back, she kissed us both and sat down.

Sal surprised her by pushing her along the sofa and laying over her. Her hand went between Lucy's legs. Lucy went to say something, but Sal kissed her and started to roughly rub her. I watched as her fingers slipped in and pushed. I moved nearer, switched the vibe on, and placed it gently on Lucy's perineum. She moaned and lifted her legs, giving me better access. I placed the length of the vibe between her pussy and ass, pushing it firmly against her skin, as Sally finger-fucked her quite hard.

Lucy was breathing hard, little grunts and moans as her orgasm neared. Her hips lifted off the sofa as she let out that familiar groan. Her legs twitched as she came. Not as powerfully as earlier, but the odd chuckle showed her enjoyment. As she went over the peak, I removed the vibe and Sally stopped, with her fingers still in Lucy. She kissed her gently, and I stroked her tummy and breasts. She slowly looked from Sally to me.

"Don't you two ever stop?"

"Complaining?" Sally asked.

"No. Just curious."

Chapter 15 – Lucy

As I headed to my appointment with Jenny, I still hadn't decided how honest to be. It was only a few days since I'd returned from the holiday, and those days had been filled with different emotions. On our last full day, we didn't leave the villa, spending the day eating, drinking, lounging around the pool and … well, enjoying each other. Holidays with Sally were proving dangerous; last year, she and I became lovers. And this year …?

"Hello, Lucy. Come on in."

"Hi, Jenny. Thanks."

I followed Jenny through the house, and we settled into our usual chairs.

"I'm sorry I had to cancel the last meeting at short notice," I said. "But I had a chance for an unplanned holiday."

"No problem, Lucy. Did you have a good break?"

"Yes … I did … thanks."

The hesitation in my reply gave me away. Jenny didn't say anything, but she had noticed.

"Did you have any time to think about what we discussed last time?" she asked.

"Yes, but I still shy away from it. I don't want to think about it. I'm afraid, I suppose."

"Afraid of what?"

"I'm not sure. I guess I didn't think I'd have to deal with this. My family were neatly in a box marked 'the past'."

"But you still feel you need to deal with it?"

"If I'm going to continue seeing my mother, I have to."

"Have you seen her since our last meeting?"

"No. She's visiting me again on Saturday."

"Are you looking forward to it?"

"Honestly, no. I'm not dreading it, but it's something to endure."

"Well, many people feel like that about relatives, even without the history between you and your mum."

I hadn't thought of it that way, but what she said was true. I had friends who weren't close to their parents or siblings.

"How is she taking your father's death?"

"In some ways, very well. After all, in her view, he's gone to heaven, or a better place, or whatever she believes in. Annie and Tim tell me she's coping well with the practicalities."

"That sounds hopeful."

"Yes. We'll have to wait and see. I'll be able to get a feel for it on Saturday, I hope."

"Are you more comfortable with her now?"

I pondered the question for a while before answering.

"I suppose I am. I don't think we're going to shout or fight, and we're feeling our way. But I've decided I'm not going to pretend to be something I'm not. I've tried to shield her from the real me, but not anymore."

"What made you decide that?"

"Talking to Sally." I'd told Jenny about the relationship early on, but a couple of sessions ago, I'd given her Sally's name. It seemed odd not to. I was sure Jenny remembered Sally, but she didn't confirm it; professional etiquette, I suppose. "I was digging a hole for myself. At some point, I'd either be unable to keep the act up, or I'd resent having to do it."

"Good points."

"Yes. She'll have to accept me as I am."

"Do you want her to?"

The question startled me. It hadn't occurred to me. We sat in silence for what seemed like ages while I thought it through.

"I'm not sure. Part of me doesn't care. But there is a bit of me that wouldn't object to having a family."

I'd seen how other people related to their parents and siblings. How they supported them and could rely on them in difficult times. I'd had to rely on friends for that.

"The problem is my family have never been like other families."

"What are you aiming for? Perhaps that's what you need to think about."

"Yes. I don't have a clear view at the moment. It's a bit unsettling."

"I'm sure it is. It's never easy when our established truths are shaken."

Jenny was surprised when I laughed.

"Oh, Jenny. That's not the half of it."

I made a snap decision and told her what had happened on the holiday. Not the details, but the essence. It came tumbling out in a somewhat random order, but she got the gist. I was breathless when I came to a halt. Since the holiday, I'd run events through my mind so many times, but this was the first time I'd had to make some sense of it all.

"That was quite a holiday," Jenny said.

"It certainly was. To use your phrase, that's another of my established truths shaken."

"Are you finding that difficult?"

"No. I'm not one to regret my actions. I enjoyed it as much as the others. But I've been gay most of my adult life; not looked at a man for fifteen years. It's come as a bit of a surprise."

"Do you want to include all this in our discussions or leave it aside?"

"I have no idea, Jenny. I guess there's not much point looking at one bit of my life and excluding others, is there?"

"No," she replied. "It's usually best to look at the whole."

We set the next appointment and Jenny suggested I allow myself to let my mind wander in the meantime, rather than try and concentrate on one thing. There was too much going on.

***

After Sally left on Saturday morning, I spent an hour tidying the flat. Putting away anything which might betray the activities of the previous night. Then chastising myself for still trying to be someone I wasn't. I had been nervous before Sally arrived. We hadn't had a chance to discuss the holiday and there seemed a lot to discuss. We had a chat about it, but only while we recovered after falling on each other when she arrived. In the end, we didn't concentrate on it long. Sally made clear she and Marcus had loved it, but it would only happen again if I wanted it to.

When Mum arrived in the afternoon, she was brighter than at our last meeting.

"I've brought some cakes," she said, laying a box of doughnuts on the table.

"Thanks, Mum."

I made some tea and we went through to the living room.

"You're very tidy, Lucy. This place is always spotless."

I kicked myself for my earlier diligence.

"It's not always like this. I've often got lots of drawings and sketches lying around. I thought I'd better tidy up a bit."

"I'd like to see some of your work, if it would be okay."

"Of course. How about I dig some out for next time?"

"Thank you."

"How are you getting on, Mum?"

"It's not been as difficult as I thought it would be. I miss your father …" she paused and shifted uneasily in her chair, "… but I feel more in control now."

I wasn't sure how she meant that, and I wasn't about to ask.

"Are you going to your church?"

"No. I … I go with Annie and Tim to theirs."

I already knew this, but I wanted to hear it from her.

"Is it different?"

"Oh, yes. Very different. It was a bit of a shock at first. Everything is much more relaxed, and it's a mix of all sorts of people. I gather there are even some people like you who attend." I bit my lip hard. "Everyone is friendly, and I've been invited to lots of things."

"Have you been to any?"

"No, not yet."

"Will you? You might make some new friends."

"I know. I'm scared, I suppose."

"I understand, Mum." I did now. She had spent her whole life mixing only with people like her and Dad. People with narrow minds, and rigidly similar outlooks on life. "But why not try it? You might surprise yourself and learn new things."

"I might. Annie's offered to go with me if I want."

"That's nice. You'll have some support."

"Yes. I'll wait until I've moved."

"You're moving?"

Again, I already knew this from Annie.

"Yes. I thought about what you and Annie said. If I stay where I am, I'm always going to be thinking about your father."

"Is that a bad thing?"

She looked at me hard, her face for once unreadable. I began to regret such a direct question.

"No. But I want to start afresh. Away from too many memories."

I left it there. But after she'd gone, I wondered if there was more in those brief statements than met the eye.

***

For the first time I could remember, I was nervous as I waited for the door to open. I normally loved visiting Sally and Marcus and spent an evening with them at least two or three times a month. But even after my discussion with Sally the night before, I wasn't sure how I'd feel meeting Marcus for the first time since the holiday.

"Hi, Luce," Sal said, giving me a big hug. "Come in."

"Hi, Sal."

I paused in the hallway; Sal knew why.

"Come on, Luce. He's not going to jump you."

Marcus was standing by the dining table and smiled as I walked towards him.

"Hi, Luce," he said, as I gave him a slightly awkward hug and a kiss on the cheek, which he returned.

"Hi, Marcus."

"Darling," Sally said. "I've told Lucy you aren't going to jump her."

"What if I want him to?" I asked.

"Then you just need to tell him. I'm sure he'll happily oblige." The grin on her face told me she meant it.

"Sal, behave," Marcus cut in. "Lucy, as far as I'm concerned, nothing has changed. If you want to put it down to holiday high spirits, that's fine. You're still Sal's bit on the side," I laughed at that, "and you and I are friends."

Those few words took all my tension away and I gave him a more relaxed kiss on the cheek.

"Thank you."

"Now, like a drink?"

I readily accepted and we chatted while they prepared dinner.

"How was your mum?" Sal asked.

I told them about the visit.

"What are you going to show her?" Marcus asked.

"I was worried for a moment. Almost all the stuff I've done lately would have been unsuitable. I'll have to dig some older things out, I've got plenty lying around."

"But you're supposed to be showing her the real you," Sal said. I knew she was winding me up.

"Yes, but most of my recent work I wouldn't even show friends. You're the only ones who see them." I wagged my finger at both of them. "You're the ones leading me astray."

They both turned their heads slowly and looked at me, eyebrows raised. It was so funny and perfectly in unison, I burst out laughing, as did they.

"Alright, alright. That might not be strictly true."

"I love the 'people like you' remark," Marcus said. "She's not going to change there, is she?"

"No. But at least she said it openly."

"True. I suppose that's a hint of progress."

Over dinner, we talked about the holiday, leaving the more salacious aspects unspoken. Even without that, it had been fun. We got on well. The adage about two being company and three a crowd contained a lot of truth, but we were comfortable together. Complicated, but comfortable.

Once we settled on the sofas after dinner, it was no different to all the other evenings I'd spent there. Sal and I had both drunk quite a bit, as usual.

"So, Marcus," I said. "I'm just a holiday fling."

Sally sniggered into her glass as Marcus fixed me with a stare, which I held.

"No, Lucy. First and foremost, you're a friend. And my partners best friend and lover. If you want me to, I'll bend you over this table and fuck you senseless. And Sal will happily rip your clothes off to get a better view."

I heard Sal laugh again.

"But I'll only do it if you want to. I don't want you to be uncomfortable here. I don't want you to think something is expected whenever we invite you. It isn't. I know this is an odd situation, but I want it to work for all of us. And if it means you and I never do anything again, that's fine by me."

His words gave me mixed feelings. Relief he was being level-headed about what had happened, and not making assumptions. But also, I had to admit, more than a tinge of disappointment.

"You wouldn't want to continue?" I asked him.

"Oh, I'd love to. Two beautiful women to play with? Both as sexy as hell? It was amazing. Yes, I'd love it to continue. But I'm conscious of how this must be for you. Not the fact you had a threesome, but that the third person was a man. I'm guessing that hadn't been on your radar."

I looked quizzically at Sal; she gently shook her head and Marcus picked up on this silent communication. She clearly hadn't told him about the conversation which had led to our show for him. I told him now; about my fantasies, about looking at the pictures they'd given me, about using them to get off.

"Even so," he continued. "You've tried it now. If you want to play again, you'll be welcome. Yes, Sal?"

She smiled. "Oh, yes."

"But if you don't, that's fine too."

We sat quietly, each with our thoughts. I watched the wine swirl in my glass as I rolled it around. My head was mildly confused. Partly by the amount of wine I'd drunk, but also by my indecision. I'd enjoyed what we'd done on holiday, I wouldn't have changed a thing. Part of me wanted to do it again, perhaps right now. To have him bend me over the table and take me while Sally watched or, better still, joined in.

But a part of me was uncertain. Uncertain because this was a man I was talking about and I hadn't fully accepted it yet; I didn't understand what had changed in me. And uncertain because of our situation. It had been complicated enough when Sally and I became lovers. But if the three of us were going to play, how many more opportunities it presented for it all to go wrong.

Chapter 16 – Sally

I sat in the doctor's waiting room. It was something I'd become more accustomed to, accompanying Marcus to hospital appointments. They were depressing places; usually decorated in a bland, boring way, and there seemed to be only one supplier of furniture to all medical establishments.

I was apprehensive. Marcus had cajoled me into seeing the doctor about the times I'd passed out during orgasms. It had only happened a few times and always after an intense, prolonged experience. It only lasted a few seconds, but it had unnerved him, and I realised it possibly made him hold back; that was something I didn't want him to do. And I had to admit, it worried me more than I'd let on. So, I'd seen my doctor.

I was relieved when I saw it was a woman. When I hesitantly explained the problem, she booked a few blood tests, an ECG, and X-rays. I'd had them all and was waiting to be told the results.

"Come in, Miss Fletcher."

"Thank you, Doctor."

"I've reviewed all your test results, and there's nothing there that worries me. Has it happened again?"

"Just once since I saw you."

"And was that after one of your more … intense sessions?"

I'd given her a few hints about our sex life.

"Yes."

She leaned back in her chair.

"I don't think we need to worry about it. Your tests are fine, you're not getting any other symptoms and it's not happening at any other time. I've come across a few women with similar experiences in my career."

"Is it dangerous?"

"Not in itself, but you don't want to pass out in a risky position. Just make sure your partner is watching out for you."

"Oh, I know he is."

"Well, he sounds like a keeper to me."

"A keeper?" Marcus said, a grin on his face.

"That's what she said."

"Not sure that's strictly a medical term."

"I burst out laughing when she said it. But I'm obliged to follow my doctor's advice, so you're stuck with me now."

I was standing in the kitchen, a glass of wine in my hand, watching him prepare dinner.

"Do we need to do anything about it?"

"No," I replied. "It's probably sensory overload, and my body saying, 'too much'."

"So, if it happens, we stop, relax and allow you to recover."

"Yup, that's about it."

"Perhaps I shouldn't push as hard?"

I put my glass down, walked the few paces to him and turned him to face me.

"Please don't let it change anything. It doesn't hurt and it's not dangerous. We carry on exactly as before. It just means we're too good."

"Okay. But promise me you'll tell me if it gets too much."

"Promise."

As we sat down to dinner, he filled me in on his day.

"Eva called. She's happy with my final edits and wants to publish."

"Wow. That's wonderful, darling. Are you pleased?"

"Yes. I must admit, I am."

"When's it being released?"

"Haven't got a date yet, but sometime in the autumn, I'd guess."

"Why does it take so long?"

"God knows. I'm sure there's a commercial reason for it. We'll find out in a couple of weeks. Eva's coming here for a book launch and suggested meeting up. She'll have some cover ideas and a contract and who knows what else. I invited her to dinner. Hope that's all right?"

"Of course, I'd love to meet her, after what you've said about her."

"I'll be interested to see if she ever switches off. The times I've met her, she's very much in 'control' mode."

As we cleared away the dinner things, I wasn't sure how Marcus felt about one of his books being commercially published. Sometimes, he could be a bit closed, emotionally. Since we'd been together, I realised it was a part of his defence mechanism, and he never hid his feelings from me now. But if I were going to be published, I'd be ecstatic. He seemed unfazed by the whole thing.

"It's Lucy's birthday at the end of the month," I said, as we sat down for the evening.

"Decided what you're going to do, yet?"

"We could go away for a weekend again. We'd have a choice of dates because her birthday's in the middle of the week."

"Where do you fancy taking her?"

"I'll have to ask. I did have one idea though."

"What was that?"

"The weekend after her birthday is the next play party. I wondered if she might like to come along."

"That might be pushing it a bit, Sal."

"I know, but do you mind if I ask her?"

"Of course not, but don't be disappointed if she isn't interested. I'd better check with Matt if it would be okay to bring her."

***

"What would you like to do for your birthday?"

Lucy chuckled and I felt the vibrations in my breasts which were currently a pillow for her head. We were laying on her bed, having spent the previous hour using it as the platform for our lust. Luce was tracing her nails lightly over my tummy and thighs. If she carried on, I wasn't going to be responsible for my actions.

"More of this will do," she replied.

"That's not a problem. But where?"

She lifted her head and looked at me.

"Are you planning something?"

"No, but we could go away somewhere. Fancy it?"

"We've only just got back."

"So?"

She dropped her head back on my chest.

"Sal, I …"

"Lucy Halstead. If you're going to mention money …"

"Okay, okay. I won't."

"Where would you like to go?"

"Nowhere."

I heard the cheeky defiance in her voice.

"Come on, Luce. I thought we'd got past this."

"Alright, New York."

"Great. When do you want to go?"

She sat up and screwed her face up, looking at me.

"You would, wouldn't you?"

"Yes, of course. Do you fancy New York?"

She looked away, trying to hide a grin.

"I've always wanted to go, but a weekend might be a bit short."

"Agreed. We'll go when we have more time."

She slapped my thigh.

"I can't win, can I?"

"No."

After a long discussion, interrupted by some extremely pleasant exercise, she decided what she wanted to do.

***

"Sal, this is Eva. Eva, my partner, Sally."

As we made the necessary small talk, I assessed our visitor. Marcus had already told me a little about Eva. Although she had long dark hair, her look was androgynous. A tall, slim figure, with few visible curves, dressed in a trouser suit with what looked like a silk shirt and a skinny tie, knotted loosely at the collar. She had an assertive air, almost arrogance, but I found myself agreeing with Marcus's assessment it was a bit of an act.

"Did the launch go well?" Marcus asked.

"As well as they ever do," Eva replied. "We'll have to wait and see when the figures start coming in."

"Is your business all about the figures?" I asked.

She looked at me as if I'd asked her for a kiss, then her face softened.

"Well, yes, it is, Sally. I'm afraid the reality for us is if books don't sell, we don't make any money. That's not good business."

"Don't worry, darling," Marcus said. "I told Eva I'm not in it for the money, but she didn't understand the concept."

For the first time, Eva appeared to relax and smiled broadly.

"Oh, I do, Marcus. I understand writers very well. But most are not as realistic as you. I see them all the time. Some have spent years writing their masterpiece and are convinced it will make them rich. Convinced someone will give them a six-figure advance and the money will roll in. They haven't even done some basic homework. Others are possessive of their creation and won't allow even the smallest change.

"To come across someone who does it for fun and isn't looking to become a superstar is refreshing. Particularly when they tell me that at our first meeting. And then tell me they won't do any publicity."

She was teasing him now; I was enjoying it. I think he was, too.

"That's your job," he threw back.

"Okay," she conceded. "We'll have to discuss that at some point. I'm hoping I can persuade you to put in an appearance or two. It would help."

"I know," he conceded. "I'll consider any proposal."

"Meanwhile, I've got some potential cover mock-ups. I could have emailed them, but it's better to see them in person."

She opened a small box and took out a bundle of dummy books with the covers stretched over them. Laying them on the table, she lined them up in a row. I watched Marcus as he studied them and could immediately see he was affected by finally seeing them. He'd gone quiet, for a start. There were four, and I was surprised by how different they were.

"I think they all reflect the story well," Eva said. "But I'm guessing you'll have your own ideas."

She was teasing him again. I went to finish off dinner and left them to it. I heard quiet conversation but couldn't make it all out. As we ate, Eva asked Marcus about his writing history, why he wrote, what he got out of it. When Eva found out what I did, she laughed.

"I trained as a librarian, as well," she said. "I found myself in a job in the public library system and it bored me. I wish I'd thought of following your path, Sally. It sounds fascinating. But I was offered an opportunity at a small publisher and I've worked up from there."

"Do you enjoy it?" I asked. "It sounds frustrating."

"Oh, it can be. But find the right book or the right author and it can be so rewarding. I love books and I love creative people. The benefits outweigh the frustrations."

As dinner progressed, Eva noticeably relaxed. Marcus had been right; she put on a work face. We were seeing the person behind it. At around eight, she looked at her watch.

"I'd better think about leaving soon. I don't want to get back to London too late."

"Are you driving?" Marcus asked.

"No, I don't drive. I'll get a taxi to the station."

"We've got plenty of room," he said. "You're welcome to stay the night and we can take you to the station in the morning."

She thought for a few moments, weighing us up.

"If you're sure it's not a problem. I don't have to be in the office too early."

"I can drop you off on my way to work," I said.

"Then, yes, thank you."

Eva proved to have a wicked sense of humour and told us some memorable stories about authors she had worked with; no names mentioned, of course. At one point when the conversation paused, she looked around the room.

"This is a beautiful flat. Have you been here long?"

We told her the story of finding and renovating it.

"I've always fancied taking on a project like that. What was it like when you bought it?"

We showed her the pictures we'd taken, and she took up my invitation for a quick tour as it now was.

"Well, you've done a wonderful job," she said after we re-joined Marcus. "It's much bigger than I first imagined. Your bathroom is something else."

"Yes," I said. "We didn't know what to do with the vaults, but Marcus suggested the bathroom idea."

"A man of many talents," she replied.

"Of many suggestions," he said. "Not all of them feasible."

By the end of the evening, I decided I liked her. Something was intriguing about her; something hidden I couldn't fathom. When it was time for bed, I discovered why Marcus had felt free to invite her to stay. She had a small case in the hallway. It turned out she had stayed in a hotel the previous night and had everything she needed, so I didn't have to find things to lend her.

The next morning, after breakfast, we set off; me taking Eva to the station on the way to work.

"Thank you for putting up with me," she said. "It did save a night-time journey through London."

"Not a problem, Eva. You're welcome anytime."

"I have to say, a couple of the pictures were interesting."

I thought for a moment, and when the penny dropped, I turned to her. Her face was a picture. She was teasing me now, smiling broadly.

"Eva, I'm sorry. I'd forgotten about those."

We'd not given her the room beside ours. After Lucy's warning, it was reserved for her. But I'd forgotten we'd hung a couple of Lucy's pictures in the room we'd put Eva in. They wouldn't be as explicit as those in the playroom, but I couldn't remember which ones they were.

"Don't worry," she said, "it's not a problem. They're similar to the large picture I noticed in your bedroom. Don't tell me Marcus paints as well? Or you?"

"No. They're by a friend of ours."

"They're very talented."

"Yes, she is. We like them."

"Did she do the portraits as well?"

"Yes."

"Does she have a website or anything?"

"No, I'm afraid not. She only does them as a hobby."

Eva laughed.

"Another one who doesn't need the money?"

"She does put a few in a local gallery from time to time, but more of the portrait style than those in the bedroom."

"Mmm. Pity."

"I told you there'd be a market for them."

"I guess there is," Lucy replied. "But I couldn't do it under my own name."

"Use an alias. There's lots of websites which sell art. You ought to try one and see what happens."

"I'll think about it."

"Promise?"

"Yes, miss. Promise."

We were on our way to a spa. Lucy had decided she fancied a weekend being pampered; I'd looked around and found what I hoped would be the perfect place. It was. We had a wonderful time being pummelled, massaged, and beautified. This was interspersed with eating, drinking, and enjoying each other.

"What are you doing on Wednesday?" I asked.

She groaned.

"Ah, it's as you suspected?"

"Yes. Annie and Tim are taking me out for dinner with Mum."

"It might be okay."

"It probably will, but it wouldn't be my first choice."

"Know where they're taking you?"

"Not yet, it's a surprise."

"Will your mum have chosen it?"

"I doubt it. Mum and Dad never went out to eat. You know, in case they found something to be offended about."

We shared a look and laughed.

"Annie or Tim will have booked it?" I asked.

"I guess so."

"Where would they go?"

"I have no idea. Somewhere family-friendly, I suppose."

"Do they drink?"

"Annie and Tim do a bit, but I don't think Mum does. She certainly didn't when Dad was alive. Alcohol was another thing on his long list of evils."

"Perhaps she will try a few forbidden fruits now he's gone."

"It'll be interesting to find out. It might tell me a few things."

Chapter 17 – Lucy

Friday evening and I was waiting for Sally to arrive. I'd been surprised when she said she was coming this week as we'd spent the previous weekend together, but wasn't going to say no. She had something planned; she wouldn't tell me what, but I'd been told I didn't need to get anything for dinner.

When she arrived, she was struggling with several bags.

"Happy Birthday," she said. I laughed at that. She'd indulged me with a spa weekend and she and Marcus had given me things on the day – and both called me with birthday wishes. I wasn't expecting anything else; I should have known better.

"Thank you, Sal. But that was Wednesday."

"I know, but it's not finished yet." I narrowed my eyes at her. "Oh, don't worry. We're just going to have some fun. First of all, we're going to have a quick shower and get dressed up. We need to be ready in less than an hour."

We were back in the bedroom in ten minutes and Sally handed me a present from one of the bags. I frowned at her, but she laughed and retrieved some clothes from one of the others. I opened the present to find a beautiful set of underwear. Silky, soft, and sheer. Red and black, with a pair of black stockings, also with a red seam down the back.

I was more used to dressing up now, thanks to Sally. I understood what she meant. Yes, it might work for your partner, but it made you feel good as well. It made me feel special.

"Shall I …?"

"Yea. I hope it fits."

We watched each other as we put similar sets on. Hers had green highlights, instead of red. When we finished, we stood in front of the mirror.

"Well?" she asked.

I liked what I saw in the mirror; both myself and Sal. I turned and gave her a kiss.

"Thank you. I feel great."

"Good. That little red dress of yours would finish it off nicely."

"What are we doing?" I asked.

"Dinner and a bit of a dance," she replied.

"A dance?"

"Why not? Oh, one final thing."

She handed me two small presents. I opened the first. A small butt plug with a red jewelled end. She held out her hand and gave me a wicked grin.

"Bend over."

"No, Sal. I've never worn one out."

"Well, it's about time you did."

She got some lube from my bedside drawer and when I bent over, she lifted my dress, lowered my briefs and I flinched as the cold gel hit my ass. With a quick twist, she put the plug in place. I re-arranged my clothes and she handed me the other present. I knew what it would be and in a short time, I'd inserted a similar plug in her.

Her phone pinged as we were straightening our clothes; the taxi had arrived.

We went to Cranes, the restaurant we'd visited briefly before our trip to the ballet last year. This time, we were in no rush.

"How was Wednesday?" Sally asked.

"Not too bad, in the end. Not as bad as I feared."

"Where did you go?"

"A nice pub near Annie. Quiet, but the food was good."

"How was your mum?"

"Uncomfortable. Apparently, it's the first time she's ever been in a pub."

"Really?"

"Yes. But she warmed to it. She even had some wine."

"And …?"

"Not sure she enjoyed it, but she tried it."

"No arguments or dramas, then."

"None at all. I even got presents."

"Ooh, what?"

"Annie and Tim gave me some craft shop vouchers. They were apologetic about not knowing what to give me, but I was surprised to get anything. And they gave me two cards which Nathan and Sarah had made. I was quite touched."

"Dare I ask what your mum gave you?"

"A pair of earrings."

"Nice?"

"Well, they're well made."

"But?"

"Fish."

"Fish?"

"St Peter fish."

"Ah …"

"Exactly."

"She's still trying to redeem you."

"Seems like it."

"That's a shame."

"Yea, but I wasn't surprised. I thanked her nicely and she seemed pleased. After all, it's the first present she's given me in a long time."

"Still got them?"

"Of course, Sal. How could you think I'd dispose of them?"

"Sorry."

"I'll need to wait at least a month before I lose them."

By the time we finished dinner, we'd both unwound. After Sally paid the bill, we prepared to set off, although I still didn't know where. We decided to pop to the ladies, and that was when I was reminded of the plug. During the meal, I'd occasionally felt it when I shifted in my seat, but as I walked to the loos, I was aware of it with every step. As we left the restaurant, I stopped Sal.

"Do you really wear a plug to work?"

"Sometimes."

"Doesn't it … you know … have an effect?"

"Yes," she replied, that wicked smile on her face. "That's why I wear it. Sometimes, Marcus doesn't know what hit him when I get home. Why? Are you feeling an effect?"

"God, am I."

"That's the idea. And you're not allowed to take it out; that's my job."

With that, she walked down the stairs and I had to run a few steps to catch up. She put her arm through mine, and we walked quietly for a while. As we took a left turn, I guessed where we were going.

"Juvenals?"

"Yup."

"I haven't been there for years. Last time I went, it had gone downhill."

"I know. But a little bird told me it's changed recently."

Juvenals was a nightclub in a basement. Many years ago, it had been one of the places to go. Quite expensive; not a place you went every week but reserved for special occasions. A friendly atmosphere and great music. But something changed and it got a reputation for drugs and violence.

As we descended the stairs to the door, a couple of large bouncers came into view.

"Good evening, ladies."

"Evening, lads," Sally replied and showed them two tickets. They gave us the once over and opened the door. We walked to the desk, where the tickets were inspected again by a lad who paid regular visits to a piercer.

"Welcome to Juvenals. Please go through."

As we walked through the door into the main club, I was astonished at how much the place had changed; I didn't recognise it. The layout, the décor, even the size were all different. It was busy, but not heaving. But what struck me were the people. A bewildering array of styles; some dressed in eveningwear, as we were. But there was a heavy sprinkling of alternative styles, and I saw immediately this was a far from straight crowd.

"Wow, Sal. What a transformation?"

"Isn't it? Come on, let's grab a drink."

We went over to the bar and found one thing hadn't changed; the prices. But it didn't faze Sal, so I tagged along. There was a shelf around the dance floor, and we found a couple of high stools and perched on them.

"It's an interesting crowd," Sal said.

"It sure is."

As we looked around, the floor cleared, and I saw there was a small stage at the far side.

"Is there something happening?" I asked Sally.

"It's burlesque night."

The next couple of hours were a mixture of the sublime to the ridiculous. Comedians, fire-eaters, dancers, and a couple of strippers. All controlled by a drag MC who was hilarious. We watched, we laughed, we drank. And all the time, the plug gave me reminders of its presence.

When the show finished, the dancing started. We were both pleasantly well-oiled and took to the floor with most of the others. As I moved around, the plug gradually worked its magic, and before long, it was all I could think about. The floor was crowded, and everyone was pressed close together. Sal and I were virtually hugging, I could feel other bodies pressing into me and I felt a few touches which weren't accidental. And all the time, the heat was building around my groin.

"Want to go?" Sal asked.

"Why?"

"Because you're breathing like a bitch on heat."

I looked into her eyes.

"Are you ready?" I asked.

She leaned in and put her lips to my ear.

"Ready for what?"

"Whatever you want."

"I want to replace that plug with something bigger."

We left the club and climbed the stairs with almost indecent haste to hail a taxi. When we got to my flat, Sally slammed me against the wall in the hallway, and pressed herself into me, kissing me hard. She pulled my dress over my head in one movement. My breathing was ragged; I was burning between my thighs and my ass was screaming for attention.

She grabbed my wrist and dragged me to the bedroom, throwing me onto the bed. Going to the toy drawer, she pulled out the double-ended strap on. We held each other's eyes as she rolled her dress over her head, slid her knickers off and pushed one end into her pussy, quickly doing the straps up. As she lifted a wand from the drawer, she turned to me.

"Knickers off and on your knees. Give me your ass."

I obeyed, getting on all fours, and sticking my now naked bum up. She jumped onto the bed and knelt behind me. My breath left me as her hand clamped over my pussy and roughly squeezed it. Her fingers invading me as she pushed them between my lips. Before I could recover my composure, she drove the dildo into me and started fucking me.

I was already panting, my whole body reacting to her force. It exploded into stars as the wand touched my clit. My arms gave way and my shoulders landed on the bed. My ass joined in as she tugged the plug and began to move it in and out.

Then it started. I heard a disembodied cry, my voice echoing around the room as my orgasm overtook me. A dildo fucking me, the wand working its magic and my ass being stretched was all too much. I gave in. My body was in control, pushing back to meet her thrusts which didn't stop. I felt dizzy, my body tingling all over.

As my orgasm peaked, I heard a cry as our mutual frenzy brought her climax as well. But she didn't stop. While I was still recovering, I felt a cold sensation around my ass, followed by pressure. The pressure of the strap-on as she pushed it into my ass.

I shrieked as it broke through and slid in deep. I stopped trying to make sense of it. My clit was still throbbing, almost painful. I could feel my pussy still tense and spasming. She knew it needed a rest but had found a way around it. She began to fuck my ass instead. Long, deep strokes while she held my hips and pulled me back to meet each thrust.

She spanked me. I was no longer sure where each sensation was coming from. What I was aware of was a deep feeling in the centre of my being. A warmth spreading from my ass, through my groin, up to my tummy and down to my legs. I started to shake; gentle tremors, over which I had no control. I vaguely heard her cry out again and was aware of her action slowing for a moment, but it resumed, and my body slumped.

I lost control as a massive orgasm spread over my body. I vaguely remember collapsing onto the bed. Sally followed me and continued to fuck my ass as I reached the peak.

My next memory is of lying on my front with a weight on top of me, my brain slowly re-establishing contact with various parts of my body. I was still shaking slightly and light-headed.

"Okay?"

Sal's voice brought me closer to reality.

"Mmm."

"Sure?"

"Mmm."

We lay like that for a while as we got our breath back. I became aware the dildo was still buried deep in my ass. The pleasure it had given had passed and it felt strange. I rocked my hips.

"Hold still," Sal said.

She lifted herself slowly and gently slid out of me. As it popped out, I let out a gasp. I heard her undo the straps, and she lay back over me.

"That better?"

"Yes, it was getting uncomfortable."

"Better when it's a real cock."

"Why?"

"It goes down."

"I hadn't thought of that."

Eventually, Sal rolled off to one side and I turned to face her.

"You okay?" she asked.

"That was … incredible. Did you …"

"Three times."

"I think I noticed one."

"Well, you were away with the fairies."

"The fairies?"

"It's what Marcus calls it when I'm not really there anymore. When I let my body take over."

"I've never believed in fairies until now."

As we had a leisurely breakfast the next morning, I was still smiling. So was Sally. Hardly a word was spoken, but the looks said it all. As we put the dishes in the kitchen, she put her arms around me and gave me a gentle kiss.

"I'm going to see Helen this morning."

"Helen? Oh, the redhead?"

"She's going to make me a corset."

"Really? Is that what she does?"

"Yes. She made the outfit she was wearing when you met her."

"Wow. She's good."

"Want to come?"

"Why?"

"She can make one for you."

"Seriously?"

"Why not? I'd like to see you in one."

"Well, I don't know."

"My treat."

I opened my mouth to object; she frowned. I closed it again.

"Hello, Sally. Hello, Lucy. Please, come in."

"Hi, Penny. Thank you."

Penny led us into the hallway and closed the door. I'd been surprised by the address. One of the most select roads in the city, all large detached Victorian villas. The inside matched the exterior grandeur; immaculately finished and furnished. We followed Penny through a corridor to the back of the house and into a large brightly lit room with a worktable, material neatly stacked on shelves, and an old treadle sewing machine in the bay window. Helen was sitting at a small desk against the wall and rose as we entered.

"Good morning, Sally. And you've persuaded Lucy to try something as well."

"Hello, Helen. Yes, but we may need to convince her."

"I'm sure we can do that."

I'd only met Helen once, and she was as impressive today as she had been then. She was one of those people you noticed; it wouldn't matter where you were. If you saw her, you'd look. I couldn't decide if she enjoyed the attention or was possibly even oblivious to it. Having talked to Sally about it on the way, she wasn't sure either.

"The first thing I do with new clients," Helen said, "is a complete set of measurements. You'll need to strip to your knickers, so if you prefer, we can do that in a more private space."

"I'm fine here," Sal replied. "You've all seen most of me. Luce, how about you?"

"I'm fine here, as well."

I'd never experienced anything like it. I'd had a bra fitting and measured my waist and hips, but Helen measured everything. Arms, legs, neck, height, several different levels around the chest, tummy, and thighs. Helen measured and Penny wrote everything down. Helen asked if it was okay to take some pictures.

I found myself looking at Penny a few times. She was even more gorgeous than I remembered her. A natural, unaffected beauty with a body to die for. She caught my look on more than one occasion but just smiled before I averted my eyes.

When the measuring was finished and we had our clothes back on, we discussed what we wanted.

"Well," Sally said. "Let's start with a corset. Something like you wore when we first met?"

"And Lucy?" Helen asked.

"I … I'm not sure," I replied, stumbling a bit. "I've only recently started wearing this sort of thing."

"This sort of thing?" Helen said, with a haughty tone.

"Sorry …" I said. "I didn't mean …"

Helen's face broke into a gentle smile and she waved her hand in dismissal. She was playing with me; I felt as if I was in front of the headmistress.

"Don't worry, Lucy. I'm happy to show any woman how good she can feel in some handmade corsetry. And you have the perfect figure for it. Why don't we try something similar to Sally? At least to begin with."

We spent the next hour choosing what we might want. Helen showed us pictures of things she had made, pictures of other styles. We looked at materials; the choice was bewildering and when she said they could be embroidered with anything we wanted, my head nearly exploded. Sally was struggling to choose as well. Finally, she gave up.

"Helen, I've got a suggestion. We've more or less chosen the style and shape. How about we leave you to choose the colour and materials. You're the expert. Agree, Luce?"

"Yes. I'm going around in circles. It reminds me of trying to choose the right colour when I'm painting."

"You're an artist?" Penny asked.

"It's only a hobby," I replied.

"She's good," Sally said. "We've got a few pieces."

We agreed to let Helen use her experience and surprise us. We set a date to go back in a couple of weeks for the first fitting, which would be for the basic structure.

As we got into the car, I turned to Sally.

"Sal, just out of interest …"

She raised her eyebrows at me.

"… out of interest, how much would one of these corsets be?"

She started the car.

"From a thousand upwards."

"What?"

"Depends on the material and embroidery."

"Have you agreed a price with Helen?"

"Nope, I told her to do whatever she wanted."

"Sal …"

"It's a birthday present. Is that okay?"

I shook my head and sighed. She'd caught me out again.

"Thank you," I said.

"Right, got anything planned?"

"No, a quiet weekend. I probably need it after last night."

"Coming back to ours?"

"I don't want to disturb you."

She frowned at me.

"Coming back to ours?"

"Yes, please. Thank you."

Chapter 18 – Marcus

I'd spent quite some time looking at the mocked-up covers Eva had brought. In truth, I liked them all and was finding it difficult to choose a favourite. I'd been surprised at my reaction when she first laid them out on the table. I'd published several books now, and although I'd paid for professional covers, they were only available as e-books. To see physical examples of how my book would look in a bookshop had proved surprisingly emotional.

I'd read the contract Eva had left and talked to Peter about it briefly. He was happy with it; 'a standard deal', he'd called it. I had no qualms about signing it. I'd been honest; I didn't need the money. But I was interested to see how the book was received compared with those I'd published myself.

If it sold well – and it was a big if – she'd want a new book from me. And in a hurry. Fortunately, I was already halfway through the first draft of a sequel, but I hadn't told her that.

I was still looking at the covers when I heard the front door, and female voices. Sally was back, presumably with Lucy.

"Hi, darling," Sal said as they came in from the hallway. "I've brought Lucy back. Hope that's okay."

"Of course. Hi, Luce."

"Hi, Marcus. Are those the covers for your book?"

They both joined me, looking at them.

"Decided yet?" Sally asked.

"No, not yet. Lucy, which does your artist's eye prefer?"

She studied them for a while, turning them over.

"God, it's hard, isn't it?"

"Be brutally honest, because I can't decide."

"Well," she said, picking one up. "I'm not sure which I prefer, but I do know I'm not keen on this one. There's too much going on."

I'd been of the same opinion, thinking the one she was holding was the weakest. We put it to one side.

"We're going for the elimination method, then?" Sally asked.

"Looks like it."

As we ate lunch, they told me about their adventures the night before, along with a few hints those adventures continued when they got home.

"We must go to Juvenals," Sally said to me. "It's completely changed, and the burlesque was good."

"Did you go to Helen's this morning?"

"Yes, Lucy came as well."

"Oh?"

"Helen's going to make one for her, too."

"She forced me, Marcus," Lucy said. "You know what she's like."

"Don't believe her, darling. She's getting into the whole dressing up thing."

"I'm beginning to see the attraction," she said.

Sally looked at me and winked. I knew what was coming.

"Luce?"

"Yes, Sal."

"We're going to a play party tomorrow afternoon."

"Going naked, this time?"

"No, I haven't decided what to wear yet."

"From what I remember, you've got plenty of options."

"Want to come with us?"

Lucy froze; then looked from Sally to me and back to Sal.

"Seriously?"

"Yea. It'll be fun."

We fell silent as Lucy considered. The offer had surprised her.

"Well, I ... I mean ... What would I ...?"

"Would you like to?" Sally asked.

Lucy gave a nervous smile and a faint blush coloured her cheeks.

"I don't think I could. From what you've told me, I'm not sure I'd be comfortable."

"But would you like to?"

Once again, she looked from Sally to me and back again.

"I'm intrigued, I won't deny it."

"Okay, Lucy," I said. "Don't let this devil force you into anything. But the two of you went into a lap-dancing club on your own. A lot of women wouldn't. We were nervous when we first went, but everyone is really friendly. There's a huge mix of people and nobody judges anyone else."

"Am I allowed to go?"

"Yes," I said. "We can bring guests, but we're responsible for their behaviour. You'd need to promise to be a good girl."

"And if I'm not?"

"Well," Sally said. "You remember what Marcus does to naughty girls?"

Lucy looked at the table. I could see she was in two minds. She wanted to go but was nervous.

"There's no pressure, Luce," I said. "It's your choice. Think about it. If you do, fine. If not, we can drop you off at home on our way."

After lunch, we sat and chatted, but Lucy was distracted, clearly thinking about tomorrow. At one point, she took a deep breath and turned to Sally.

"If I did choose to come tomorrow, what would I wear?"

"Anything you want. You can go in ordinary clothes; we did, the first time."

"Until you took your dress off," Lucy said with a grin.

"True, but that was my choice."

"You said most people dress up."

"Yes, but there's always a few people who don't."

"Do they stand out?"

"I suppose they do, a bit."

Lucy lapsed into thought again.

"Look," Sal said. "Why don't we go downstairs? You can help me decide what I'm going to wear, and we can look at something for you. If you decide to come."

They were gone for two hours.

***

As we drove, Lucy sat quietly in the back of the car. She'd made her decision and she and Sally had spent ages getting ready. As usual, I was banished from the bedroom. I would only see what Sally was wearing when we got there. Lucy was wearing one of Sally's more conventional wet-look dresses, although I'd noticed she was wearing stockings and high heels. The dress was short, but she looked great and seemed comfortable in it.

"Happy with the rules, Luce?" Sally asked.

"Yes."

"And if you want to leave at any time, you tell us," I said. "Promise?"

"Yes, I promise."

As we walked from the car to the entrance, Sally kept up light conversation to bolster Lucy's confidence; she was jittery and a bit breathless. Going through the door, we encountered Dave.

"Hello, you two," he said. "Oh, three."

"Hi, Dave. This is Lucy, a friend of ours. She's come along to see what it's all about."

"You're very welcome, Lucy. Enjoy yourself."

We headed to the changing area and grabbed a locker.

"Won't be long," Sally said, heading to the changing room with a small bag.

A couple of guys I remembered talking to briefly came in and we exchanged a casual greeting as they headed to change.

"Is all the talk about … well, the fetishes and stuff?" Lucy asked while we waited.

"No, talk about whatever you want. Treat it as a social gathering."

"Where everyone is half-naked."

"You'll soon forget that. No, 'forget' is the wrong word. You'll notice it; it's a big part of the whole thing. But it soon becomes normal."

"I hope so. I'm shaking."

"I know. But you look amazing. There will be plenty of people who will want to know who you are and have a chat."

"I feel like a fraud. I don't know anything about all this."

"Tell them. There are people here from experts to beginners. Tell people you're a novice and they'll be fine with it."

The changing room door opened, and Sally walked out. She raised an eyebrow as she spotted my lustful look. She had a mesh body stocking on. It covered her from neck to toe and clung to every curve. It was semi-transparent, but you had to concentrate to see through it. She was wearing a tight PVC mini skirt to cover her modesty, but as she approached, I could see her bare breasts through the material.

"Well?" she asked.

"You look sensational." An image flashed through my head. "Was that expensive?"

She gave me a quizzical look.

"Not particularly. Why?"

"I might show you later."

"You don't mind me flashing my boobs?"

"Nope. They're yours to flash."

Lucy laughed.

"You two are … well, I need to find a better word than wicked."

"Come on," Sal said. "Let's go."

She took Lucy's arm and we went through to the main area. It was early yet, but quite a few people were milling around. A glance confirmed we knew some of them, at least to nod to. I dropped our food and drink off and we went through to the play area as Sally explained the different sections to Lucy. Looking at the schedule, we found a couple of things we wanted to see.

"Anything take your fancy, Luce?" Sally asked.

"All these things happen right here? In front of everyone?"

"Yup."

"I'm not even sure what half of them mean," Lucy said.

Between us, Sally and I managed to explain everything, but Lucy decided she'd stick with our choices. I wasn't sure she was as naïve as she was making out but kept quiet.

"Hi, Sally," a voice behind us said and we turned to find Yas. "Hi, Marcus."

"Hello, Yas," Sal replied. "This is Lucy. Luce, Yas. She's one of the organisers."

They exchanged a greeting.

"Your first time?"

"Yes," Lucy said. "Never attended anything like this before. It's a bit of an eye-opener."

"Ah, so these two have been leading you astray?"

"Sort of."

"Good." She looked Lucy up and down. "I'm pretty sure you'll find plenty of people keen to lead you anywhere. Relax and have fun."

As she left us, I saw Lucy had noted the clear compliment.

"Sal, I do believe Lucy's blushing."

Lucy turned away as Sal laughed.

"Oh, Luce. You'll get used to that. People aren't afraid to tell you when you look good. No-one's creepy, but the compliments will come. By the end, you'll feel a mile high."

We spent some time doing the rounds, talking to several people we knew and introducing Lucy. The tension gradually left her, and she became herself, rather than being on her guard. We took a break to get something to eat and drink.

"Well?" Sal asked.

"I don't know what to say," Lucy replied. "It's unreal. You were right about everyone being friendly."

"There's always something good to look at, too."

Lucy let out a deep chuckle.

"There sure is. What you're wearing is quite restrained. Some of the outfits are …"

She left the sentence unfinished, but the look on her face told us she'd seen a few which met with her approval.

"Time for a gag, I think," Sal said, and we headed for the demo area.

A guy we didn't know was giving a talk about gags and hoods. We were interested because we hadn't had much luck with gags. We had one which was okay but were interested to see if there were better alternatives.

The guy knew his stuff. He had a lad and a girl who he demonstrated the different styles on, and we did see one or two things of interest. The hoods and masks also made us think, and Sally and I shared a look and a smile on a couple of occasions. Lucy laughed when she noticed. The most interesting thing came at the end, when he told us he made most of the items he'd shown us.

"Marcus, get his details before we leave."

"Yes, ma'am."

"Do you like being gagged?" Lucy asked.

"We haven't found anything I find comfortable yet. Looks like that might change."

"I need the loo," Lucy said; not moving.

"I'll come with you," Sal offered.

"Thanks."

"Will you be alright, darling?"

"I'll manage," I replied.

As they left, I looked around. Since our first visit, we'd come a long way. We were comfortable here; part of it. We were still novices but were accepted. People wandering by nodded or greeted me, asked how we were or where Sally was.

As I turned back to the break in the hangings, I experienced one of those déjà vu moments.

Sally and Lucy were coming towards me, but Lucy's dress had vanished. She was wearing one of Sally's basques; deep purple and opaque with a short lace skirt hanging from the waist. The picture was completed by black stockings.

"What do you think?" Sally asked. Lucy did a nervous twirl.

"Wow. You look ravishing, Luce."

"Thanks."

"How do you feel?"

"Sexy and terrified."

"It's certainly sexy," a soft voice said behind us. We turned to find a smiling Penny but all three of us were rendered momentarily speechless. She was wearing a scarlet PVC catsuit. I'd never seen one as tight. It was shaped over her breasts highlighting hard nipples and had a zip from the neck to the midriff. Sally was the first to recover.

"Hi, Penny," she said. "Sorry. That suit is incredible, don't you think, darling?"

"I'm not saying a word; it'll only get me into trouble."

Penny laughed; her gentle, warm laugh.

"Thank you. I always feel good in this."

"I've never seen one shaped around … here." Sally waved one hand over her chest.

"They're made by someone Helen knows. Shaped to the wearer."

"That would explain it. You couldn't get that fit off the shelf. What do you think?" she said, turning to me. "Could I get away with something like that?"

"You bet, but you might not have it on long."

"Is it easy to get on?" Lucy asked.

"Once you get the hang of it, it's okay," Penny replied. "Getting it off again can be a different matter."

"Ah," I said.

Penny picked up on my meaning.

"Don't worry," she said, her smile now taking on a cheeky edge. "You can have it made with the zip going all the way from front to back." She paused. "For easier access."

My turn to feel a slight flush on my face. She saw it and her smile broadened.

"I must go and get something to eat," she said. "Are you watching the clamps demo?"

"Yes."

"Can you save me a place?"

"Of course."

We all watched her walk away. The suit showing every movement of her gorgeous bum as she went. I suspected she was exaggerating her gait, knowing we were watching, but I wasn't complaining.

"That's just about perfection," Lucy said in a whisper.

Sal chuckled.

"I can't argue with that. Marcus?"

"Mmm."

"Marcus …?"

One or two explicit images faded from my mind as I was brought back to reality.

"Yes?"

I turned to find them both looking at me with smiles on their faces.

"Don't worry, Luce," Sally said. "I'm guessing he was away somewhere giving those cheeks some colour. Am I right, darling?"

"It may have crossed my mind."

She leaned across and gave me a kiss.

"And I'd buy a ticket to watch," she said.

"So would I," Lucy added. We both turned to look at her and she blushed, before breaking into a beguiling smile.

Chapter 19 – Sally

"How are you feeling?" I asked Lucy when Marcus had gone off to the loo.

"I'm glad I came," she said. "It's fascinating."

"Feel good?"

She knew what I meant.

"Yes," she replied and leaned nearer to me. "And if I'm feeling it, you must be gagging for it."

"Don't know what you mean." She raised an eyebrow. "Yea, okay. It can get frustrating."

"What can?" Marcus asked as he re-joined us.

"Oh, nothing darling. Girl talk."

He sat beside me and gave me a kiss. Lucy was right, I was feeling it. The body stocking was tight and as I moved, rubbed gently over my skin. That had had its effect; my nipples were aching and although it was crotchless, things were warming up between my thighs. Marcus leaned close to my ear.

"Fancy a challenge?" he asked.

I looked at him; there was a gleam in his eyes.

"What?" I replied.

"Yes or no?"

"Yes."

"Are you wearing knickers?"

"Yes."

"Go and take them off."

"Marcus, I – "

"Go and take them off."

I went to get up, but he laid one hand on my arm, while the other hand went to his pocket. He slipped something into my palm. I knew instantly what it was and sat back down.

"Darling …"

"Do it," he said, holding my gaze.

"Do what?" Lucy said, having overheard the last remark.

"Sal's chickening out, Luce," Marcus said. I bridled at that.

"Out of what?"

Marcus was still staring at me and I was finding it harder to hold his gaze.

"Are you going to tell her," he said. "Or shall I?"

I was torn. I wanted to do it – needed to do it – but here? Now? With Lucy here? Before I could decide, he leaned nearer to Lucy and lowered his voice.

"All I've asked her, Luce, is to remove her knickers and put a plug in her ass. Is it too much to ask?"

Lucy stifled something between a gasp and a giggle.

"Really?" she said.

"Yes. And she won't do it."

He made a few quiet clucking noises. I couldn't help laughing and when I turned to Lucy, she was grinning.

"Come on, Sal," she said. "You don't normally refuse a challenge."

"Lucy, you're supposed to be on my side."

"I'm not the one chickening out."

I stuck my tongue out at her and turned to Marcus.

"How come you haven't set Lucy a challenge?"

"With what she's wearing, it would be a bit obvious if Lucy took her knickers off."

"Exactly," Lucy said, enjoying my indecision. "I would if I could, but I can't."

"Oh, you can," he said. His hand went back to his pocket and he held his fist out to Lucy. I grinned at her as a puzzled look crossed her face. She held out her hand and Marcus dropped a plug into it. She closed it quickly and reddened.

"I thought I was supposed to be on my best behaviour," she said.

"So be a good girl, and go and put that in."

Lucy and I shared a look.

"I'll be checking, of course," Marcus said, as we got up and headed for the changing area. He'd given us the smallest of our butt plugs and they were simple to put in without drama. As we left the loos, I was conscious of the air around my swollen pussy. And conscious my skirt was short. I'd have to be careful how I sat from now on.

When we got back, Marcus had been joined by Penny, and we sat either side of them.

"All done?" he asked.

"Yes, thank you, darling."

"Good."

Penny looked quizzically from Lucy to me and then to Marcus.

"Oh, I set them a little challenge," he said. "Just to spice up the afternoon."

I was keen to change the subject, and Lucy was too.

"Penny, can I ask a rude question?" she said.

"Try me."

"Do you wear anything under that suit?"

Penny flashed a wicked grin.

"No, you can't wear any underwear; it would show. But you can hide other things."

She was playing with us now. We all wanted to ask, and she knew it. I couldn't resist.

"Such as?"

Without looking at any of us, the reply came.

"Today it's a nice plug and a set of Kegel balls."

Marcus laughed.

"Not vibrating, I hope."

She turned to him with the sexiest look I'd ever seen.

"Oh, no, Marcus. Who would I find to control them?"

Well, there would be three volunteers here, for a start, I thought.

"Do you tease your mistress, Penny?"

"Not often. Not unless I want to take the consequences. I'm sorry, have I gone too far?"

"Not at all," I said. "If you ever want anyone to look after the remote …"

She looked at each of us in turn.

"That might be fun," she replied.

Marcus shook his head.

"Down girls, please."

I shoved him gently.

"You wouldn't want a go?" I asked.

"I'm not saying a word. I don't know, Penny. What happened to the shy girl we first met?"

"She's still here," she replied. "If you'd prefer her …?"

"Oh, no. You're fine as you are. You just make us all wish we were twenty years younger."

He wasn't wrong.

"Oh," Penny said, as the demo started. "I've always preferred older partners. I guess Helen is older than all of you."

After the demo, I needed to go home and jump someone, but I realised it might be difficult today. We'd all be horny, but one of us was going to be disappointed. Perhaps we should have thought it through better.

When we got to the car, I pulled the handle, but the door didn't open. Marcus hadn't unlocked the car. He was standing next to us on the passenger side.

"What?" I asked him.

"You're only getting in if you pass my check."

Lucy laughed as he turned me around and pushed me against the car – like a cop, frisking a suspect. And he did frisk me. His hand went straight under my skirt and I gasped as it found my pussy. Bare and exposed to the air. He fingered it for a few seconds, sending shivers through me, before running his fingers over my perineum and reaching the plug in my bum. Pressing his weight onto me against the car, I felt his breath by my ear.

"Good girl."

I pushed my bum back against him, his cock pressing into me. He stood back and turned to Lucy.

"Wearing yours, Luce?"

"Why don't you check?"

She had a challenging look on her face, which quickly changed to a little shriek as he grabbed her and turned her to face the car. I watched his hand lift her dress and go down the back of her knickers between her cheeks. I heard a low groan as he found the plug and started moving it. Knowing Lucy, she'd be extremely sensitive by now and she wasn't objecting to whatever Marcus was doing.

He leaned nearer her and repeated the 'good girl' before replacing her clothes and opening the car. As he walked around to the driver's door, I gave her a wink and we got in.

On the way home, we asked Lucy for her impressions. They were positive, as I thought they would be. She was still unsure of how she might fit into this scene, but she was unfazed by it and clearly interested.

"Did you leave early because of me?" she asked.

"No, Luce," Marcus replied. "We haven't stayed for the whole thing yet. The first time it was because we were nervous. Now, it's normally because Sally gets desperate for a fuck."

"And you don't?" I said.

"Well, possibly."

"I'm glad it affects you in the same way," Lucy said.

"Horny, Luce?" I asked.

"God, yes."

When we got home, I was trying to work out what to do. I needn't have worried. When we got in from the garage, Marcus turned to us.

"Right. I'm going to leave you to it for as long as you want."

"Oh, Marcus," Lucy said, looking embarrassed. "That's not right. I should go home."

"Luce, we invited you and knew this might happen. You're horny as hell and your lover's standing here. No doubt, even hornier." He wasn't wrong. "And one thing we know about Sal is she can manage both of us with ease."

As Marcus turned away, she stopped him. Looking from me to him, she shifted uncomfortably.

"If I wasn't here," she said. "What would you be doing?"

"By now," I replied, "I'd be tied down waiting for him to ravage me. Or the other way around."

There was a long pause, as Lucy looked at the floor.

"Can I watch?" she said quietly.

Hot shivers went through my body from head to toe. Lucy hadn't watched us play a scene, but it was one of my fantasies. I turned to Marcus and raised a questioning eyebrow.

"Sure you want to?" he asked.

She raised her head slowly and looked at each of us.

"Yes."

"Sal?" he asked.

"Yes," I shot back.

"Okay. What's the setup?"

"You're in charge," I said. It was what I needed tonight.

"Into the playroom and wait for us," he said to me.

I went through, adjusted the lighting, and put on some low background music. As I waited, kneeling on the rug, I took some deep breaths and cleared my mind. My body was ready for anything; the play parties always turned me on and being there with both Marcus and Lucy had been a dream. The encounters with Penny had also been interesting.

The door opened and they came in.

"Make yourself comfortable, Luce," he said, and came and stood in front of me. Close enough that I was staring at his cock, stiff under the mesh boxers he had stripped down to. I wanted it; I didn't care how, I wanted it. I knew I'd get it, but when? That was totally in his control.

"Stand up."

I rose until I was level with him, his eyes burning into me. Lowering the bar from the ceiling, he positioned me under it and raised my arms. I grasped it as he attached the cuffs locking me to it. He raised the bar slowly until I was fully stretched, and my feet just touched the ground.

I was facing Lucy and our eyes met. She smiled a little shyly, not realising how much her presence was turning me on and adding to this experience. Marcus came up behind me. In one movement, he pulled my skirt over my hips and I stepped out of it. He pressed against me, his cock pushing against my bum, and his arms coming around my midriff and resting there.

"Comfortable?" he asked.

"Yes."

"Lucy and I have had a little chat. There are one or two things she'd like to see. I'm going to show Lucy what a little slut you can be."

One hand slid over my breasts and I shuddered at the touch.

"Do you mind me calling you a slut in front of your lover?"

"She knows what I can be."

Lucy chuckled.

His other hand slid down my tummy and I jumped as his fingers rolled over my clit and continued over my pussy. I wanted him to use it; to rub it, finger it, slap it. Anything; I wanted to come. He pushed two or three fingers into me and moved them around, then brought them to my mouth. I opened my lips and sucked them as he pushed them in.

"You're enjoying Lucy watching this, aren't you?" he asked. I mumbled in the affirmative. "I think Lucy will be in charge of your orgasms tonight. You only get to come when she says you can."

A big grin appeared on Lucy's face; I was in trouble.

"But you know the rule, Sally. Pain before pleasure. Lucy is very keen to see you suffer. I can't disappoint her."

He went over to the racks and took down a flogger. I knew he wouldn't do too much warming up. I was horny as hell, and my pain threshold would already be high. As the first swing came in, I was ready; needy, even. He played the fronds over my body, moving around me, hitting a different area each time. This was the set-up; getting my body used to the impact.

He switched up. The impacts got firmer, and I let myself react; letting the gasps and moans come out freely. Enjoying the touch of the leather and letting my body move and react as it wanted. My nipples were hurting, and my pussy was pleading for attention, but they'd have to wait.

He came to stand in front of me.

"Something's not right here," he said, lifting a section of the mesh over my chest between his fingers. "This bodystocking is protecting you. I want to hear the leather on bare breasts."

I gasped as he yanked his hand down, ripping the mesh and pulling it away from me. Going around my back, he leaned into my ear.

"And I want to hear leather on this gorgeous ass."

A tearing sound as he tore the material again, my body being pulled about as he destroyed my outfit. It was a huge turn-on; as if I were being violated.

"That's better. Now, let's start again."

Before I was ready, the flogger came down. On my breasts, my back, my thighs, and my bum. Firm regular strokes, with no break; my body rippling as the impact sent nerve impulses firing everywhere. But my groin was on fire; hot, wet, and needy.

When he stopped, I let my body relax and opened eyes which I hadn't realised I'd closed. I was looking straight at Lucy who was watching me, transfixed. Even from this distance, I could see she was breathing heavily. Marcus followed my eyes and laughed.

"I'm not sure which of you is enjoying this more."

He put the flogger down and picked up a leather strap. Turning me around, he placed me so Lucy had a clear view of my bum. Then lowered the bar a little so I could spread my legs and stick my bum out. All of which I did without instruction.

"Good girl."

Before I had a chance to reply, I cried out as the strap landed across both cheeks and almost knocked me forward. It came again and again. I had no chance to steady myself between each impact. The strikes rolled into one long ecstasy of pain and I felt myself building towards a climax. I was desperate and just went with it, but my moaning must have given me away. He stopped and I slumped down, letting out a cry of exasperation. All I got was a wicked chuckle.

My bum was stinging, my pussy was throbbing and leaking down my thighs. I could feel sweat on my face and running across my breasts. And he was standing in front of me with a smile on his face. I loved this bastard so much.

"What do you think, Luce?" he said. "Does she deserve a reward?"

"Why not?" she replied. "After all, she'll need a lot more."

He leaned into my face.

"Say thank you."

"Thank you, Luce."

He moved over to the drawers and took out a wand. Turning it on, he stared into my eyes and brought it closer and closer to my pussy. Just as it touched, he pulled it away. I almost screamed as he turned around. Then my heart missed a beat as he held it out.

"Want to, Luce?"

She hesitated for a second, then got up and took it from his hand.

"One moment," he said, and my feet left the floor as the bar rose. I was left dangling in mid-air.

Lucy switched the wand on and brought it close to me. I didn't see the strap until it bit into my bum and made me shriek. At that very moment, Lucy pushed the wand into me, and I lost control. The strap coming down on my exposed bum and the vibrations rushing through my groin all melded into one.

My body was jerking violently; I had nothing to steady myself against as I was hanging free. I trembled as a massive rolling orgasm enfolded me from head to toe. Weird noises were echoing in my throat and I could see coloured flashes.

As I gradually made sense of the room around me, I realised they'd stopped. I was coming back, my head hanging loose in front of me. I felt myself being lowered and guided gently to the floor.

I saw Lucy squatting in front of me, a slightly worried look on her face. I smiled at her. Marcus undid my wrists and lowered my arms gently. He came and sat beside me, holding me close and I laid my arms around his shoulders.

As my breathing slowed, I lifted my head and he kissed me. I leaned forward and kissed Lucy as well.

"Thank you," I whispered to her. She still looked a bit shell-shocked.

"Wow," she said. "Was that … normal?" All I managed was a throaty chuckle. "I've never seen anything like it. Are you in pain?"

"That's the idea."

She shook her head.

"No, I mean … I'm not sure what I mean."

"I'm on a high, Luce. That's what pain does. It gets me high, then I can take more, and my orgasms are more intense."

We sat on the floor for a while. I drank some water and tried to explain to Lucy how I felt. But I'd never managed to explain it fully to Marcus, so it was a feeble attempt.

"Did you enjoy it?" I asked her.

She blushed slightly; I knew the answer.

"I'm a bit ashamed to say yes."

"Don't be."

"Then yes, that was one of the hottest things I've ever seen."

"Horny?"

She nodded and grimaced.

"Yes, as horny as I can remember."

Marcus chuckled and whispered in my ear.

"Ready for more?"

"Anything you want."

"Good, because your sensitive lover here would like to see a caning."

I looked at Lucy, her face now full of concern again.

"Oh, no," she said. "That's enough, surely."

"Not yet, it's not. Remember your picture?" I pointed to the painting of my bum with the six welts. I turned to Marcus. "Think you can recreate it, darling?"

"With pleasure."

Chapter 20 – Lucy

Marcus stood and gave Sal his hand, pulling her to her feet. Between them, they removed the remains of the body stocking, still hanging from her like a torn second skin.

"You choose," he said.

She walked over to the rack and picked a cane, handing it to him.

"On the horse?" she asked.

"No, bending over the end."

As she settled in position, I wondered whether to stay on the floor or return to the sofa. I stayed put; it was comfortable sitting on the thick rug, and I was nearer the action. I was desperate to do something to satisfy my own need but couldn't quite summon up the courage. Marcus solved the problem for me.

"Here," he said, handing me the wand. "I think you need this."

Sal looked around and smiled; I had the permission I needed. Spreading my legs, I settled back against the edge of the table behind me.

"Move to the left," Marcus said. "Then she can see you."

I moved and saw Sal's face in the mirror, watching me. Making myself comfortable again, I turned the wand on and touched it to the material covering the edge of my pussy. I didn't want to come before I'd seen some of the action. I saw Sally pouting.

"What?" I mouthed.

"Off," was her only reply.

I quickly wriggled out of my knickers and threw them aside.

"Are we all ready now?" Marcus asked with exaggerated sarcasm.

"Yes, thanks," I replied.

He started sliding his hand gently over Sal's already red bum, the little plug now exposed. I'd been very aware of the one I was wearing all afternoon.

"Legs together."

She snapped them shut.

He took up position to one side and gently tapped the cane against her skin. Initially, I saw her body tense at the touch, but it gradually relaxed and when it settled, his arm came out and I winced at the sound of the cane coming down across her cheeks. Her body flinched and she let out a curious sound; something between a cry and a giggle.

The welt was already visible, a clear line across the top of her bum. Marcus stood still, letting her recover from the first stroke, her body slowly resting back on the padded top of the horse. Then in one movement, his arm swung again and repeated the strike. The same crack, the same cry.

I had tensed up; my body was reacting to what I was seeing. My heart was beating faster, and I was willing him to strike again, wanting to see him inflict pain on her body. I wasn't sure about this reaction but couldn't resist any longer. I let the wand touch my wet flesh and let out a sharp moan as it began its magic. Both of them were watching me, but I didn't care. It spurred me on.

As I guided the wand where I needed it, he gave her another stroke, then another. At each contact, the muscles in my groin tightened. The fifth stroke followed. Sally and I were watching each other in the mirror, her mouth falling open as the cane struck. But her eyes were firmly fixed between my legs.

The final stroke forced her to look away. This time, the sound was harsher, her cry louder, and her body shook from the pain. I could see tears on her face. I couldn't understand how that made me even hornier. I was near now; Marcus was gently stroking her bum and watching me. Looking in the mirror, I saw Sally was too. The audience was enough, I pushed the wand hard onto my clit and my orgasm rolled through me.

I lost sight of them and let my body do what it wanted, my head falling back, my bum and thighs twitching as I kept the wand going as long as I could bear. Eventually, I had to remove it, and the climax slowly ebbed. As it did, I heard a low moan. Looking up, Marcus was delicately running his fingers between Sally's now spread legs. She was loving every second, but desperate for him to finish it.

"Pleeease …"

A long, pinched plea left her, but he ignored it. He was watching me and calmly continued his teasing. Then I realised why. He was waiting for me to recover; when he thought I had, he removed his fingers and walked over to the drawers. Turning back, he held up a double-ended strap on, offering it to me.

I couldn't resist. Sally was bending over, her bum covered in welt marks and as horny as hell. I stood up, still a little shaky after my orgasm, took the strap-on, and placed it between my legs. I didn't need any lube this time. I inserted it and did up the straps. We were doing this out of Sally's view, and he held his finger to his lips and winked.

He squatted in front of Sally and stroked her hair, giving her small soft kisses.

"Need anything?" he asked.

"Your cock in me." Her voice was strangled, pleading.

"No."

She slumped, letting out an exasperated cry. He motioned to me.

"Will this do?"

I moved into her vision in the mirror and her face filled with joy. She let out a depraved chuckle and grinned. He stayed still, watching her, as I got behind her and slowly slid the dildo into her pussy. I couldn't see her face as Marcus was between her and the mirror, but her long moan told me she needed this. I looked down and felt a renewed lust as I took in my strap-on stretching her lips. But what really thrilled me was her bum. Red and glowing with those angry welts. They rippled slightly as I slid slowly in and out.

"Is that good?" he asked. So quietly, I could hardly hear him.

"Mmm."

"More?"

"Yes."

He came around and stood by me and they shared a look in the mirror.

"Fuck her, Luce. Let's see how needy she is."

The scene had affected me in a way I didn't understand. I wanted to use her. I wanted to fuck her until she couldn't take any more. I set to it, holding her hips, and driving into her. Her moans instantly increased. She was looking into my eyes reflected in the mirror as I used her, building to a climax.

Marcus produced the wand and before she had time to react, he turned it on and pressed it against her butt plug. She let out a scream and her body started to shake. Her head drooped as she came hard, her hips jerking so much I struggled to hold on. Little cries and whimpers echoed around the room. As she fell from the peak, I slowed, but Marcus handed me the wand.

"Keep going, Luce. She's not finished yet."

He walked to the other end of the horse and she raised her head slightly. He stood in front of her and pushed his boxers down, releasing his cock. I'd never quite got over his patience, but he needed something now. He gently wrapped some of her hair around his hand and lifted her head. When it was in the right place, she opened her mouth and he slid it between her lips. Her hands went around his hips and pulled him towards her.

"Right, Luce, do your worst."

I was a bit light-headed. My need was rising again as the dildo in me was doing its work. But the scene was taking me to places I'd never been before. We were using Sally, but she was enjoying it as much as we were; probably more. I went with it and started to fuck her as hard as I could, pressing the wand onto the plug.

She built quickly to another orgasm, her cries and moans muffled by his cock deep in her mouth. I went to slow, but Marcus urged me on.

"One more," he said, "one more."

She didn't come down from the first orgasm; her body still shaking, the moans uninterrupted. There was a sudden moment of stillness, followed by her body writhing on the horse, her legs trembling. Marcus slipped out of her mouth and her moans and groans filled the room, interspersed with odd words, mostly obscene.

He held up a hand to me and I slipped slowly out of her. Marcus was stroking her back and hair, and I gently ran my hands over her hips and bum as she came down. I was breathing hard and it wasn't all from the exertion of fucking Sally. We stayed like that for some time before she took a couple of deep breaths and stretched. Marcus squatted in front of her.

"Okay?"

She let out some disjointed chuckles.

"Wow. Yes."

I moved aside as she went to stand up and we helped her to her feet. She pulled us both to her, wrapped her arms around us and kissed us wildly. She looked at Marcus's cock.

"Time we did something about that," she said, and turned to me with a questioning look. "Want it?" she asked.

I knew the answer; I'd known as soon as I saw he hadn't come in her mouth. I looked at his cock, looked at him.

"Yes."

"Sure?" he asked.

"She's desperate for it," Sal replied. "Just fuck her."

Before she'd finished the sentence, she pushed me over the horse in the position she'd been in. I spread my legs slightly and relaxed onto the padded top. I wanted this; wanted it so badly. His cock split my lips and his whole length slid into me, making me groan.

"See," Sal said. "Now fuck her like she fucked me."

I wanted it; he wanted it. We were both close and didn't waste any time. The force of his thrusts banged my thighs against the edge of the horse, but I didn't care. I cared even less when the wand hit my plug. That was it; I laid my head on the leather, closed my eyes, and left him to it.

My body had one of those moments when it hasn't got a clue what's happening. Random muscles were twitching, my pussy and ass were producing their own fireworks and my brain was passing the time drawing stars and coloured lights.

I vaguely heard him cry out and felt his explosion somewhere inside me, but I was only aware of my own feelings. The movement slowed; he'd stopped, and my body was gradually relaxing. With a shock, I realised tears were running down my face. I panicked briefly, but let it go. If it worked for Sal, why not me?

As my body returned to normal, I felt hands gently stroking me and heard Sal's voice.

"Okay?"

"What ... the ..."

"Relax, breathe."

I don't know how long I lay there before they helped me up and led me to the sofa. When I sat down, they sat either side and wrapped me in their arms.

"Have a drink," Sal said. "That was something else."

I sipped the water slowly. I realised I was sitting on a towel, leaking, and giggled.

"What?" Sal asked.

"I think I may need to clean up."

***

On my way to Jenny's a few days later, I had so many things bouncing about in my head, I didn't know what to tackle first. In the end, it all came tumbling out while she sat opposite me, listening calmly, and making an occasional note. When I finished, I sat back in my chair and realised I'd been quite animated as I told the tale.

"Well, Lucy. Another interesting weekend."

"Interesting? I'm surprising myself all the time, Jenny. I think I may be having a mid-life crisis."

"Does it worry you?"

"Honestly, no. Well … I'm a bit confused by it all, I suppose. My life was quite stable until recently. Now I find myself acting like a teenager let loose on the world. I thought I was past all that."

"But you didn't have to do any of it."

"Oh, I know. I did it all willingly." We both smiled at that. "But I guess I feel a bit vulnerable."

"In what way?"

"I'm the outsider, I suppose. Not quite a full member of anything. My family have got on fine without me for years, and for Sally and Marcus, I'm the bit on the side."

"Do they see it like that?"

"Not in those words; they always make me so welcome and included. But let's be honest, if anything went wrong, I'd be the one left on my own."

"Don't be so sure, Lucy. Relationships are never as straightforward as they seem."

As I drove home, I thought about that remark. I knew she was right. My relationship with Sally and Marcus was complicated. There were so many strands to it, and we seemed to be adding new ones all the time. The question Jenny had asked me kept echoing in my head. How did they see the relationship? How did they see me?

Chapter 21 – Marcus

Sally was happier than I'd ever seen her. Work was good, we were good, and Lucy was the icing on the cake. But it all seemed to have happened a little too easily. If Lucy had been someone we'd met at the munch and had a few fun sessions with, it could have ended as easily as it started.

But she wasn't. If anything went wrong, there would be a lot of pain for all of us. I didn't want to spoil our fun and couldn't decide what to do. If I kept on talking about it, they'd think I was unhappy with the situation. Perhaps I was thinking too deeply about it; it wouldn't be the first time.

***

"What would you do?" Sally asked.

We were sitting at the table after dinner and the subject had got around to her father. He hadn't been discussed much since we got back from France. I knew she'd been pondering whether to pursue the search.

"What do you want to achieve?" I replied.

"I want to know who he was, what he was."

"Then you need to make contact. But you need to be prepared for a strong reaction. They may not reply, they may not believe you. They may get angry. Anything's possible."

"I've thought of that."

"And, I suggest you keep quiet about anything to do with what he left you."

"Agreed."

"If they were left in the lurch when he died, we don't know how they managed. As far as they're concerned, he just disappeared. They probably have no idea what happened to him."

"It must have been hard for them."

"Very possibly, but I'm only thinking of you. I don't want to see you hurt again."

She took my hand and slipped her fingers between mine.

"I know. But I don't want to give up yet."

"So …?"

"I've got an address and an e-mail. I guess we compose a letter."

"There is an alternative."

"What's that?"

"Go through a third party. Martin, or some sort of private investigator. Get them to make contact. You could stay out of it."

"That's possible."

"But you want to do it yourself, don't you?"

"There's enough deception around my father, I don't want to create more. If I contact them and they don't reply or tell me to stay away, fine. That'll be the end of it."

We spent the next few evenings composing draft after draft of the letter. Every time, we didn't like what we'd written. We tried to see it from their point of view, but that complicated things even more. In the end, we put together a few paragraphs giving the cold facts, as we knew them. We didn't hide anything, except the details about the legacy.

"Now we need to translate it," Sally said. "I'm not sure my French is good enough."

"Know anyone who could do it?"

"Not anyone I'd trust enough with this information."

"You'll have to do the best you can and apologise at the beginning."

She spent a couple of evenings tutting and swearing as she made the best translation she could and sent it to the e-mail address we'd been given. As the days passed and no reply came, it looked like the trail had finally gone cold.

***

"October the eleventh."

"Excited?" Sally asked.

"Yes, but nervous. I'm going to have to speak in front of loads of people."

Eva had scheduled the launch of my book. She'd also persuaded me to have a launch event, where I'd be the centre of attention. I knew I'd have to do it, but I was dreading it.

"You'll be fine," Sal said. "I'll be there for you."

"I know, but I'll be glad when it's all over."

"I've got some news, too."

"What's that?"

"All the archives are packed away ready for the library move. I'm at a bit of a loose end for four or five months."

"What are you going to do?"

"I'll have to help out around the library."

I thought for a moment; I'd been mulling over an idea for a while.

"Why not take three months leave?"

"What?"

"Take some time off."

"Why?"

"How about going away for a couple of months?"

She looked at me, wide-eyed.

"Seriously?"

"Why not? I can write wherever I am. If you haven't got anything to do, surely they'd give you the time?"

"Where would we go?"

"I did think about the south of France again. But anywhere you like."

I could see the idea instantly appealed. She had that fidgety edge, thinking through the possibilities.

"What about … Lucy?" she asked.

I'd expected the question.

"She can join us whenever she can. It's only a short flight, and it'll be summer break, so she should be able to get holiday."

"Mmm …"

The look on her face told me she knew something I didn't. I waited for her to tell me.

"Well," she said. "It's just … Lucy told me at the weekend she's taking a few weeks off in the summer to write her part of a book she's collaborating on."

"Ask her if she can write in the south of France."

"Really?"

"Yes, of course."

"You wouldn't mind?"

"No. I might get some rest."

"Or be permanently exhausted."

"I'll take that chance."

"I'll ring Luce."

"See if you can get the leave first."

"David agreed immediately," Sally said when she got home the next day. "He was struggling to know what to do with me until we move to the new library. It solved his problem."

"Well, that's stage one."

"And stage two. I popped over to see Lucy. She jumped at the chance after I convinced her she wouldn't be in the way. I did tell her she might have to pay rent in kind."

"And?"

"She's going to try and take more time off."

"I might have guessed. Where would you like to go?"

"I'm leaving that to you."

"Really?"

"Yes, surprise us."

"Thanks. No pressure, then."

I spent the next couple of days trying to find the right place. I considered going back to the villa we'd rented before but decided to look for something special. I had a picture in my mind but wasn't sure if it was just a fantasy. On the third day, I found it.

"How long for?" Sally asked when I told her I'd booked somewhere.

"Seven weeks and three days."

"Wow. I've never dreamed of going away for so long. Why the three days?"

"Because it wasn't free for any longer. Don't have a heart attack when you see the credit card bill."

She waved my warning away. Even though I was now comfortable spending her money on things for us, I had swallowed hard before spending over thirty thousand on a holiday.

"Is it a villa again?" she asked.

"Wait and see."

She poked her tongue out.

"Where is it?"

"Wait and see."

"Okay, I give up. Are we hiring a car?"

"Why don't we drive? We'll have our own car and we'll be able to take all the stuff we need without worrying about weight limits. The journey can be an extension of the holiday."

"That makes sense."

"Will Lucy be coming for the whole time?"

"Not sure yet. Now I know the dates you've booked, I'll talk to her and see."

***

"The structure will be finished a week before we go away," Sally told me.

"Pleased with them?"

"So far, but then they've got to be embroidered."

"Is Lucy happy?"

"She's come around to the idea. Mind you, I think she quite likes Penny helping her try it on."

"And you don't?"

"Hadn't thought about it."

"Liar."

"Me?" She put on her best innocent look. It never worked; whenever she did, it made me want to ravish her. Perhaps that was the idea.

"I have a confession," she said.

"Oh?"

"Lucy and I told Helen and Penny about our relationship."

"Fair enough. I'm guessing they weren't exactly shocked."

"No, I think Penny suspected anyway."

"There's more to her than meets the eye."

"You don't know the half of it."

"Really?"

"How old do you think she is?"

"Not quite as young as I first thought. She looks about twenty, but she doesn't act twenty; perhaps twenty-five."

"Thirty."

"Wow."

"She's a freelance web designer."

"Okay."

"And she's a judo black belt."

"I'd better not upset her, then."

"I don't think that's likely."

"Why not?"

"I get the feeling she quite likes you."

"Well, I'm such a likeable guy."

"Helen asked if we all got together."

"She's not one to hold back, is she? I bet you didn't find anything about her."

"Not a thing. She's very guarded."

"Well, she's probably got a good reason for that."

"Yea. Anyway, I've invited them to dinner next Friday. If I'm honest, I was a bit surprised when they accepted. Well, when Helen accepted for both of them. She's going to bring the corsets for a final fitting before they go off to be embroidered, so Lucy's coming as well."

"That could be an interesting evening."

We took bets beforehand about what Helen would be wearing. We'd never seen her dressed down and she didn't disappoint. When she arrived with Penny, she was sporting a long pencil skirt with a silk blouse and a tailored jacket with square shoulders. Penny was more casually dressed.

They decided to get business out of the way first, and disappeared downstairs for the final fitting, leaving me to get on with dinner. It was half an hour before they returned.

"All okay?" I asked.

"Yes. They fit perfectly," Sally replied.

"They have been interesting to do," Helen added.

"Why interesting?" I asked.

"Well," Helen replied. "Some of my creations are purely for effect. TV, films, photographers, and the like. They don't need detail. They want something that will make the wearer look good, often from a distance. They also tend to want something for nothing. Many of my customers are on a budget. You gave me carte blanche with these, and I'm enjoying myself. I haven't made anything as elaborate as these for some time."

"Except for yourself," I put in.

"True. I am my own best advertisement, after all."

After some small talk and a drink or two, we sat down to dinner. Helen fascinated me; I still couldn't work out if the person sitting in front of me was real or an act. She wasn't pompous or pretentious, but everything she did was precise. The way she dressed, the way she talked, even the way she ate and drank.

Penny was as much fun as always. It was interesting to see that although she deferred to Helen, she wasn't afraid to bring a subject up or disagree with her mistress. As I expected, she wasn't flirty in this setting, as she had been at the party.

I wondered what their attraction was. They obviously clicked as a couple; they'd been together for three years. Presumably, their sexual and D/S needs complemented one another, but it was difficult to see how such different characters lived harmoniously. It was a puzzle.

"I'm told you're going away for the summer, Marcus," Helen said.

"Yes. Seven weeks in the south of France."

"Sounds like something from a bygone era."

"I suppose it does, but we're fortunate enough to be able to do it. So why not?"

"Why not, indeed?"

"You'd be welcome to join us for a week or two," I said, hoping Sally and Lucy weren't silently cursing me.

"I think it would be too short notice for us but thank you. And the three of you are going together?"

I had picked up on one of her tells. When she was playing with you, her eyes widened slightly. She was playing with me now.

"Yes. I believe you're familiar with our somewhat complicated set-up."

"From our point of view, it's not complicated."

"No, but it's unorthodox in the wider world."

"Indeed."

The others were silently watching our gentle sparring match. I realised Helen hadn't worked me out yet, either. She was testing me; seeing if I would go too far or take offence. Looking at Penny, it was clear Helen was being her normal self. I assumed she was used to her mistress's ways and her face showed not a hint of concern about the situation.

"But I forgot," I said. "You have a third party, in Ben."

Penny glanced in my direction, but her face had an amused air. Helen gave a slight nod and smiled briefly.

"Of course," she said. "You met him at The Rocky Horror Show."

"Yes, Sally liked his bum."

Sal chuckled quietly.

"I seem to remember," Helen said, turning to Lucy and Sal, "they both liked Penny's, as well."

"Oh," Lucy said. "You heard that? Sorry."

Helen smiled indulgently at Penny.

"No apology necessary, Lucy. I can't deny the truth of your words. Although I'm not sure 'juicy' would be my word of choice."

Lucy looked a little awkward for a moment before Sally looked at Helen and me.

"Okay, you two," she said. "You've duelled enough."

"Oh, pity," Helen replied. "I rarely find someone willing to take me on and I do so enjoy it."

Her manner had changed; she'd lightened.

"I remember what happened to that guy in Chad's," I said. "I'm not going to push you too far."

"He was such an immature youth. I prefer something more intellectual."

"I have to say, it was one of the best things I've ever seen."

"I don't like doing it, but he was pestering a friend."

"And now I hear Penny is a judo black belt."

"As is Helen," Penny chipped in. We all looked at her mistress, who was unfazed by the attention. "It was Helen who introduced me to judo."

"I don't practice much now, but Penny and I still spar occasionally."

I knew Sally and Lucy had joined me in imagining that. I also knew Helen knew what we were thinking. Sally came back first.

"Helen, do you mind me asking about Ben? I haven't seen him when we've come for our fittings."

"Ben isn't with us permanently," she replied, fixing her eyes firmly on me. "After all, who needs a man hanging around all the time?"

"No," I said. "We're not good for much."

"Marcus, I'm disappointed. I was hoping for a stronger response."

"I know you were."

She laughed and turned to Sally and Lucy.

"Is he always this smart?"

"Not always," Sal replied. "Only when he's having fun. He enjoys a verbal challenge."

Helen returned her gaze to me, studying me for a moment.

"I think you and I are going to get on, Marcus."

"I hope so, Helen. I'm too scared of you not to."

Penny laughed and for the first time in the evening, Helen's face relaxed completely.

"That," she said, "I don't believe."

The sparring came to an end and Helen told us about Ben. She shared him. He worked in London and lived with a male dom, an old friend of Helen's. He spent time with Helen and Penny occasionally.

"He's with us for a few days each month. If it weren't for this one," she nodded towards Penny, "I probably wouldn't bother. But she seems to need a man every so often."

Penny blushed but turned to look at Helen with a raised eyebrow. Helen held the gaze for a moment.

"I suppose he is quite a pleasing distraction," she conceded. "And very obedient."

A second or two of silence was followed by a laugh from Sally.

"Careful, Helen," she said. "You'll be giving away too many secrets."

"Indeed. I'm supposed to be a woman of mystery."

"Have you always lived the lifestyle?" Sally asked.

"Most of my adult life, yes. In one way or another."

"And always dressed so elegantly?" Lucy added.

Helen gave her one of her gentle nods.

"Thank you, Lucy. I started dressing like this for one of my … business ventures. I found it suited me."

"Do you make all your clothes?"

"Oh, no. I only make underwear and corsetry. Most of my clothes are made by a friend of mine."

"You have some interesting friends," Sal replied.

"When you've mixed in the circles I have, you meet all sorts of extraordinary people."

"We're beginning to see that. We've only been with this group for a few months and some of the people are incredible. It's given us a whole new world to explore."

"And you've lured Lucy in, as well."

Sally turned to Lucy.

"As long as she wants to be lured."

Lucy had a shy moment, and Helen laughed.

"When you start," she said, "it can be overwhelming. Always remember, you only need to go as far as you want. Avoid anyone who tries to push you further."

She turned to me.

"How did you get into all this? If you don't mind me asking."

Sally and I briefly told her how we'd met and what had happened since. Lucy hesitantly told her how she fitted in. Both Helen and Penny listened intently.

"That sounds like a fairy tale," Helen said when we finished. "It often takes years to find the right person, let alone two. Some people never do."

"We have been lucky," Sally said.

"You have. And I hear you have your own playroom?"

"Yes." She looked at me; I nodded. "Like to see it?"

We led them downstairs and into the playroom. Helen slowly walked around, looking at everything.

"Matthew and Yasmin?" she asked.

"Yes," I replied. "I found him on the net. It was them who introduced us to the group."

"Good man, is Matt. This is impressive for a private house. I've seen some professional dungeons less well equipped."

Penny was standing close to her, looking around with a grin on her face.

"Don't get ideas, Penny," Helen said.

"No, Helen. But it is wonderful."

Helen went over to look at the pictures on one wall.

"These are rather good."

"All Lucy's work," I replied.

"Really?" Helen turned and gave Lucy an appreciative look. "I assume you had willing models?"

"Something like that," Lucy replied.

Helen took her time going around the room, inspecting the furniture and the racks of equipment. I wondered if she'd open the drawers, but she resisted the temptation, if it existed. She paused in front of each of the pictures, as well, clearly taken with them.

Penny stood in the centre, slowly turning to take everything in. Her rapt expression led me to imagine having her here under entirely different circumstances. She caught me watching her, and briefly raised one eyebrow. I smiled sheepishly and turned away, only to see Sally smiling, having caught the whole exchange.

As they left at the end of the evening, I was relieved when Sally reiterated my offer.

"If you are able to join us, Helen, you'd both be most welcome. Even if it's only for a few days."

"Thank you, Sally. I suspect I'm going to be too busy, but we'll see."

We settled after they left, and Sal refilled our glasses.

"That went rather well," she said.

"It did, didn't it?" Lucy replied.

"I think Helen likes you, darling."

"I think she likes anyone she can play mind games with," I said. "I think she's lonely."

"She's got Penny."

"Yes, but has she got anyone else? I get the feeling her life hasn't been easy."

"That's funny, I thought the same when she was looking around the playroom. And she's clearly seen a few professional dungeons."

"Do you think she'll join us?" Lucy asked.

"No," I replied. "She's not even considering it."

Chapter 22 – Sally

When we drove away from the flat, it seemed strange we wouldn't be back for eight weeks or more. By the third day, we were approaching the Mediterranean coast and I'd forgotten about home altogether. Marcus still hadn't told me where we were going; 'surprise us, you said' was all I got. He could be infuriating at times.

We by-passed Marseille and headed along the road to Toulon, which we also sped past. But shortly afterwards, we entered Hyères and he found what he was looking for. I stayed in the car while he went into a building with several business plates by the entrance.

On his return ten minutes later, he threw me a plastic wallet.

"Nearly there," he said.

We left the town and drove a few miles before he turned into a driveway fronted by tall stone pillars. The drive meandered for a while, passing some sparse vegetation and rocky outcrops. At one point, I glimpsed the sea; much nearer than I had expected.

The road now hugged the side of a hill rising above us. As we turned a corner, we were confronted by something out of a fairy-tale. In front of us was what looked like a miniature castle, its stone walls hugging the cliffs, tumbling to the sea. It was difficult to see where the natural rock ended, and the built structure began.

Driving through a crenellated gateway, we found ourselves in a small courtyard. Around the edge were flowerbeds with climbing plants covering the rock and stone alike. The most striking thing was a large wooden door in the wall; the only sign there might be some sort of dwelling here.

He got out of the car, and I followed. Taking the wallet from me, he opened it and took out what looked like a small car key fob. Handing it to me, we walked towards the door which gave a gentle clunk as I pressed the largest button. He pushed it open and ushered me in. The hallway we entered had bare stone walls, wooden floors, and a vaulted ceiling. There were pictures and eclectic pieces of furniture dotted around.

We wandered to a doorway at the other end and went through to a room in a similar style. But the similarity ended there. It was massive; at least twenty metres square, an immense stone fireplace occupied a large part of one wall. The walls were panelled to shoulder height and there was a sweeping staircase at one end leading upstairs and a smaller one going down. There were enormous sofas dotted around, along with a couple of cannon.

But what caught the eye was the wall facing us, which had six large glazed doors in it, through which the sea beckoned. Opening one, we stepped outside onto a terrace. It was large and divided into discrete areas. One shaded at the moment by overhanging rock, with dining furniture. Then another with loungers and tables, leading to an infinity pool clinging to the edge.

When we reached it, we could look down and see the sea, only a few feet below us. A set of narrow steps led to a ledge almost at the water level, with benches cut out of the rock. I pulled him to me and kissed him.

"You do have a knack for finding these places."

"We haven't finished yet."

He led me back inside and we spent twenty minutes exploring. It was suitable for a much bigger party, but the thing that struck most was the attention to detail. All the furnishings matched the age and style of the place and much of it looked antique. But hidden everywhere were thoroughly modern touches. Everything was wired and automated.

I'd noticed the huge fireplace in the main room was now home to an equally large screen and the sound system turned out to be out of this world. It was installed everywhere; inside, outside, even in the pool. It took us two days to fully understand how it all worked. There were more bedrooms in the lower level, as well as a wine cellar and various utility rooms.

We chose the biggest bedroom upstairs; a vast room with windows formed from old gun-ports. Two of them had cannon in place. We spent the next hour bringing everything in from the car and unpacking it, finally sitting on the bed and grinning at each other.

"Pool?" he asked.

I beat him to the door, and he chased me down the stairs. We shed our clothes as we crossed the terrace and jumped in. We splashed about like a couple of kids; laughing as our voices echoed around the terrace, bouncing off the stone and the rock. I eventually wrapped myself around him and he held me tight. We felt the same need and he carried me to a lounger, laid me on it and took us both to a very happy place.

***

"Is it far?" Lucy asked as she kicked her shoes off into the footwell. I'd met her flight into Marseille airport.

"About an hour and a half," I replied.

"Oh, sorry to make you come that far."

"It's nothing. We'll have to do it again in a week."

"Why? Are you sending me home again?"

"Mary and Ken are coming for a few days."

"That's great. I haven't met Ken."

"He's a nice guy. This will be his first time abroad."

"How old is he?"

"I'm not sure. I guess about sixty."

"And he's never been abroad?"

"Apparently not."

"Wow."

The traffic was heavy around Marseille but cleared as we headed south.

"Are we in a villa again?" Lucy asked.

"Not exactly."

"What, then?"

"Wait and see. Marcus has surpassed himself this time."

At several points, we could see the Mediterranean and Lucy let out several sighs of satisfaction along the way.

"I've never been on holiday for more than two weeks," she said.

"Me neither, but I could get used to it."

"Yea, too used to it."

When I finally turned into the driveway, Lucy was looking for a building.

"Don't tell me, we're in a tent."

"Patience, Luce."

"God, Marcus has affected you, if you're telling someone to be patient."

I smiled to myself. She was right. As we turned the final corner and went through the gateway, I turned to see her looking around, puzzlement on her face.

"This looks interesting."

After parking the car, I led her to the front door and as we went through the hallway, she had the same reactions we had. When we got to the main room, she let out a little shriek.

"Is this all ours?" she asked.

"Yup. The whole place."

I called out to Marcus and we found him out on the terrace, writing. He closed his laptop as Lucy went to greet him and they hugged each other.

"I'm going to show Luce around," I said. "Have you eaten?"

"No, I was waiting for you. It's all ready."

I took Lucy upstairs and showed her the bedrooms.

"This is your room," I said. She turned and gave me a disappointed look. "Marcus insisted."

She looked puzzled.

"Don't worry," I said. "Whether you use it or not is up to you. He thought you and I might want the odd night without him." Her face brightened. "Or you might want a rest."

She laughed at that.

"Fair enough."

"And, Luce ..." I went over to what looked like one of the wardrobe doors. "... this leads into our room next door."

We'd brought a lot of Lucy's clothes with us in the car and I'd already hung them up. She unpacked her carry-on and we went back downstairs. I quickly showed her the lower level before returning via the kitchen to join Marcus on the terrace.

The dining table was covered with food and we ate as we brought her up to speed about our home for the next few weeks. Marcus had found a folder giving its history and seemed to have learnt it by heart. But with us, he was on safe ground when it came to history.

It had been built centuries ago as one of a series of forts to protect Toulon, then turned into a bit of a folly in the nineteenth century, before a Marseille businessman had renovated it recently to its present form.

"I've been thinking what it reminded me of," Lucy said, as she sat back, having had her fill. "And I've just worked it out."

"Well?"

"The lair of a Bond villain."

We had to agree; it could have been. Over a couple of glasses of wine, we told her what we'd been doing. It wasn't much, in truth. We'd been here a week and only been out three or four times, mainly to stock up on food and wine.

"I'm surprised you haven't got staff to do all that," Lucy joked.

"It was an option," Marcus replied. "Maids, cooks, anything you wanted. But I thought we'd prefer to do it ourselves. I didn't fancy having people around all the time. I've arranged for a cleaner to come in twice a week who'll also change the beds and towels and stuff. I hope that's all right."

"Oh, yes," she replied. "Particularly if we're having the same rules as last time."

"What rules?" I asked.

"Exactly."

A few minutes later, we were all naked and Lucy and I were in the pool. We lounged around for the rest of the afternoon, had dinner, and spent an evening enjoying one another. Six weeks of this was going to be heaven.

***

"You realise the rules will have to change," Marcus said. We were due to pick Mary and Ken up in the afternoon.

"Yes," I replied. "Pity, that."

"Oh, I don't know," Lucy said, her eyes twinkling. "It'll mean we're keener when we go to bed."

"I've put them in the bedroom at the other end of the landing; there's no way they'll hear anything from our rooms. But we'll need to be a bit careful."

"It'll be fine, they're only here for five days," Marcus said and turned to Lucy. "But you'll need to remember not to jump Sal and me all the time."

"Me?" she said. "Little me?"

"Yes. Little you."

"Good flight?" Marcus asked Ken.

"I guess so, Marcus, I don't really know. It's the first time I've flown, but it was quite exciting."

He was like a kid in a sweetshop. As we drove through Marseille, he was constantly looking out of the window, taking everything in. Mary and I were in the back and she looked at me and rolled her eyes.

"He expected to see aliens or people with two heads," she joked.

"Now, Mary," Ken replied. "This is all new to me and I'm going to enjoy it."

The exchange was tinged with a humour and softness which made me realise how close they'd become. Before we left, I'd haltingly asked Mary if they needed one room or two.

"If we needed two rooms, I wouldn't be bringing him," she'd replied. The more I thought about it, the more I agreed with Marcus; Mary's memoirs would make interesting reading.

When we arrived at the fort, Lucy greeted Mary who introduced Ken. He was back to kid in sweetshop mode, absolutely blown away by the place. After we finished dinner, Marcus gave him a tour of the entire site. When they returned, he was buzzing.

"Well," he said. "I've seen everything now. I never thought I'd stay somewhere like this."

"It must be even older than you," Mary replied. Ken shook his head and turned to me.

"Do you know, Sally, she's three days younger than me. Just three days."

"But those three days make all the difference," Mary added.

The next two days we all went out together. We visited Toulon and the Navy Museum, which was a hit with every member of the party. We took a boat trip to three beautiful islands a few miles offshore, all with beaches to die for.

On Friday, we decided to spend the day at home, relaxing. For the first day or so, Ken had been a bit bashful when we were laying around the terrace and pool. I think it was because Lucy and I were wandering around in bikinis. But he soon joined in and any shyness disappeared.

In the afternoon, Marcus revealed a plan.

"Everyone up for an evening out?"

"What have you got in mind, darling?"

"I thought we could go to Hyères for dinner, and on to the casino. See if Mary can break the bank again."

Ken looked at Mary.

"Don't believe them, Ken," she said. "We went to the casino at home once, and I was lucky."

"We'll see."

Mary took easily to any situation, but Ken was wide-eyed at the restaurant Marcus had chosen and when we got to the casino, he could hardly contain himself. I wanted to let everyone enjoy the fun again, but limited it to five hundred euros this time, trying not to embarrass anyone.

We watched with amusement as Mary carefully explained the different games to Ken. As we had been the first time, he was curious as to how she knew, but she waved an arm and dismissed the question.

We wound our way around the various games, and I was miffed that by the end of the evening, the results were similar. Ken and I had lost money, while Lucy had a modest profit. We ended up once more watching Marcus at the roulette wheel, and this time, Mary had joined him. They seemed to be doing well but there were some chips on the table I didn't recognise. When we went to exchange what we had left, they waited until last, whispering together, conspiratorially.

As we drove home, they still refused to disclose their winnings. Marcus would tell me when he was ready, but I couldn't work out why they were being secretive.

It was late when we got home, but we weren't tired and settled on the terrace with a couple of bottles of wine.

"Come on," I said. "Spill the beans."

Mary looked at Marcus and they shared a silent agreement.

"Well," he said. "The roulette wheel seems to quite like me. I came out just under ten thousand up."

Lucy gasped and Ken's face was a picture.

"What?" I said. "You've only played twice before. How did you do that?"

"I couldn't have done it without Mary."

I looked over at her; she had a strange look on her face. Halfway between a contented smile and pure cunning.

"Mary," I said. "What have you been up to?"

"Me, darling? she replied. "Nothing."

"Mary …"

"I told you I once had a boyfriend who was a croupier?"

"Yes."

"He taught me a thing or two about roulette."

"Do you mean how to cheat?"

"Not exactly cheat; it's not possible. Just ways to even the odds. They're technically legal, but most casinos will spot them eventually. I suggest you don't return to that particular establishment."

"Mary!"

"I gave Marcus a few suggestions as well."

"You worked together? Is that allowed?"

"We happened to be playing at the same time. How could anyone possibly think we colluded?"

Her face was a picture.

"All right. How much did you win?"

She didn't immediately reply, and I could see she and Marcus were enjoying our impatience.

"Thirty thousand."

A moment's silence was followed by gasps and laughter. Ken was sitting stock still, staring at Mary with something approaching awe.

"Well, Ken," I said. "She never ceases to amaze, does she?"

He recovered and turned to me with a growing smile.

"That's what I love about her, Sally."

I could see he meant it.

"Now," Mary said, looking at me. "I know you, Sally Fletcher. You won't take the winnings, will you?"

"Nope."

"Okay. But I am paying you the thousand you stood for Ken and me. No argument; fair enough?"

We shared a moment of deep affection. I always met my match in Mary.

"Fair enough," I conceded.

The afternoon before Mary and Ken were due to fly home, she went up to their room to do some packing and invited me to help. I knew that meant she wanted to talk.

I sat on the bed as she put a few things in a case before sitting beside me.

"Thank you for inviting us, darling. It's been wonderful and Ken's loved every minute."

"He seems to enjoy anything you throw at him."

"He does. Making up for lost time."

I knew she was building up to something.

"Come on," I said. "Spit it out. You're not going to try and give me the winnings back, are you?"

"No, it's not that."

She sat looking into my eyes until I felt a tad uncomfortable.

"You're happy, aren't you?" she asked.

"Yes, Mary. Happier than I've ever been."

"I can see it in everything you do. It makes me happy too."

"You got me here, Mary."

"I've helped. But you've got two wonderful people in your life there."

I went to agree, then gradually understood what she'd said. As I raised my head to look at her, she had a warm smile on her face.

"And," she continued, "thank you for being discrete in front of Ken. He's learning, but I'm not sure I'm ready to explain a ménage a trois to him just yet."

I froze and felt myself flush, my face hot. She smiled at my discomfort.

"I don't know what to say, Mary."

"Then don't say anything, darling."

But I couldn't stop myself.

Chapter 23 – Marcus

"She already knew?" Lucy asked.

"She'd guessed," Sally replied.

We were having dinner after Sally and I had returned from seeing Mary and Ken safely onto their flight.

"But we were on our best behaviour."

"She's a smart cookie, Luce. She put a few things together, and we confirmed it by the way we look at each other."

"I told you," I said. "She's got a few tales to tell. I wouldn't be surprised if she's done it all years ago."

"No, darling, but she wishes she had. She used to have a gay best friend and went out with his circle for years. She got lots of offers and rather regrets not taking any up."

"So, she knows all about us now," Lucy said.

"Yes, well nearly everything."

"Nearly?" I said.

"I was honest. I told her how good you and I were together and how you encouraged me to explore new things. And how that led to Lucy and I getting involved."

"She's all right with it?" Lucy asked.

"Yea. 'Enjoy yourselves while you can' was all she said."

"Wow."

"She had also guessed about some of the kinkier stuff."

"Really?"

"She didn't think we met Helen at a Tupperware party." Lucy laughed. "She thought Helen was very impressive but wouldn't want to be at her mercy. Then she looked at me and said, 'though some might like it'."

"What did you say?"

"I was so flushed by then I didn't need to say anything. But she'd worked it all out; she knew what Penny's collar was."

"Perhaps we should take her to the next play party," I said.

"She'd probably go, given half a chance. But that's one area where I'm not having my aunt steal the limelight, however much I love her."

After dinner we gratefully returned to our nakedness now we were alone again. The next day, we decided to alternate our time; one day we'd go out and explore, the next we'd stay at the fort. Lucy and I could write, and Sal could relax.

"You mean do all the work and cooking," she said.

Two days later, Lucy and I were writing at opposite ends of the dining table on the terrace. I heard Sally's phone ring somewhere inside; I wondered if something was wrong. None of us had received many calls since we'd arrived. Ten minutes later, she came out with a jug of fresh lemonade.

"Well, I've got good news and bad," she said, putting three glasses on the table and filling them. Lucy and I stopped working and waited for her to tell us.

"The bad news is our peace is going to be shattered again in a few days."

She looked at each of us in turn, enjoying the suspense.

"Come on," I said. "Out with it."

"The good news is Penny's coming over."

"With Helen?" Lucy asked.

"No. It was Helen who called me. She can't make it herself."

"Didn't want to," I said.

"Possibly, but Penny would like to. She didn't like to ask, so Helen has on her behalf."

We all sat quietly with our thoughts.

"When's she coming?" I asked.

"Don't know yet; they'll let us know. I hope you don't mind me agreeing?"

"No, we made the offer. But I hadn't anticipated Penny coming on her own."

"Me neither. We'll have to change the rules again."

"Definitely. Knowing Penny, she's out right now looking for the tiniest bikini she can find, just to tease us."

"I'm surprised Helen agreed," Lucy said.

"Yes, but she said something about Penny having a couple of weeks to herself each year. She's going to email me about it."

According to Helen's mail, her contract with Penny was for fifty weeks a year. Penny was a free agent for the other two. This year, she was coming to stay with us, starting the day after next.

I was slightly nervous about the whole thing and got more nervous the more I thought about it. We'd have a gorgeous woman among us who we all fancied, who knew all about our relationship and our interests. If she wanted to, she could drive us crazy.

Sally and Lucy went to pick her up from the airport. While they were gone, my conscience got the better of me and I texted Helen to make sure she was happy with the situation. She was and hoped we all had fun. I wasn't sure how to take that. When they returned, Penny came over and kissed me on the cheek.

"Hi, Marcus. This place is amazing."

"Hi, Penny. It's rather special, isn't it?"

Sally gave her a quick tour and came back downstairs.

"I've left her unpacking; she'll be down in a minute."

When she returned, Penny was wrapped in a sarong and went to sit on a lounger by the girls.

"Penny," Sally said. "Just so you know, we have one or two rules when we have guests. We won't be going around naked or doing anything in front of you. Just relax and do what you want."

"Meaning you do walk around naked and do things when no-one else is here."

"Something like that, but we don't want to make anyone feel uncomfortable."

"Sorry if I've spoiled your fun."

"Penny," I said. "I'm adding another rule."

She looked at me, not sure what to expect.

"No apologising or deferring to any of us." She smiled and her face relaxed. "You're our guest and our friend; don't take orders from any of us. Relax, have fun. Do whatever you want, you don't need to ask."

She lowered her head slightly, displaying that hint of shyness which was so alluring.

"Thank you. I'm not used to all this."

"Neither are we, but you'll find you soon get used to it."

By the time we sat down for dinner, she had relaxed and joined in the conversation and banter. Intriguingly, she hadn't removed the sarong all afternoon. As we ate, we told Penny what we'd been doing since we arrived and began to plan the next few days. Occasionally, I saw she was uneasy when we asked what she wanted to do, or where she wanted to go. Whether she was uncomfortable making decisions or just wasn't used to it, I couldn't decide.

After dinner, we ended up in the pool, and Penny finally removed her sarong. We all took a good look at her in a stunning red bikini. Contrary to my prediction, it wasn't a string, but it fitted her perfectly. I guessed Sally and Lucy were thinking similar thoughts to me.

The next day, we took Penny around the area near the fort, showing her the sights. She was good company and the shyness had disappeared. It only returned when we paid for things; that was a feeling which Lucy and I could sympathise with.

"You should have a couple of girl's days out," I said in the evening.

"Trying to get rid of us, darling?" Sal replied.

"No, but it might be nice."

I could see the suggestion was popular and there was no further argument, and they went off early the next morning.

"We spent the day in Toulon, sightseeing," Sally said when they got home in the evening.

"And shopping, by the looks of it."

They were all carrying bags.

"A bit. We thought we might dress up and go out on a couple of evenings."

"Sounds good to me. I may need to go and buy another suit."

"Who said anything about inviting you?"

The next day, we stayed at the fort. Sal and Penny relaxed, chatted, swam, and drank. Luce and I did some work, but the company, the setting and the heat were too distracting.

"Fancy going out tonight?" Sally asked.

"Yup. Where?"

"How about St Tropez?"

The girls took an age to get ready, but when they came downstairs, it was worth the wait. They made me feel shabby; not for the first time.

"I suppose you've used the time to book somewhere?" Sally said.

"No, but I've found two or three places that look good. Let's see where we can get in."

After we parked the car in St Tropez, we joined hundreds of others strolling about, seeing and being seen. One of the restaurants I'd found was full, but the second had a free table and we enjoyed a leisurely meal, before taking another stroll on the beach.

"Is this a nudist beach?" Penny asked.

"I don't think this one is, but there are a couple further along."

"I'm not sure I'd have the nerve," Penny replied.

Sally and Lucy looked at each other.

"Oh," Penny said. "I know I dress up and stuff, but taking everything off in such a public place …"

"No, Penny," Sal said. "It's not that. We stayed at a villa up the coast earlier in the year and Lucy and I ended up on a nudist beach."

Penny stopped and looked at them.

"How did it feel?"

"Liberating," Lucy said.

"Why don't you find out?" I asked. They all turned to me. "On your next girls-only day, you can come back here and try it."

Sally and Lucy looked at Penny.

"I dare you," I said.

"Well, that's it, Penny," Lucy said. "We never turn down a dare in this group, do we Sal?"

Penny looked confused, and as we drove home, they explained the lap-dancing clubs and the various dares which now formed an occasional part of our relationship. When we sprawled out on the sofas at home and the wine flowed, Penny asked us more about how we'd all got together. We told her; we had no reason to hold anything back, and by the time we were ready for bed, she knew most of our secrets.

As we climbed the stairs, I had my arm around Sally, and Lucy was talking to Penny a few steps behind. Penny split away to go to her room, but when we got to ours, Lucy went over to the drawers where we'd put our toys, took out a wand and left again.

"Seems like she's had a better offer," I said.

"You'd turn it down?" Sally replied.

Before I could answer, Lucy returned. She saw our curiosity and smiled.

"She told me she wished she'd brought a toy, so I thought I'd lend her something."

"Now we all have the same image in our heads," I said.

"Yup. What can we do to take our minds off it?"

The next morning, the girls got into a huddle and decided to take up my dare.

"Do you mind?" Sal asked.

"Not at all. Go and have fun."

I sat down to a quiet day's writing. When I broke for lunch, I sat back and thought about my life. Two years ago, I had nothing. I was struggling to pay the bills and scraping by on whatever my writing brought in. My health was poor, and I was lonely, although I wouldn't admit it.

Now, I was sitting on a terrace in the south of France, outside a beautiful old fort, staring out over the Mediterranean. Waiting for three beautiful women – two of whom I was in a relationship with – to return from their day parading naked on the beach at St Tropez. I couldn't help smiling. It had all been chance and luck, but this new life sure beat my old one.

They returned in the late afternoon, laughing and joking.

"Had fun?" I asked.

"Wonderful," Sally replied. "Quite a day." I fetched a couple of bottles of wine and we sat around the table. "We started on the main beach and Lucy decided she wanted to try a jet-ski, so we hired some."

"They're harder than they look," Lucy said. The other two were grinning.

"She kept falling off," Penny said, laughing.

"I couldn't get the hang of it. Every time I speeded up, I slipped off."

"The hire guy came to the rescue," Sally said, winking at me.

"Did he hell," Lucy replied. "He offered to give me a lesson."

"What he really wanted," Penny said, "was to get close to Lucy."

"Close? He sat on the thing and got me to sit on his lap. All I could feel was his hard cock under my bum."

Penny and Sally were in hysterics. Lucy was seeing the funny side now, but I knew how uncomfortable it would have been for her.

"Were you okay?" I asked her.

"Oh, yes," she said. "I got him to speed up until the thing was bouncing about. When we hit a wave, I lifted myself up and dropped down hard."

I knew what she was going to say. I could picture it.

"His cock was squashed between the seat and me. He screamed so loud, these two heard it."

"We didn't know what had been happening," Sal said. "We followed Lucy as her hero steered to the shore. She jumped off and he staggered onto the beach holding his groin."

"What happened?"

"We all followed Lucy as she walked away," Penny said. "The last thing I saw was the guy bent double on the sand with a couple of his mates around him."

"I must remember not to cross you, Luce," I said.

"I wouldn't hurt you," she replied.

"Not unless you ask nicely, darling," Sal added. Penny laughed, as Sally continued. "We decided to have a break and went to one of the cafes for lunch. That was where we heard what had happened. Luce was quite animated."

"I was, but I have to admit, I'd enjoyed my revenge."

"Did you get as far as the nudist beach?" I asked.

"Yes, we spent the afternoon there."

"And?"

"And what?"

"How did you feel?"

"Naked."

She was teasing me and the other two were enjoying it.

"Fair enough."

"There's not much to it. Everyone else is naked, so it's no big deal."

"You didn't attract any attention?"

They looked at each other, smiling.

"Let's say we felt quite good by the end of our time. We weren't the worst bodies on the beach."

"I bet you weren't."

"And we had some fascinating conversations."

"Did you?"

"Mmm. We'd like to talk about the rules."

"Oh, yes."

"Well, we've all seen each other naked now, so no need for us to cover up here, is there?"

Penny was watching me with an amused air and Lucy looked as if she was trying not to laugh. I was in a quandary and they knew it. Finally, I shrugged.

"If that's what you want. But I'm keeping something on."

"Spoilsport," Lucy said.

"It wouldn't be fair on Penny," I replied.

They looked at each other.

"If you say so."

They went over to the loungers, while I switched my laptop off. When I looked up, I shook my head. They were standing in a line, with their backs to me, completely naked. As I looked from bum to bum, taking in Penny's last, Sal looked back over her shoulder.

"This is better, isn't it?" she asked.

"From this angle, it's perfection," I replied.

"So, what's the problem?"

"Sal …"

"I'm fine with it, Marcus," Penny said. "Honestly."

I stood up, went over to them and slapped Lucy's bum before giving her a kiss, then did the same with Sally. When I got to Penny, she winked and stuck her bum out. I gave her a light smack and a kiss on the cheek.

"You're not escaping, darling," Sal said.

She took a couple of steps towards me and pushed her hands into the waist of my shorts, gently easing them over my hips and dropping them to the floor.

"There, that's better," she said.

"We'll see. If you three try anything …"

"Us, darling? Perish the thought."

214

Chapter 24 – Lucy

We hadn't been sure how Marcus would react. Penny had the same effect on him as she did on us, and it was more difficult for a man to hide those effects. It had made us giggle talking about it. And he was cautious. Always aware of the complexity of a situation and never wanting to make people feel uncomfortable. I'd seen that from how he'd dealt with the relationship I had with Sally and now him.

We lay on loungers and took in some early evening sun. Marcus had his eyes closed, perhaps asleep, or trying not to let his eyes wander over us; well, over Penny. I had no such reluctance. She was on the lounger between Sally and me, and we were both studying her body, as we had on the beach earlier. I'd not seen such perfection for a long time. Penny wasn't shy about showing it off, but she didn't flaunt it, either.

"What are we doing for dinner?" Marcus asked, turning on his side to face us.

"Penny's cooking, darling. She picked up loads of stuff at the market."

"Is everyone getting hungry?" Penny asked.

When we agreed we were, she got up and walked across the terrace leading inside, with three pairs of eyes following her every movement. When she disappeared, Marcus rose.

"You two are dangerous," he said. "I need a swim to cool off."

A few minutes later, Sally followed him.

"Coming?" she asked.

He was at the edge overlooking the sea, his arms along the ledge, his body floating behind him. We went over and settled either side of him, our arms around each other.

"This reminds me of the villa," Sal said.

"Yea, remember the thunderstorm?"

"Yes, I'm surprised we haven't had any here."

We looked out over the sea, the sunlight reflecting off the gently rippling water. If there was a paradise, it couldn't be much better than this.

"We had an interesting chat with Penny this afternoon, darling," Sally said.

"Oh, yes."

"Mmm." She looked at me, then at Marcus. "She wants to have some fun."

"What sort of fun?"

I saw her hand move between his legs.

"She wants to join in."

He looked at her, then at me, half-heartedly pushing her hand away from his rising cock.

"Sal," he said. "Be serious for a moment. Is that a good idea?"

"You mean you don't want to get your hands on her?"

"I didn't say that."

"No, because I know you do. We do too, we all want her."

"And," I said, "she wants us."

"She must be mad," he said.

"Then thank God for madness."

Penny came out with her sarong wrapped around her.

"Dinner will be ready in about ten minutes," she said. "If you need to do anything, now's the time."

We wandered to the steps and climbed out, Penny letting her eyes rest on Marcus's partial erection.

"Behave, you," he said as he walked past her.

"Yes, sir," she replied with a smile.

"We always put something on when we eat, particularly if it's something hot," Sally said. "Marcus had a bit of an incident with a grilled sardine, didn't you?"

"Mmm. I still carry the scars."

216

Penny had excelled. Plump langoustines in garlic butter, followed by slices of Camargue lamb, cooked in a tomato and olive sauce. Eaten alongside some excellent bread and local wine. Penny insisted on fetching and carrying, so we relaxed as she cleared the table.

"I'm afraid I didn't make the desserts, but the shops were too hard to resist."

We'd seen a fabulous patisserie and gone mad. She brought out several plates loaded with meringues, cream cakes, little chocolate mousses, fruit marinated in alcohol. Along with a bowl of crème fraiche and a plate of little biscuits and chocolate sticks.

"Are we expecting more company?" Marcus asked.

"We did rather overdo it," Sal said.

"Well," he said. "I'm going to have one thing, then wait a bit before I eat any more."

We all did the same and chatted quietly about anything and nothing over a glass or two of wine.

"Penny," Marcus said when the conversation died at one point. She looked over to him. "I'm told you're keen to get your hands on our bodies."

She was briefly taken aback by the question but quickly recovered.

"I'd like to … play, yes."

"Sure?"

"Yes."

"Okay. But one rule."

"Mmm."

"You're not our sub."

"I will be if you want."

"You're our friend and play as an equal. Do whatever you want, but say no if you want to, as well. Promise?"

"Yes, sir," she replied. Sally laughed as Marcus shook his head.

"Everyone happy?" he asked.

We all nodded; it was real now.

"Right," he said. "Will you do me a favour, Penny?"

"Of course."

"Can you get a towel from one of the loungers?"

Sally and I looked at each other, puzzled, as she complied.

"Now spread it on the table."

217

She laid it over the clear end.

"Strip."

A flash of excitement crossed her face as she removed her sarong to reveal her nakedness. She was concentrating solely on Marcus, the sub in her very much in control.

"Lie on the towel."

She used a chair to climb up and dropped down, lying with her feet towards us, giving us a glorious view straight up between her legs.

"Good girl," Marcus said in a voice which even made me shiver. I saw her body react to the tone.

When he picked up the bowl of fruit, I knew what he was going to do. I turned to Sally, only to see she'd understood as well. She looked at me and slowly shook her head. I heard Penny give a little gasp as the first juice landed on her skin. Marcus was slowly tipping the fruit and alcohol over her, from breasts to thighs, her body moving as she felt it running over her, an occasional giggle escaping her lips.

He put the fruit down and picked up a meringue. Holding it over her, he crushed it and let the little pieces fall onto the fruit.

"Come on, you two," he said to us. "Help me create this work of art."

We didn't need to be asked twice. Penny's body was soon covered in chocolate mousse, cream, crème fraiche and anything else we could find. Penny's face was a picture; she was loving it. Marcus bent towards her.

"Comfy?"

"Yes, thank you," she replied.

"Good, because we're going to lick you clean."

As we discarded our clothes – well, they'd have got very messy – I looked at the picture in front of me. Memories of gelato floated through my head, but this looked even better. We took positions around her and started to enjoy dessert. Her body reacted to our touch, her muscles twitching as a tongue skimmed her skin, or fingers scooped up a blob of cream.

When I looked at her face, her eyes were closed, but her dreamy smile was intensely erotic. This was turning me on, God knows how she felt. Marcus and Sally were working around her breasts, her nipples now hard and clear of the mousse they'd licked off. She had one hand between Sally's thighs and the other was cupping Marcus's balls.

I moved towards her groin, licking, and giving her tiny kisses. As I got nearer, I was rewarded by seeing her legs slowly spread open. Her pussy was still covered in alcohol, juice, and cream. I ignored Marcus and Sally and headed for it. Her groin came up to meet me as I reached her clit and slid my tongue over it. I heard her moan and let my tongue trace her lips, spreading her apart.

I tensed as Marcus's hand caressed my bum and headed between my legs.

"Can I have something to eat?" Penny said, her voice a mix of innocence and seduction. Sally climbed onto the table and lowered her pussy onto Penny's face, whose arms came around her thighs, pulling her down. I could see her tongue flicking into Sal's soft flesh, and she had to put her hands on the table to steady herself.

I had to adjust my stance as Marcus's fingers reached their target and I groaned as they slid into me and slowly stretched me apart. I turned back to Penny and gently enclosed her pussy with my lips, using my tongue to explore her wet folds. The fingers between my legs were pushing me higher and my mouth was getting rougher the further I went.

My head came back with a groan as Marcus slid his cock into me, forcing me to lift away from Penny and take a deep breath. He bent over me.

"I'll go slow," he whispered. "You deal with her."

It was glorious; sucking and licking Penny while Marcus was deep inside me, hardly moving. There were noises all around us, Sally was moaning as Penny brought her close, but little whimpers told me my attentions were working as well.

Sally came first, letting out a long whining cry as she pushed herself onto Penny's mouth. I sucked Penny's clit between my lips, and the response was immediate. A series of soft whimpers followed by a strange giggle which was the start of her orgasm. It was followed by her whole body tensing up, arching from the table, and flopping back as the moment passed and she came down.

The moment I released her from my mouth, Marcus began to fuck me, his fingers reaching and rolling over my clit. I gave in, the groan starting deep inside me as my orgasm rolled through me. My legs shaking as I struggled to maintain my position. He slowed and ran his hands gently along my back. I laid my head on Penny's tummy and looked at Sally. She'd moved off Penny to kneel beside her and they'd both watched my orgasm.

When Marcus pulled out, Penny's eyes went to his cock, still hard and covered in my wetness.

"Turn over, Penny," Sal said.

When she was lying on her tummy, we all looked at that gorgeous bum, now streaked with the runoff from the fruit. Sally picked up the bowl of cream and used her fingers to smear it over those firm cheeks.

"Darling," she said. "Lucy and I are going to lick this clean. Why don't you give Penny something to lick?"

As Marcus moved in front of her, Penny grabbed his cock and pulled him towards her. He groaned as she closed her lips around him. We set to work on her bum, occasionally kissing each other. Sal's fingers went between Penny's legs and the reaction surprised us. In one movement, with Marcus's cock still in her mouth, she pushed upwards until she was on her knees, her bum in the air.

We happily followed, our fingers sliding into her, our mouths cleaning off all the cream. Her body was moving gently from side to side, and little moans were coming from her throat. She was building again.

"Darling," Sal said. "Want to try this end?"

He groaned and slowly pulled out. Penny didn't waste any time. She hopped off the table, and bent over it, holding a hand out to Sally and me. We shuffled across so we could hold her and stroke her body as Marcus stood behind her. She squealed as he drove his cock into her, his need clear on his face. He grabbed her hips and started to fuck her. A grunt coming from her every time he drove in deep.

The hand gripping mine was getting tighter and tighter as she began to whimper again. Her body started to tense as her orgasm came, her head dropping onto the table. Just as she reached the peak, Marcus changed gear. Shorter, deep strokes, pressing her against the edge of the table. She was shaking now, little whimpers flowing from her, her breathing fast and shallow. Her body tensed again, and Marcus cried out, pulling her back onto him, his climax finally coming.

He drove into her hard a few times as he came, her body meeting the thrusts. Sal and I watched as they both relaxed, her body dropping onto the table, his draping over her. He looked up to us and we both bent and kissed him.

"Are you okay?" he whispered to Penny.

There was a moment's silence, which made me pause, but then we heard a low sound; chuckles. Very quiet, but gradually getting louder. We looked at each other and grinned. Marcus gently pulled out of her and stroked her bum. We helped her turn over and sit on the table, her eyes heavy, but there was still a huge grin on her face. She looked at each of us in turn.

"Did you enjoy dessert?"

"How's the writing going?" I asked Marcus at breakfast the next day.

"Not too well. Too many distractions. You?"

"Same. How about we put it away for a while?"

We agreed to stop working while Penny was with us. After a day sightseeing in Marseille, we spent the following day at the fort. It was fun seeing how Penny had relaxed. There wasn't a hint of reserve or shyness unless she put it on to tease Marcus.

Sally and I knew why. She wanted to push him; she wanted him to punish her. She'd asked us if it was okay and we were more than happy. We wanted to watch, but we hadn't told him.

As I wasn't writing, I started drawing. I'd brought some pads, pens and paints with me and I settled down to sketch. I found myself sketching my companions, as well as parts of the fort and the views from the terrace. In the afternoon, we were all on loungers after a good lunch. Penny got up to walk to the pool.

"You ought to draw that, Luce," Marcus said. In truth, I already had. "Perhaps give Penny one or two to take home for Helen."

Penny looked over her shoulder.

"I'll happily sit for you, Lucy."

"That wasn't the position I had in mind," Marcus replied.

Penny stopped a few feet away with her back to us. She slowly spread her feet apart and bent forward until her palms were on the floor in front of her. It was an amazing sight, her bum tight and her legs straight with her sex invitingly displayed between them. It was also an incredible feat of flexibility.

"Is this more like it, Marcus?" she said, looking back between her legs.

"Not bad," he conceded. "How long could you stay in that position?"

"I don't know," Penny replied. "Quite a long time. Why?"

"Just wishing I'd brought a cane."

Penny gracefully stood up, closed her legs, and turned to look straight at him.

"So do I, Marcus." Her eyes flashed. "So do I."

She turned, walked over to the pool, and dived in, leaving the three of us to imagine the scene. It obviously appealed to all of us, because shortly afterwards we joined her and ended up having our own poolside orgy.

Later in the afternoon, Penny did strike a few poses for me; she liked the idea of taking some sketches home for Helen. At some point, Sally and Marcus disappeared, but I didn't pay any attention, I was focussed on the naked body in front of me. It was a pleasure to draw, and she seemed to enjoy being looked at.

"Lucy?" Marcus's voice interrupted my concentration.

"Yea?"

"Can I borrow you for a minute?"

"Of course."

I put the sketchpad down and got up.

"You can bring the pad," he said. "Penny, you might want to come as well."

We trooped indoors after him and climbed the stairs. I looked at Penny, she gave me a querying look, but I had no idea where we were going. He led us to the bedroom and opened the door. As we followed him in, Penny and I saw what he'd been doing.

Sally was tied down tightly over one of the cannon, naked with her bum and spread legs facing us. It was the perfect prop; she looked vulnerable and inviting, her head over the barrel and her thighs either side of the breech. Her bum had been given a little colour.

"I thought that would make a good picture," he said.

We sat on the end of the bed and I started sketching.

"This metal's bloody cold," Sal said.

For no reason, her comment gave us the giggles and we collapsed into hysterics.

"Oh, fine," she added. "I'm glad I'm so bloody funny."

It took us a few minutes to recover.

"Have you got her?" Marcus asked. "Or shall I leave her there?"

"I've got enough. We can let her warm up."

Marcus untied her and helped her up. She was grinning but rubbing her nipples which had been affected by the cold metal. As she came over, we could see goose-bumps all down her front. Penny held out her hand and, as Sal stood in front of her, she clamped her mouth over a hard nipple. Sal stroked Penny's hair and let out a little groan. I looked at Marcus, he nodded towards the door and we left them to it.

Chapter 25 – Sally

Penny fitted in easily; she was intelligent and as eager to learn as we were. She never seemed bored by our visits to galleries and old buildings and proved a lot of fun.

After the night she first joined in, we all slept together, but agreed the beds weren't big enough for the four of us to sleep comfortably. So, we swapped partners each night, although we normally ended up messing around in one bed in the morning, ostensibly to plan the day.

Lucy, Penny, and I fancied another day on the beach. Marcus wasn't keen and suggested we make it a girls-only day. When we discussed where to go, he suggested Île du Levant, one of the group of islands off the coast. We'd taken Mary and Ken to one of the others and the beaches were exquisite, so we agreed.

It was a beautiful day and the water was flat calm as the boat took us the few miles from the coast. The island loomed larger as we approached the harbour, and we spotted a couple of small beaches.

"Umm. Have you noticed anything?" Lucy asked, as the boat moored at the quay. Marcus had set us up; everyone we could see was naked.

"Okay with it?" I asked.

They grinned and headed for the gangplank. On the harbour wall was a guide to the island. Most of it was out of bounds, some sort of military site. But the public part was a naturist area; clothes were optional everywhere. Looking around, we couldn't see any clothes at all, and we felt conspicuous. So, we stripped off and that was how we stayed until we came back to the harbour to catch the boat home in the evening.

We wandered around the small town, making a note of cafes and restaurants for later, and headed for one of the beaches. There were plenty of people around, but it wasn't crowded, and we soon found everyone chatted and greeted you, regardless of any language barriers.

The sand was almost white and the sea a translucent blue. It seemed more tropical than Mediterranean. We looked for a spot and noticed there seemed to be an unwritten rule; nobody sat too close to anyone else. We walked along the beach until we found a clear spot, backing onto some low rocks. It was perfect.

"Funny, isn't it?" Lucy said. "There are some great bodies here, but no-one cares."

"It's liberating," Penny replied. "It reminds me of the fetish community."

Lucy looked at her, puzzled.

"Alright," Penny said. "There are differences." We both laughed. "But it welcomes all ages, all shapes, all sizes, and no-one's made to feel ashamed. It's the same here."

She was right. People were sunbathing, swimming, playing beach games. Some were attractive enough to make you take a second glance; a few made you look for the opposite reasons and turn away fast. But no-one cared.

After lunch on the terrace of a restaurant overlooking the harbour, we headed for a different beach. As we passed a shop, Lucy darted inside. A few minutes later, she came out with a beachball, three racquets and a shuttlecock.

"What?" she asked, as we looked at her with our hands on our hips. "We might have some fun."

Penny was athletic and, it turned out, extremely competitive. She wanted to get to the ball first, smash the shuttlecock at your feet where you couldn't return it, and win the race to the water or back to the towels.

"It's because you're younger than us," Luce said, as we reached our spot sometime after Penny, both gasping for breath.

"You're both in great shape," she said, cheekily adding, "for your age."

"Watch it you," Lucy said, "or we'll get Marcus to sort you out."

A strange expression briefly crossed her face, almost wistful. "I wish," was all she said.

Sally

I was lying on my front, almost asleep, relishing the heat on my back when Lucy nudged me. I turned to her and she nodded towards a guy approaching us along the beach. When I saw him, I whispered to attract Penny's attention. We all tried to watch without being seen.

He was in his thirties; well-built and heavily tanned, with a few tattoos over his body. But what was attracting our attention, and of our neighbours, was between his legs. He had the biggest cock I'd ever seen.

He wasn't showing off or doing anything to draw attention to himself, but it was unmissable, gently swinging from side to side as he strolled along. You couldn't stop looking at it, and the men around us were as fascinated as the women, though possibly for different reasons.

"Wow," Lucy said after he'd passed us. "My eyes are watering."

"I know," I replied. "It must have been fourteen or fifteen inches."

"You don't want one that big," Penny muttered.

"Really, Penny," I said. "Personal experience?"

She looked away briefly as she always did when she'd embarrassed herself.

"Yes," she replied, looking up with that sweet smile.

"Ooh, do tell," Lucy said, moving closer.

"I had a fling with a guy who was equipped with something like that. When I first saw it, I could hardly wait."

"And?"

"It was too big. The girth was okay … provided I was ready. But it was too long. I couldn't take it all. He was used to it and controlled his depth, but he could never let himself go and … well, you know."

"Hammer you."

"Something like that. And giving him a blowjob made my jaw ache."

Lucy spluttered.

"Size does matter, then," she said.

"Yea," Penny replied. "But not in the way most guys think. Marcus's is just about perfect."

I raised my eyebrow and she looked away again briefly.

"Don't be shy," I told her. She looked thoughtful for a moment.

"I bet he can keep you happy without even using it."

"Yea. He often does."

"Exactly. Sex is about more than a cock."

"Certainly is," Lucy put in.

"You know what I mean," Penny said. "You use dildos and strap-ons?"

"Yes," Lucy replied.

"Are any of them bigger than Marcus?"

Lucy thought for a moment.

"No. One or two are about the same."

"There's a good reason for that."

"I fancy a drink," I said. We'd brought bottles of water with us, but they were nearly empty.

"I could do with something to eat, as well," Lucy replied. It was nearly five o'clock and we hadn't eaten since lunchtime. "Let's go and find somewhere."

As we walked back towards the town, we discussed whether to leave now or stay on. We went to the information centre by the harbour.

"Right," I said. "The last boat leaves at eight, and we can't miss that. How about we find somewhere for dinner?"

"Will Marcus be all right?" Penny asked. We both looked at her and she gave a bashful little smile. "I mean … will he be okay with it?" She blushed as we both stared at her in silence until she looked away, still smiling. I put my hand on her shoulder.

"He'll be fine, Penny," I said. "He's a big boy and can get his own dinner."

"Besides," Lucy said. "He set us up today."

"Yes," I replied. "What are we going to do about that?"

Over dinner, we decided to keep our revenge simple. We were going to put him to work.

"Hello, darling," I said. He was laying on a lounger and put his book down as we walked out onto the terrace. We'd already stripped off.

"Hi," he replied. "Had a good day?"

"Yes, thank you. Very good. You may not be surprised to hear everybody on the island was naked."

"Were they?" His fake innocence never worked. "Well, you enjoyed St Tropez so much, I thought you might like it."

I gave him a kiss and sat sideways on his lounger.

"We did, it was great."

"And," Lucy said, "we saw the biggest cock we'd ever seen."

227

"Apart from Penny," I added, looking at her. "She's had a bigger one."

We all looked at her and she turned away, smiling.

"Really?" he asked.

"Mmm. But enough of that now. You're going to pay for your little deception."

"Am I? How?"

"You've got three nicely warmed up women here. You're not going to bed until you've satisfied all of us."

A look of pure desire appeared on his face.

"But you can't use that," I added, pointing between his legs.

He slowly looked from me to Lucy and then to Penny, his eyes devouring our bodies. I knew he'd relish the challenge.

He spent most of the next two hours between our legs or on his back as one of us settled over his face. Orgasm followed orgasm.

At one point, he suggested getting a strap-on, and we took it in turns to fuck each other, while he concentrated on the third.

"Well," I asked, as we recovered, "has he made amends?"

Lucy and Penny looked at each other, then at me.

"I think so," Lucy said.

"Yea," Penny added, looking at his cock. "He may need some help with that."

He'd been hard most of the time. We'd agreed we wouldn't let him use his cock, but we determined to keep him on edge the whole time. Stroking his thighs, sliding our fingers over his balls, our nails along his shaft. All accidentally, of course.

"Aching, darling?"

"What do you think?"

"Like some relief?"

"If I'm forgiven."

Lucy was still wearing the strap-on and I had an idea. I went over to him, knelt in front of him and took his cock in my mouth. He let out a loud groan, almost a shout and it confirmed that after the previous two hours, he was incredibly sensitive. Lucy and Penny had joined me and had their arms around him.

"Will you last a bit longer?" I asked him.

"I can try."

228

"Good."

Minutes later, he was lying on his back on a lounger with Penny riding his cock, me sitting on his face and Lucy fucking his ass with the strap-on. We'd given up any thought of our enjoyment, we wanted to give back a part of what he'd given us.

He was normally quite vocal, but this was something else. His body was twitching and moving, his arms wrapped themselves tightly around my thighs.

We took it slowly; I wanted him to enjoy it. Penny was rocking gently on his cock, with Lucy behind her, holding his raised legs apart while she slid in and out of his ass, working his prostate.

His body began to tense, and his moans and groans became louder and louder. His eventual orgasm was the most violent I'd ever seen him have. He let out a long, loud cry as his hips arched off the table, almost a scream. Penny let out a little shriek as the force of his ejaculation surprised her, but she pushed back, forcing him onto the table and grinding on his spasming cock.

He was shaking and his grip on my legs was almost painful. I lifted myself slightly away from his face so he could find the great gulps of air his lungs were demanding. His whole tummy and groin were in spasm, and we all slowed at the sight, Lucy slipping out and coming around to watch. Penny sat still, and slowly his body calmed. The only sign now of the experience was his irregular breathing, a little grunt accompanying each outward breath.

As his arms released my thighs, I moved off him and looked down. His eyes were closed, but his expression told me everything. Penny gently lifted herself off, eliciting another round of little spasms from him and I handed her some tissues. We were all now kneeling on the floor around him, gently stroking his body. We shared a look and a smile. He opened his eyes and looked at me.

"Was that good?" I asked.

"Good?" He was still struggling for breath. "I can't even begin … to describe it."

He put out his arms and we helped him sit up. He pulled us all into a group hug. He was still coming down. I'd never seen him affected this way for so long. I cuddled him as Penny went to the bathroom and Lucy took the strap-on off. When she came back, Penny looked at him in wonderment.

"Do you often come like that?" she asked.

"No," he replied, looking at us with eyes still hazy. "I've never come as strongly as that. Perhaps I got a hint of what it's like for you."

Lucy laughed.

"It *was* more like a female orgasm."

"Then I'm bloody jealous."

***

The last few days of Penny's stay flashed by. We spent one day driving along the coast road as far as Cannes. It brought back memories of our holiday earlier in the year. We managed to eat in the same restaurant and took Penny into the casino. None of us had much success this time and as we drove home, we decided we needed Mary whenever we tried again.

The final day was spent at the fort. Lucy finished off a few pictures for Penny to take home for Helen. Most featured Penny herself, but one featured three female bums nestled against one another. Marcus immediately demanded Lucy produce a copy for him.

We decided to make a special evening of it and dress for dinner. Penny insisted on cooking, and I took her to the nearest market where she picked up what she needed. On the way back, we hatched a plan.

Penny set to work preparing dinner and Lucy and I set the table. We were going all out for the formal look and Marcus sorted out the wine, as well as a bottle of champagne.

"Everything's prepared," Penny said, coming onto the terrace. "It'll take about twenty minutes whenever we want it."

Marcus opened the champagne and handed us each a glass.

"To friends," he said.

"To lovers," Lucy added.

"To us," I said.

"To the three of you," Penny said quietly, "thank you."

We clinked glasses and sipped.

"Don't give me too much of this," Penny said. "For some reason, bubbly makes me giggly."

Marcus immediately picked up the bottle and before she could stop him, filled her glass until it was overflowing.

"I think we might like you giggly," he said.

After we drained our glasses, we trooped upstairs. I waited for Marcus to shower and dress, then shooed him away while I got ready. He was used to it now.

When I came down, Marcus was on the terrace. I heard activity in the kitchen and headed that way. Penny and Lucy were already there. We'd thought about going the whole hog with sexy underwear and stockings. But it was too hot; we'd bake. So, it was loose summer dresses all round; short ones.

Penny insisted she didn't need any help, and Lucy and I joined Marcus. She was an impressive cook and very organised. She produced six courses; all light and delicious and didn't panic once. She had plenty of time to sit and enjoy the food before disappearing to fetch the next. I wasn't sure how she did it.

By the time we got to dessert, we were pleasantly full. When Penny brought out a raspberry tart she and I had fallen in love with on our shopping trip, we all looked at it and knew it was going to have to wait.

"But we're eating this one off plates, darling."

Chapter 26 – Marcus

"Do you do the cooking at home?" Lucy asked Penny.

"Yes. I do all the housework."

"Is it part of your role?"

"Not formally, but I love cooking and I do the rest because I like to please. Besides, Helen's a terrible cook."

"I'll tell her that," I said.

"She'd be the first to admit it. She has many skills, but domestic chores aren't among them."

"You're very good," I continued. She raised an eyebrow. "Cooking, Penny."

"Thank you. We don't entertain much, and I rarely get the chance to push the boat out and the markets here are amazing."

We eventually found room for dessert and finished off the tart. Penny cleared up and offered to make coffee, but we were all happy with wine and the rest of the champagne. She did produce a huge box of chocolates she and Sal had picked up.

"Right," Sally said. "How about a game?"

"We should have brought some," I replied.

"Yes, but we can still think of something."

"How about truth or dare?" Lucy said.

"Good idea," Sal replied.

"I'm not so sure," I said.

"Why?"

"Well, what dares can we give each other after what we've been doing?"

"True," Sal replied. "You're right, as usual."

"What about we each ask a question, and everyone answers it?" Lucy said.

We spent the next hour and a half telling each other our intimate secrets. The questions were clichés; first sexual experience, best, worst, and funniest. But some of them were hilarious, while many were highly erotic. We were comfortable with each other, and not shy to relate every explicit detail. By the end, I guessed they were feeling as horny as me.

We took a break, and Lucy went to the loo while Penny fetched some coffee. Sal came around and sat on my lap. She'd been drinking slowly through the evening and was pleasantly merry. Just at the stage where she was up for anything.

"That was fun," she said, putting her arms around me and leaning on my shoulder. Her dress was short and as I slid my hand up her thigh, she opened her legs. My fingers continued until they encountered moisture on her inner thighs, followed by her naked pussy. She shivered as I stroked it lightly.

"Oops," she whispered. "I must have forgotten my knickers."

I moved my hand over her hip, and she raised a cheek to let me stroke it. My finger encountered the end of a butt plug and she tensed as I moved it slowly, letting out a long sigh as I pulled my hand away. We heard Lucy and Penny returning and Sal put her mouth to my ear.

"They're bare and plugged, too," she whispered. "Just in case you're interested."

I groaned as she got up and went back to her seat next to them on the other side of the table.

"It's normally you who dares us to do things," Sal said. "How about we do it the other way around?"

"Okay," I replied.

A notepad had appeared from somewhere, and I waited as they each took a slip off and wrote something. Sally took the three notes and slid them across the table.

"How do I know which is which?"

"Read them," Sal said.

I opened the first; 'dare you to spank Penny'. It was Sal's writing; I looked at her and frowned. Opening the second, I was faced with the same message. I opened the third; the same five words. I put the notes down and looked at them. Lucy and Sally had smiles on their faces, but Penny's expression was entirely different. Hesitant, tight, almost pleading.

"Really?" I asked her. She nodded and Sally laughed.

"She's been wanting it all week, darling. And if I remember rightly, Lucy and I were willing to pay to watch."

Penny grinned, she'd clearly heard the story.

"Why didn't you say?" I asked her.

She looked away, shyly.

"I didn't like to. I didn't know if you wanted to until Sally told me about the catsuit."

I surveyed the three of them.

"So, I've been set up."

"Yes," Sal said. "But what a prize."

"Okay," I said. "I'll show Penny how much I want to spank her. But on one condition."

They all looked puzzled.

"What's that?" Sal replied.

I looked at Sally and Lucy.

"I get to spank you two first. Just to get my arm warmed up."

Sally looked at Lucy; I'd never spanked her properly before. Just some slaps when I'd been fucking her, but she nodded eagerly.

"Right," I said, taking control. "I want all three of you inside in front of the fireplace."

When I followed them in, they were standing in a row, waiting to see what I was going to do.

"Turn around."

They turned to face the massive stone mantle.

"Dresses off."

As they slid them over their heads, I saw Sally had been right. They were all now naked except for their butt plugs, winking at me.

"Hands on the top."

The sight was exquisite. Three beautiful women, naked, stretching up to the mantle. I walked over and adjusted their stance, making them stick their bums out and stand straight. Their giggling showed they were up for this. I stood beside Lucy and stroked her bum.

"I'm going to enjoy spanking this. Sure you want it?"

"Yes."

I moved to stand by Sally and squeezed her bum.

"You, you little minx. I won't be gentle with you."

I moved over to Penny and stood close. Stroking her bum, I put my lips by her ear.

"Sure you want this?" I whispered.

"Yes," she shot back.

"I don't know your limits, so stop me when you need to."

She turned to me with a fierce look on her face which almost made me step back.

"Spank me as you would in your fantasies," she said, her voice low and husky. "Let go, let it all out. Give me everything you've got."

I made myself comfortable in the centre of a sofa and chose Lucy first. Laying her securely over my lap, I began to spank her. I took it gently, but her feedback was more positive than I expected.

As she began to moan slightly, I allowed my finger to slide between her legs. She was enjoying this. After a good spanking for a first time, I brought her to orgasm with my fingers, and let her come down for a few minutes.

"Okay?" I whispered.

She chuckled.

"I am now."

I let her go and sit on the sofa opposite me and called Sally to me. This time I was firmer, I knew what she could take, and I gave it to her. Her bum was red and burning by the time I let her come.

As she joined Lucy and they cuddled up, I called Penny. I was looking forward to this; I'd wanted to do it for so long. She made herself comfortable over my lap and I rested my hand on that gorgeous bum. She'd told us she was a pain junkie. She could take more than I could give her; more than any spanking could do. I took her at her word. I would let myself go; thrash those tight cheeks until she squealed.

For the next ten minutes, I let my hand warm her skin, watching her flesh buckle under my strikes and wobble as I pounded it. It slowly turned pink, then red areas appeared. Penny lay still most of the time, but her breathing quickened and little whimpers started to greet the harder strokes.

I was so turned on, my cock confined under her body. After a prolonged series of hard strokes, I slid my hand between her legs, and she jumped as I found her sex. She was soaking wet, the moisture covering her thighs and my trousers. I pushed three fingers into her and fucked her with them. She began to pant, and her body froze for a moment before shaking violently as she came, emitting random noises. I heard an orgasm from the other sofa.

I made her stand up. She obeyed instantly and I rose, stripped off and sat back down. She laid back over my lap without being asked. I gently stroked her bum, surveying the result of my actions. For the first time, I looked over at Sally and Lucy. They were laying back on the sofa, watching intently, their hands between each other's legs.

I settled myself for a final flurry and began to spank her as hard as I could. The muscles in my arm were beginning to ache and I wasn't sure how long I could carry on. Penny was moving more now, her body responding to each stroke. Her feet occasionally coming off the floor.

"Still," I ordered her, and she obeyed as much as she could.

My hand was striking hard; I was lost in what I was doing. I'd shut Lucy and Sally out. My world consisted of my hand, the beautiful bum it was spanking and the writhing body it was a part of. She was whimpering now, interspersed with an occasional 'yes', 'more', 'harder', muttered through gritted teeth. It spurred me on.

Her bum was red and angry, the colour spreading over her thighs as I sought new areas of pale flesh to warm. My body was tense, revelling in the experience, needing to spank her harder and harder as her body demanded it. I was vaguely aware of a loud groan nearby but kept going.

Penny was quieter now, low moans and groans continually coming from her mouth. I knew I wanted her; I needed her. My cock was hurting, still trapped under her tummy. I wanted to fuck her. After a final set of strikes, as hard as I could manage, I stopped.

"On your knees."

She rolled off my lap and bent over the sofa. I jumped behind her and plunged into her, crushing her against the cushions. She was louder again now, whimpering. I was oblivious to everything but her responses. Her hand reached back and searched for mine and when she found it, she put it on her head, holding it there until I got her meaning and grabbed her hair. She let herself slump onto the sofa and I began to fuck her. No finesse, no control. I fucked her like a man possessed, pulling her hair until her head was forced back.

She wailed as her orgasm came, spurring me on harder. Her climax carried on as I used her, getting more and more powerful. Raucous cries coming from her mouth along with a wild array of obscenities. I slowed for a moment, pulled the plug out and rammed a thumb into her ass, before attacking her pussy again. She began to shake violently; I could feel her thighs trembling against mine.

Then she screamed; a scream which filled the room and went right through me. Her pussy seemed to devour my cock and pull my orgasm from me. My hips hit her hard, time and time again, as my cum spilled into her. She was clawing at the back of the sofa, seemingly trying to grab something to hold onto.

As my orgasm waned, I slid my thumb out of her bum and released her hair. Her head flopped onto the cushion and her arms slowly stopped their flailing. I collapsed onto her, and sought her hands, interlacing my fingers with hers. All that could be heard was our ragged breathing, along with the occasional groan or moan as her body twitched and jerked.

I kissed her cheek and nibbled her ear, getting a deep rumble in response. I have no idea how long we stayed like that.

"Okay?" I eventually whispered.

She gave a little whimper.

"No," she said, in a soft, sultry voice. I was alarmed; had I gone too far?

"What's wrong?" I asked.

"You could have done that a week ago."

The tension disappeared as I heard a laugh behind me. Sal and Lucy came over and joined us. Sal knelt by me, cuddling, and kissing me. Lucy sat on the sofa and stroked Penny's back, causing her to jump. She still hadn't come all the way down.

"Well," Sal said. "That was worth the price of the ticket."

"Did you two enjoy it?" I asked.

"We sure did. Horny as hell. You didn't see anything but the two of you, did you?"

"No, I was oblivious to everything but this gorgeous creature."

"It showed."

We slowly helped Penny up and they led her to the bathroom. When they came back, she came up to me, threw her arms around me and kissed me. We all settled in a cuddle on the sofa; Sally and Lucy were keen to examine Penny's bum and I joined them. It was angry; dark red, with a few purple tinges. The occasional tiny broken blood vessel.

My face betrayed my thoughts, and Penny turned to Sally.

"Does he normally let himself go like that?" she asked.

Sal gave me a lingering look, a gentle smile on her lips.

"No," she replied.

"I think he needs to sometimes, not be so controlled. Perhaps you should too."

Sal looked at me.

"I think we might try it," she said. "What do you think, darling?"

"We'll see."

Lucy was slightly detached from our conversation and Penny noticed.

"Having the same doubts as Marcus, Lucy?" she asked.

"This is all new to me. I won't deny I enjoyed that. I did when I watched these two. But afterwards, when I see the results, it makes me uncomfortable."

"I understand, but were Sally or I unhappy with anything Marcus did?" Lucy shook her head. "And you saw what it did for us. This is about people who want to take each other to a different plane."

She paused and looked slowly from Lucy to Sally and back again.

"Who knows?" she said to Lucy. "Perhaps you'll turn out to be the one inflicting the pain."

Sal got some balm and we gently covered Penny's bum and thighs with it, as she told us how it compared to other things she did. It turned out to be relatively mild. Helen could make most of Penny's body the same colour as her bum was now.

"How long does it take you to recover?" Lucy asked.

"This will be gone in three or four days and I'll be ready for the next session."

Lucy shook her head but was smiling.

"So, you see," Penny said, looking at me. "We could have done this at least twice while I was here."

"You should have said something," I replied.

"I'm not used to initiating things."

"Perhaps you need to speak up for yourself more."

As we reached the bedrooms, Sal kissed me.

"Lucy and I are going to leave you two to it. I assume that's okay?"

As we got into bed, Penny climbed on top of me.

"Thank you," she said. "That was awesome. I need that from a man sometimes."

"Ben?"

She gave a dismissive snort.

"Ben's a nice guy, but he's as submissive as they come. Helen gets the two of us to play together, and I enjoy it. But even she can't get him to play a dominant role; it's not in his nature."

"You get a cock, but not much else."

She chuckled.

"Something like that. It's better than nothing, but sometimes I crave a session like tonight."

"Why don't you and Helen find someone other than Ben?"

"We've talked about it, but we don't want a full-time male about the house. Ben suits us fine that way."

We'd been talking softly, and I realised the warmth of her body on mine and the touch of her fingers along my side was arousing me again. She'd felt it too, and now had my stiffening cock trapped between her pussy and my tummy.

"Now," she whispered, wriggling on it. "What would you like me to do with this?"

Chapter 27 – Sally

We were quiet as we left the airport, having seen Penny onto her flight. It had been a wild ten days and my memories made me blush a couple of times. The traffic around Marseille was heavy and the journey was slow.

"Do you know," Lucy said, leaning forward. "If you'd told me a year ago, I'd be part of what we've been doing, I'd have said you were mad."

"Any regrets?" I asked, and she chuckled.

"No, none at all. But it's been a bit of a shock to the system."

"Too far, too fast?" Marcus asked.

"No, I'm enjoying every minute, but it almost seems too good to last."

We didn't speak much until we got back to the fort and prepared dinner together. As we ate, we shared our thoughts about the time Penny had been with us. They were uniformly positive and put us all in a good mood, and I was surprised when Marcus turned to me during a lull in the conversation.

"Come on," he said. "What's on your mind?"

I looked at him, briefly annoyed, before letting my shoulders sag.

"I can't keep anything from you, can I?" I replied.

"You've been brooding for two or three days."

"Sorry, I didn't mean to. Was it obvious?"

I looked at Lucy, who shrugged.

"No," she said. "I hadn't noticed anything."

I looked back at Marcus.

"I've had a reply from Jacques," I told them.

"Ah …" was his only reply. We sat silently, Marcus waiting for me to elaborate. He gave me time to think, but it was his way of pushing me to open up. It always worked.

"It's quite brief and formal," I said. "Thanking me for the information and asking if I knew anything else. I'm not sure he believes our fathers are one and the same man."

"Hardly surprising," Marcus said.

"No. Anyway, he suggested we talk over the phone or something, rather than sending stuff by mail."

"How do you feel about that?"

"It's fair enough, I suppose."

He put his hands across the table, and I grasped them.

"How about offering to meet him?" he asked.

I looked away, staring into the distance.

"While we're in France, you mean?" I replied.

"Yes. We could pop to Paris for a day or two or stop off on our way home."

"I'm not sure."

"I know, I wouldn't be. But we knocked on what we thought was their door a few months ago. We'd have met them then. It's a risk because it could go wrong. But face to face it'll be much easier to discuss the whole thing."

"It would, wouldn't it?"

"But it's up to you."

"Thanks."

"You're welcome. But if you do offer to meet him, it's going to be in the next few days."

I looked at him sharply.

"Why?"

"Because I'm not having you brooding over this for the next three weeks. Don't invite a new shadow in."

I flinched at his comment and heard a hushed gasp from Lucy. I was briefly angry to be cornered, but he was right. If we arranged to meet Jacques on our way home, I'd be thinking about it for the rest of the holiday. It would spoil it for all of us.

"Right," I said. "Let's do it."

I went indoors to get my iPad and showed them the mail.

"Perfect English," Marcus said.

"I noticed that, too."

Looking at train times, it was obvious we'd need to spend a night in Paris.

"Do you want to come, Luce?"

"I think it would be best if I stay here. Marcus will be with you, and you won't want me there when you meet him."

She was right and we all knew it.

"Will you be all right here on your own for a night?"

She looked around with an appraising air.

"I think I'll manage."

With their help, I composed a few lines, explaining we were currently in France and would like to meet him. In less than half an hour, he replied. He'd be happy to meet me and suggested a café local to him; he was free any morning.

***

As the TGV came to a halt at Gare de Lyon, we picked up our bags and followed our fellow passengers onto the platform. A short Metro journey took us to our destination. The café Jacques had chosen was in Montmartre, and we'd booked a hotel close by.

Marcus was being especially attentive, putting his arm around me on the Metro, holding my hand as we made our way through crowded areas. He was normally like this, but he knew I was nervous, and his reassuring touch never left me. Tomorrow, I might be meeting a half-brother who, until a few months ago, I didn't even know I had.

The hotel was quiet, and we didn't leave it, having dinner in the restaurant and spending the evening in our room, finalising how we were going to handle the next morning. The day ended with the softest, tenderest sex we'd had in a while. I drifted off to sleep in Marcus's arms.

We found the café easily; a typical Paris establishment, patronised more by the locals than the tourists. Going in, there was a hum of conversation, but it wasn't full. We found a table and ordered some coffee. Marcus had suggested we arrive a little early. Waiting for someone gave you a little more confidence than being waited for.

On the dot of ten, a man came through the door and I knew instantly it was Jacques. He looked around and I caught his attention, standing as he approached the table.

"Sally Fletcher?" he asked.

"Yes. Jacques Mahoney, I presume?"

He smiled at the formality, and I introduced Marcus. After we'd all shaken hands, rather awkwardly, he went to the bar to get some coffee and re-joined us. We made some halting small talk about our journey, our holiday; anything but the topic we were here to discuss. And Marcus wasn't going to help; he'd told me this meeting was mine. He would step in if anything went wrong, but he wasn't going to lead.

As we talked, I studied the man in front of me; he was beautiful. Not a word you might normally apply to a man, but he was. His movements were graceful and precise, his hair short and perfectly styled. But it was his face which fascinated. Blue eyes which smiled and shone, perfectly proportioned nose and mouth. His eyebrows were shaped, and I was sure he was wearing a hint of make-up.

"Sally," he said. "We should come to our business."

"Yes. Sorry, Jacques. I tend to talk when I'm nervous."

"It is okay. It is natural."

"Where do you want to start?"

"Do you have any photographs of your father? The information you sent me fits with what I know, but a picture should confirm it."

I opened my iPad and laid it on the table.

"I only have four photos of him," I said. I showed him the wedding picture Mary had given me, the old holiday photo, and a small headshot. "And this is the one from the passport we found in the name of Brendon Mahoney."

I sat back, letting him take his time. He swiped through them several times, as I sat tensely on my chair, my heart thumping in my chest. I realised how important his response was to me.

Eventually, he pulled out his phone. After a few actions, he turned the screen to face me. My father stared out in a picture unknown to me.

"This man is father to us both," he said. I looked at him, not sure what to say. His face was expressionless, and I couldn't read his thoughts. We sat looking at each other for what seemed like an age. Finally, his mouth broke into a delicate smile.

"Hello, sister," he said.

Without any warning, I broke down and wept. He laid his hands on the table and as I laid mine on them, he gently squeezed my fingers. When I looked up, I saw tears in his eyes too.

Marcus silently put some tissues on the table; where he got them from, I had no idea. But Jacques took one, offered it to me, then took one himself. We were laughing between our tears. I was bemused by my reaction; I hadn't expected it to be so emotional.

When we recovered, we told each other a few details. Briefly, without embellishment. The tales were remarkably similar. About a man who had no backstory, disappeared mysteriously for long periods, but always seemed to have plenty of money.

We shared memories of the elusive man who had been our father. A snippet from one of us sparking a fragment from the other. Marcus kept us supplied with coffee but otherwise stayed apart from the conversation. As we ran out of tales, we came up to date and I told him what I'd done since our father's death.

"What about you, Jacques?" I asked.

"Oh," he replied, "I've done various things. Now, I run a couple of clubs. Nothing worth talking about."

I suspected he meant he didn't want to talk about it, and I didn't push.

Marcus and I had agreed I would tell him nearly anything he asked if the meeting went well. But not about Mary or the shadow, nor my inheritance. It turned out Jacques was in the same boat.

"I confess I have not told you everything. There are some details I wouldn't divulge without my mother's agreement."

"Have you told her?" I asked.

He looked pensive.

"Not yet. I wanted to be sure it was him. We thought he had deserted us, and we were both bewildered. That turned to acceptance. We can laugh about it now. She calls him her 'scélérat'. I think it translates as scoundrel."

"Well, he probably was."

"It looks like it."

After another half an hour, we agreed we'd send each other all the pictures we had, and I'd send him the documents which Martin had uncovered.

As we parted, Jacques gave me a big hug and kissed me on both cheeks. After shaking hands with Marcus, he turned to go.

"I'll be in touch, sister. If I tell my mother, I think she might like to meet you."

As he left the café, Marcus put his arm around me.

"Okay?"

"Yes."

"Want something to eat?"

When the simple café food arrived, I was hungry, and we ate in silence. As I leaned back in my chair, I turned to Marcus.

"I have a brother," I said.

"Yes," he replied. "You know what happens next, don't you?"

"What?

"You'll find out your father was Darth Vader."

"Sounds like it went well," Lucy said after we'd told her what had happened.

"Yes," I replied. "Far better than I'd feared."

"Did he look like your father?"

"No. No resemblance I could see. But he was striking, wasn't he, darling?"

"Yes, he was."

"In what way?"

"Very graceful. Every movement was delicate. And he made up his eyebrows."

"Really?"

"Yes, I think he had other make-up on, as well. But it was beautifully done."

"What happens now?" Lucy asked.

"He's got to decide how to tell all this to his mother. Then we'll see."

"How do you feel?"

"Excited. But whether anything comes of this is up to Jacques and his mother."

Marcus and I had discussed this on the journey home. I'd done what I could. If Jacques and Genevieve let me into their lives and told me their story, it would be great. I was itching to hear it. But if they didn't, I'd have to accept it.

"Were you all right last night, Luce?" Marcus asked.

"Yes. The place was a bit spooky on my own."

"Did you get any work done?"

"Yes, quite a lot."

"How much more have you got to do?"

"I reckon two or three days. I can finish it off when we have rest days here."

He looked at me and I nodded. We'd talked about this as well.

"Then you won't get any rest."

"It'll be fine."

"How about you crack on the next couple of days and get it finished? Then we've got three weeks of pure holiday left. No work, no worries."

"Won't you get bored?"

"I can get on with some writing," he replied, pulling me to him. "And this gorgeous creature here can keep us supplied with food and drink."

"Yes, sir," I replied.

"And anything else we might want."

***

"I've had a mail from Penny," I said. They both looked up from their laptops. "She says a huge thank you for the holiday and all the fun she had. Then a few smiley faces. Helen loved the pictures and is going to send us a few."

"What of?" Lucy asked.

"No idea."

We found out later in the day.

"Thank you for looking after Penny …" I read Helen's email, paraphrasing. "Hasn't stopped talking about it … given me rather more detail than you might wish." Lucy chuckled. "Impressed by the colour of Penny's bum, but the attached will show you what she's capable of. They both hope to see us soon."

"What's she sent us?" Lucy asked.

I opened the first attachment and winced.

"You might want to see these," I said. They came over and stood behind me. There were three pictures of Penny, and Lucy gasped at each one. She was naked and covered in marks and bruises from her shoulders to her calves. There was hardly an area that didn't have some colour and her bum was purple, with livid welts. In the last picture, she was facing the camera and the smile on her face told us she'd enjoyed every minute.

"Well," Marcus said, as he returned to his seat. "It seems we're amateurs."

"Like to have done that to her, darling?"

He thought for a moment.

"No," he said. "That's too much for me. I'll be honest, I'd happily do to her what I do to you. But I wouldn't be comfortable inflicting that."

"Not even if she wanted it? What if I wanted it?"

"No. If you want that, talk to Helen. She'd happily do it to you."

I was taken aback.

"Do you think so?" I asked.

"God, yes. She'd top both of you in an instant."

I looked at Lucy who seemed as surprised as me.

"What makes you say that?" Lucy asked.

"Didn't you pick up she rather likes you two?"

"No," she replied.

"Your radar must be faulty, Luce."

"I think I turned it off when I got involved with you two. It was getting confused."

Chapter 28 – Lucy

The final three weeks of the holiday were close to heaven. I couldn't remember being so relaxed, so comfortable; so happy. Coming home was a shock and returning to work was difficult. It was the first time in years that going to a job I loved seemed hard. It was topped off by my next meeting with my mother.

"And you had all that to yourselves?"

"Yes, Mum," I replied.

I'd shown her a few pictures from the holiday; those I thought were safe to show her. The fort and some of the places we visited. She seemed absorbed by the fort.

"But it looks huge."

"It was. I think there were eight bedrooms in all."

"It must have been expensive."

"I don't know, Sally rented it."

Holidays were a bit of a mystery to her. We'd never been on holiday as children and I wasn't aware they'd been away after my banishment.

"Is Sally well off?"

I wanted to change the subject, but I needed to be as open with her as I could.

"She and Marcus are comfortable, yes."

"How did you all manage to get so much time off work?"

I patiently answered the question, but she didn't comprehend. Writing was another art form that had passed her by; she didn't see how anyone could do it full time. And as I tried to explain what Sally did to a woman with such a narrow world view, I found myself wanting to scream.

"Isn't it strange for a single woman to stay with a couple?"

Before I could think of a suitable answer, she continued.

"And they're not married, are they?"

Part of me wanted to tell her everything. How we'd walked around the fort naked, had sex whenever we wanted, with whoever we wanted. How another woman had stayed with us and joined in. But I knew I never would; she'd never be ready for it. I made a tame reply and changed the subject.

I did push the boundary a little. I told Mum about Mary and Ken coming out to stay and our visit to the casino. But my heart sank as I saw she wasn't even sure what a casino was. I was wasting my time. I returned to small talk about her new house and how she was getting on at the church.

After she left, I wondered what the point was. Why was I trying to rekindle a relationship which had been dead for so long? She wasn't difficult, she never asked embarrassing questions. But she was lifeless; never interested in anything, never wanting to learn new things. I found it energy-sapping.

I grabbed a bottle of wine and settled on the sofa. Getting back into a normal routine had produced mixed emotions. We'd been away a long time and it was good to get home and be in familiar places. But I missed being with people; the laughter, the conversation, the companionship. I missed cuddling up to someone at night. It wasn't the sex; well, not entirely. For nearly seven weeks I'd shared a bed with another person every night. Now, my bed felt lonely.

I ended up getting another bottle, and by the end of the evening, I'd got myself into a bit of a state. Thinking about my relationship with Sally and Marcus. It was something I'd never imagined, and it was wonderful. But where was it going? I was still the other woman and I was the one who'd end up dumped if anything went wrong; alone again. And possibly without my best friend. I needed Jenny's help.

***

By Saturday night, I'd pushed my doubts to the back of my mind.

"But she's harmless enough, surely?" Sally said.

"Yes, but what are we achieving?"

"I'm not sure families are supposed to achieve anything," Marcus said. "It's mostly about trying not to kill one another."

I knew Marcus's family hadn't been close, and he was cynical about the subject, but in a way which always made me laugh. We were sitting at their table after dinner on what had become our regular Saturday night date. We'd reminisced about the holiday and how hard it had been going back to work.

"At least you're getting on all right and she seems to be getting over your father's death," Sal said.

"She never mentions him. It's as if he didn't exist."

"That's a bit strange," Marcus said. "From what you've said, I expected her to have a little shrine to him."

"According to Annie, there's not one picture of him in her new house."

"Does she know why not?"

"No, and we're both afraid to ask."

I had my suspicions but was keeping them to myself for the time being. They weren't pleasant.

"Are you coming to the next play party, Luce?" Sal asked.

"When is it?"

"The weekend after Marcus's birthday."

"Why not? What could possibly happen?"

They looked at one another conspiratorially and I wondered what I'd let myself in for now.

"This one's a bit different," she said.

"Oh, yes."

"Don't worry, it's all the same sort of stuff. But this man here suggested something to Matt which they're going to try."

"Go on."

"Well," Marcus said. "There are a lot of people in the group who make stuff. You know, leatherwork, restraints, clothes. So, why not let people show their wares."

"Ooh, a kinky market."

"Yea, that's about right," Sal replied.

"Sounds fun."

"Would you like to take a pitch?"

250

My mouth dropped as I went to say something, but nothing came out.

"Luce," she said. "Everyone who's seen the pictures you did for us has loved them. They're damned good. Why not see if there's a market?"

"I don't know."

"You love doing the explicit stuff, don't you?" I had to admit I did. "But you can't put it in a normal gallery, and you're not selling it. I reckon it would go down a storm with this group."

I thought about it. I did now have a lot of explicit pictures, but I'd never contemplated selling them.

"We'd help, wouldn't we?"

"Yea," Marcus said. "Give it a try."

"I'd have to do so much preparation, though."

"What?"

"Get stuff framed and- "

"No, Luce," he said. "Don't overthink it. Take what you've got and have them mounted. Put them in plastic sleeves and display them like that. People will always want their own frames, anyway."

"Could do."

"Perhaps get a few framed so people could see the end result."

The idea appealed and terrified in equal measure. I had enough confidence now to know my pictures weren't bad and would appeal to the right person. But the thought of displaying my work was scary enough and the subject matter made it even scarier.

"Penny's persuaded Helen to take a pitch," Sally said. "I told her we might be persuaded to wear our new corsets if they're ready."

"Really?"

"If you don't mind."

"I've been set up twice in one evening here, Miss Fletcher."

"You can say no to both."

"I know. Not sure I want to."

***

Jenny listened calmly while I reeled off what happened on holiday. I told her almost everything, holding little back. I needed to tell someone, and Jenny was the unlucky one. When I'd finished, I slumped back in the chair and let out a long sigh. She said nothing while I calmed myself.

251

"How do you feel about what happened?"

"I'm a bit confused, Jenny. I loved it all, every minute. I haven't had so much fun in years; well, ever, probably. But coming back has been hard."

"In what way?"

"Coming back to reality. To my own home … alone."

"You still feel like the other woman?"

"Yes. Sally and Marcus still have each other, but what do I have?"

"You're not comfortable on your own?"

"Oh, yes. Well, I was, until my friendship with Sally changed. But if it were a normal relationship, we'd be thinking about the future. What we might do, where it might lead."

"But you can't."

"No. I don't know where I stand. I don't know how they see me. What do I mean to them?"

"Have you spoken to them about it?"

"No."

I'd thought about it, particularly in the last couple of weeks. But I couldn't face it. I couldn't think of what to say. I wasn't clear in my mind what I wanted.

"Are you going to?"

"But what do I say?"

"What do you want, Lucy?"

"I don't know, Jenny. I think I love Sally and as more than a friend. That's hard, given her situation. I'm worried that telling her will put her in an impossible position."

"Why?"

I looked at her sharply but saw a faint smile on her lips.

"Well," I said. "You can't love two people at the same time."

"Why not?"

Why not?' As I drove home, that question echoed through my head. It was still there the next morning and through the working day. It seemed preposterous; love was between two people. Except … except there were polyamorous relationships. I'd met people at the play party who were in multiple set-ups. But how would it work? Why was I even thinking about it? There was no escape; I was going to have to speak to Sally.

252

Chapter 29 – Sally

When I arrived at Lucy's, dinner was ready, and we caught up while we ate. I was buzzing because we were unpacking the archives in the new library. It was proving challenging, but we had so much space and everything was purpose-built. It was a joy.

After dinner, we settled on the sofa, and Luce produced another bottle of wine. It was some time before I realised she was unusually quiet.

"What's up, Luce?"

"Oh, nothing."

"Come on, out with it."

She looked away and didn't reply. Finally, she turned to me, her face serious.

"Sal," she asked. "What am I to you?"

The question caught me by surprise, but it shouldn't have. I'd been thinking the same thing. I put my glass on the table.

"Luce, you mean the world to me."

"But you're with Marcus."

I shifted in my seat to look directly at her.

"Come on, Luce. Spill."

She took a deep breath, and it all came out.

"I don't know where I am," she said. "I'm in a situation where I wonder if I've lost control. The holiday was wonderful, everything about it. So many things, playing and replaying in my head. Fun, laughter, sex, warmth."

She paused to catch her breath.

"But coming back to earth, thinking about it all, I feel like the outsider. I'm the one living alone while you two have each other. I don't know where I stand. If this all goes pear-shaped, I lose a lover … well, two … and a best friend. I'd be devastated. I'm not stupid; I knew it might all go wrong when we started, but the more I enjoy it, the more terrified I am about what's going to happen."

She reached out and softly took my hand in hers.

"I'm scared, Sal."

A few tears crept from her eyes, which looked directly into mine.

"Scared of what, Luce?" I whispered.

She screwed her eyes shut, and they slowly opened.

"That … I'm going to lose you."

"Why?"

"I don't know. I don't know how you and Marcus feel about me. I feel like …"

"… the other woman?" I replied.

She nodded. I wasn't sure what to say. I knew I wasn't giving Lucy up unless she wanted it to end, but I could understand her fears. Marcus and I were a unit; we weren't giving each other up anytime soon. Lucy's addition had been a bonus for both of us. But …

"Luce," I said. "Perhaps Marcus and I haven't been as thoughtful as we should have been. You're right, he and I have each other, and I guess we haven't given enough thought to your feelings. I'm sorry if we've hurt you."

"No," she said. "I'm not hurt. I went into this with my eyes open and I've loved every minute of it. I … I want more; that's the problem. I want things I can't have."

"Such as?"

She looked away, wiping a tear from her face. I knew what was coming. She turned back to me and focussed on my eyes.

"I love you, Sal."

Now it was my turn to cry; tears welled up and ran down my face. I gently pulled her towards me, and we wound our arms around each other; both now crying freely. I put my mouth to her ear.

"I love you, too," I whispered.

"But …"

She went to pull away, but I held her firmly against me.

"Ssh ..."

She surrendered, and I stroked her hair as she sobbed into my shoulder, my own tears rolling still. After several minutes, our crying slowed, and I reached to the table for some tissues. She gently pulled away, her face red and puffy, and covered in moisture. I guessed mine looked much the same. We wiped our faces, watching each other.

"But ...?" she said. "We can't ... It can't work. What about Marcus?"

"He knows."

"Knows what?"

"That you love me."

"How? I've only just admitted it to myself."

"He's been telling me for a while. He's quite amused by it all."

"How did he know?"

"I don't know. He just did."

"And does he know ...?"

"That I love you? Yes. Although he had to push me to admit it to myself."

"You ... you were scared too?"

"Yes."

"What happens now?"

"First, we wash our faces."

I led her to the bathroom, and we cleaned up as best we could. Returning to the lounge, I poured some more wine and we both sat on the edge of the sofa, saying nothing, cradling our glasses.

"Okay," Lucy finally said. "What does happen now?"

"I don't know, Luce. I've not been in this situation before."

"Me neither."

"So, we have to make it up as we go along."

"Isn't that what we've been doing?"

"Unfortunately, yes."

"Why unfortunately?"

"Because it isn't working for you."

She put her glass down, and reached out for mine, placing it on the table. Taking my hands, she turned me to look at her.

"Sal, it's not that. God knows, I'm loving it. But I was getting a bit greedy, I suppose. And shocked when I realised I loved you; that's what scared me."

"What's so scary about loving me?"

She laughed, at last.

"Nothing," she replied. "You know what I mean. If you hadn't accepted it … or felt the same way. Well …"

"It could have been awkward."

"Awkward? Our relationship, our friendship, could have ended there and then."

"Sorry, I hadn't looked at it that way."

"It's all I've been thinking about since the holiday."

I leant forward and our lips met in a soft, loving kiss.

"Good now?" I asked.

"Relieved. Although I'm still not sure if this changes anything."

"Do you need anything to change?"

She looked away for a few moments.

"No. I've got it off my chest and I feel a lot better. I guess I was feeling sorry for myself."

"You do know how much you mean to me, don't you?" I said.

"I think I may have lost sight of that for a while. But yes, I know."

"And to Marcus."

"I don't get him."

"Why?"

"Well, is he just going to accept that the woman he loves, loves someone else as well?"

"Yes."

"I'm not sure I could."

"But Luce, you do."

She thought for a moment, then burst out laughing.

"Oh, God. So I do. This is too complicated."

"It is, but there are no rules. We'll just have to make it work for us. Perhaps the three of us need to talk."

"Possibly." She picked up her glass and took a large swig.

"Luce," I said. "If you don't want to play with Marcus, you know he won't mind, don't you?"

"Yes."

"Want to stop?"

She turned to me with a wicked grin on her face.

"No. I've made my choice. I've come this far and it's proving ... entertaining."

I raised my eyebrows and she laughed.

"Alright," she said. "I'm loving it. I still struggle to understand his acceptance of all this."

"What, accepting that he gets to watch two women have sex?"

"Now you put it like that ..."

"That he gets to have sex with two women instead of one?"

"True ..."

"That he gets to spank two bums, instead of one?"

"Three, on holiday."

"Exactly. He's loving it, too. But he'd accept our situation without all that."

"I know."

"I told you, he's not a typical man."

We both went back to our wine and sat with our thoughts for a few minutes.

"Sal ..." Lucy finally said.

"Mmm."

"What do two people who've just confessed their love for each other do?"

I turned to see her smiling at me.

"Well," I replied. "I guess they find some way to express that love. To turn it into reality. To explore the meaning of love through physical acts of passion which leave them both on a higher plane and at peace with each other."

She leaned over to me, slightly drunk now.

"I love it when you talk dirty."

* * * * * * *

The story will conclude in **Kinky Companions.**

Author's Note

I would like to thank all those involved in helping me bring this story to the page. You know who you are, and I will be eternally grateful.

If you've enjoyed this book, please think about leaving a review, either on the marketplace where you bought it or on one of the many book review sites, such as Goodreads. Reviews are helpful for other readers (and authors, as well!).

The adventures of Sally, Marcus and Lucy will continue in Kinky Companions, the final book in the series. I hope you'll join them.

To keep in touch with my writing, you can visit my website, where you can subscribe to my quarterly newsletter, or follow me on social media.

Website: www.alexmarkson.com
Twitter: @amarksonerotica
Facebook: Alex Markson
Goodreads: Alex Markson

Alex Markson
May 2020

Printed in Great Britain
by Amazon

27737071R00152